At the bedside of a comatose, storm-ravaged castoff, Bruce MacAlister proclaims in desperation his fervent, secret love...

His eyes were riveted on the pale face that had haunted his dreams and many of his waking moments for the past few months. Had she moved her eyes?...Grasping the limp hand he said, "Oh, Kirsty, I'm that sorry. I should've spoken up the first time I saw you, and felt that spark between us. I'm sure you felt it too. Och, why could I not have said something then?...I want to make up to you for all the horror you've been through, this past week and before that. Come out of it. Come to me. I've such plans. We can be married, I care not what folk say. We can go far away together, and explore the world and laugh and sing together and...Oh...what am I saying? God help me! Help Kirsty, or better yet, help me to help Kirsty."

...Still gently clutching her hand, he gazed tenderly but intensely at her face. The lids flickered again, revealing the well-remembered intense green eyes, and then all at once her lips began to move...

"Where am I, and who are you?"

Share the trials and triumphs of Bruce MacAlister in these other *Isles of the Sea* novels:

The Call of the Isles   *Fires in the Glen*
My Heart's in the Highlands   *Haven by the Loch*

BY Molly Glass:

Lure
of Distant
Waters

MOLLY GLASS

Fleming H. Revell Company
Tarrytown, New York

Library of Congress Cataloging-in-Publication Data

Glass, Molly.
    Lure of distant waters / Molly Glass.
       p.   cm.
    ISBN 0-8007-5408-5
    I. Title.
PR9199.3.G572L87   1991
813'.54—dc20   91-17542
                                                  CIP

Copyright © 1991 by Molly Glass
Published by the Fleming H. Revell Company
Tarrytown, New York 10591
Printed in the United States of America

In memory of
my dear friend Jennifer Holmes.

TO
Edith and Harvey Benson, of Kelowna,
my heartfelt thanks.
To Edith, my very first reader
of Isles of the Sea, and
to Harvey, for all his encouragement
during some rough times.

And, behold, the glory of the God of Israel came from the way of the east: and his voice was like a noise of many waters; and the earth shined with his glory.

Ezekiel 43:2

Scottish Words and Phrases

Aboot: about
Ain: own
Auld: old
Babby: baby
Bairn: child
Ben: within
Besom: woman (derogatory)
Cauld: cold
Chuck: food
Claes: clothes
Cliping: telling tales
Da': dad
Doric: a broad Scots accent
Drookit: drenched
Dwam: dream or daze
Dyke: wall
Eedjit: idiot
Fashy: fussy
Girnin': whining
Glaiket: silly
Glesca: Glasgow
Greet: cry
Guid: good
Gye: very
Happed: wrapped

Hoors: hours
Ken: know
Kist: chest
Lane: alone
Mask: infuse tea
Mind: remember
Naebuddy: nobody
Off license: A public house where merchandise can be taken on the premises or "to go."
Onybody: anybody
Peasebrose: a porridge made with ground peas
Poke: sack
Polis: police
Sleekit: Crafty
Sonsy: pretty
Stane: stone
The day: today
Thegither: together
The morrow: tomorrow
Thole: endure
Thon: that
Thraw: stubbornly contrary
Thrawn: perverse
Wan: one
Watter: water
We'an: little one
Whit: what
Yin: one

$$-\cdot\circ\Rightarrow\!\!\!\Big\{\quad 1 \quad\Big\}\!\!\!\Leftarrow\circ\cdot-$$

"**W**hit's that yer readin', Kirsty?" Matt Brodie's voice faded to a hoarse whisper as he finished the question.

"Och, 'tis only an auld book I found in the press under the stairs, Da'."

"Oh, aye!" The cabin of the *Revelation* was silent, except for the noise of the water slapping on the hull of the boat and the rasping of Matt's breathing. For the past few days both sounds had been changing. First the water nearest the shore had formed a few ice crystals that had broken up during the day, making a grating sound on the boat's timbers. The man's breathing, too, had become harsher. Kirsty Brodie stole another glance at her father. Then she reached for the strand of wool she used to mark her place and closed the book, sighing mildly as the old man shuddered.

"Kirsty, I'm awfu' cauld!"

"I know, Da', but ye ken there's not a fireplace on the boat, and we finished the paraffin this mornin'. I'll step ashore, though, and stir up the ashes to make ye a toddy. 'Tis glad I am that the Reverend MacAlister's brother kept coal on board—ballast they call it—or we'd have been stuck. Thon box of candles is another thing to be thankful for."

Her father had closed his eyes again and did not answer for a few minutes. Then, "I'd be much obliged for the toddy, lass!"

Kirsty glanced at him once more before leaving the tiny cabin to heat the water. He was being far too humble, not a bit like himself. She pondered over this change as she stepped carefully along the plank that stretched from the *Revelation* to the shore. Their plan to live on Reverend MacAlister's houseboat had worked well enough when the weather was fine. Even when it rained or the fog spewed in off the sea, she could manage, but in the last few days an icy blast had swept the deck every time she opened the hatch, and that was harder to thole, especially for her da'.

Even though he only had one foot—having lost the other in a train accident—Matt's pride would never let him give in to his handicap. A week ago he had lost his balance on the slippery plank and plunged into the freezing water. He had grasped the rope quickly enough, but even so he had caught a chill. Kirsty had lit the paraffin heaters and kept them burning day and night, until the fuel had been all used up.

During their many trials and tribulations, she had never known her da' to be as meek as this, and she could not stop worrying. Yes, maybe the time had come to get some help. The big minister had told her to ask the town constable for whatever they needed, if things got hard.

Big minister indeed! His name was *Reverend Bruce MacAlister*, and in Kirsty's heart and mind, just *Bruce*. He owned this bonny house-boat, the Mains Farm, and half the land hereabouts. Habit made her glance about before dipping her ladle into the barrel of drinking water, which she filled from a spring Bruce had showed her. Would the spring freeze up in this cold wind, she wondered? The pan of water she had placed on the rekindled fire bubbled over, but she ignored it for a few more minutes. Her thoughts returned to the man. *At least be honest wi' yoursel', Kirsty Brodie. You ken fine you've not met one to equal him in all your born days and never will again. There's no law against dreaming, even when it can never be more.* The rattle of her da's stick on the cabin's paneling brought her again to the present dilemma. If she and Matt were to stay here for the rest of the winter and survive, she would need to go to the town called Aribaig for supplies.

Balancing the pan of boiled water, Kirsty made her way up the plank. She carefully placed each foot firmly on the slats formed for that purpose, holding tightly with her free hand to the strong mesh rope sides, designed to keep a child from falling overboard. Once again she breathed a silent thanks to Hamish Cormack, whom Bruce had mentioned more than once as being his brother, for all this provision. Da' had been at the end of the plank, not paying enough attention, when he had slipped.

Back in the cabin, she mixed the hot drink for him, spooning in some of her precious horde of brown sugar. Holding the mug while her father drank, she puzzled anew at the ease with which he now allowed her to tend him, another sign of the changes in him since his fall.

Pushing that thought aside, she began to tell him of her plans for next day. "If I leave early enough, I can go round the beach path and be back before the tide comes in again. We need paraffin oil and some other things. I'll bring linseed as well, to make you a poultice. That wheeze is ower—"

"Dinna fash yersel' for me, lass. I've the feelin' I'm done for, an' it's a' my ain fault!"

Kirsty showed her shock. "Da'! That's foolish talk, and I'll not listen to it. Ye've a wee touch of a cauld in your chest. Who wouldna have, after yon dip in the watter? Ye'll be better in no time."

Her father struggled to sit up. "Take the wee rowin' boat, Kirsty. Ye could be back in about two hoors that way." Her glance held horror, mixed with a spark of anger, but before she could reply, he strained to say more. "Right ye are, I just forgot." Kirsty's dread of the deep water was one of the few things that caused contention between them. But not today.

She went on to speak of her plans. "I should've took the polisman MacLeod's advice the last time he came."

"Whit's that ye say, lass? Who came here?"

Kirsty sighed. He had forgotten again. She leaned over the bunk to explain once more.

"Ye mind how the minister, Reverend MacAlister, said he would ask the constable to look in on us once in a while? Well, his name is MacLeod, and he's rowed out from Aribaig twice now. Each time I was that quick to tell him we had all we need."

Matt groaned. "Kirsty, you were richt enough! We dinna need the polis. But will ye stop yer bletherin' for a wee while? I want to tell you a thing or twa whilest I can still talk. Naw, dinna interrupt, just listen."

Amazement at what he began to say, mingled with relief that this was more like her da', rendered Kirsty speechless.

At last Matt paused to gasp for breath, and she managed to whisper. "Spanish doubloons? Och, Da', ye must be haverin'! Even if ye're not, what good are they? If they're stolen, I want none of them."

"They're a lot o' good, and they're no' stolen. I found them in yon cave I tellt ye aboot on the wee rock island oot in the sound. Nane but the birds and a seal or two go there. The coins belong to naebuddy but the finders. That's you and me, lass. I gave one to yon fellow from Gourock, when he was hidin' in the cave next to oors—ye mind o' him, Kirsty? Well, he offered to find oot whit it would bring. He never came back, but I'll wager they're worth a lot mair than a shillin' each, maybe even as much as a sovereign!"

She stared at Matt, wondering if the fever had indeed affected his brain. "A sovereign! Each! Och, Da', ye *are* haverin'."

"Maybe no' each, but they could be, an' I'm no' haverin', lass. Anyway, I wanted ye to ken where it is. Dinna let on to onybuddy else yet. I'm hopin' for enough money. . . . Think on it as found money!" His laugh brought on another fit of wheezing, but he waved her aside when she went to help him. "I want it for you lass. To gie ye a start at the dressmakin' or even in a wee sweetie shop. Whatever ye like. Ye've been a guid lass to me, an' I havena been as considerate of ye as I should, being wrapped up in masel' a' these years." He glanced up at that, to find her sitting with her eyes covered, her shoulders shaking with silent sobs.

"There now, lass. We've been through the mill, you an' me, an' I havena prized ye enough. But we've never gi'en into it, have we? I'm finished wi' the fightin', Kirsty. Onct I'm oot yer road, ye'll get on weel enough. Maybe get yersel' a guid lad to settle wi'. But whatever ye do, ye're a sensible lass, and ye'll not—" He choked again, and Kirsty lifted her head.

Tears stained her cheeks, but her fury at his words rang clear: "We'll have a lot more good times, Da'. Stop that kind of talk. In fact, stop ony kind of talk, till ye get yer breath. We'll go to Glasgow thegither, that's what we'll do. If what ye say about treasure is right, and we do sell the coins, we'll pay a cobbler to make ye a special kind of boot. But for the rest of it, I dinna want to ken. . . . Oh, Da'!" The last was a wail, as he had fallen back on the pillow, with his eyes closed. His face had drained of all color; the long talk had exhausted Matt, and he slept.

Waking at the crack of dawn, Kirsty had happed Matt up well, using every blanket out of the kist. Then she placed a dish of cold peasebrose close to his hand. She put a fresh new candle in the sconce above the bunk, making sure it was well secured before she lit it. Her da' didn't like to be left in the dark.

Only when she had finished with him did she start her own preparations for the journey to the town. She had found a heavy cape, complete with hood, among some other gear. The cape reached her ankles but no matter. Another search had produced a pair of canvas bags with rope handles and a second empty paraffin can. If she could carry all this back over the beach, they would be fine for another fortnight. She would ask the polisman to bring some things with him the next time he came. Although her da' seemed better this morning, even having a bit color in his cheeks, she still concluded that pride could cost too much. After pulling the canvas cover down over the hatch, but not securing it, she strode off at a good pace in the direction of Aribaig.

As a child, Kirsty Callahan Brodie had always enjoyed walking and playing by herself, so she had no trouble setting and keeping up the steady pace, considering how the cloak and heavy boots tried to hamper her. Twisting her neck now, to look backward, she smiled at the marks her tackety boots made on the wet sand. Quenching the feeling of dread, she forced her gaze toward the water. The tide was going out, and if all went well, she should be back long before it came in again. Maybe her tracks would still be visible.

She must not linger to admire the sky. Today, the lovely scene spreading out behind her had tinted the clouds a deep fiery red, which she saw only as beauty where they hung low over the receding water.

A rhyme came to mind, and she recited aloud, "Red sky in the morning, shepherd's warning!" An old wives' tale, she hoped, but

her honest heart reminded her of the basic truth of a lot of these
ancient sayings.

Skirting round an outcrop of sharp rocks, she noted that this
might be too steep to climb over; but if the worse came to the
worst, she could do it. The handle of the empty paraffin can
pressed into her palm, through her mittens, and her thoughts
jumped again to the return journey, when the cans would be full.
Oh, well, the mittens were made with thick wool. Her Granny
Dickson had spent all her time knitting such mittens, and after she
died, Kirsty had inherited a dozen pairs in her own size. She wore
the last pair.

"I wonder if I'll end up like my granny, sitting by the fireside,
knitting mittens?" Her laugh echoed hollowly off the sea-wet rock.

At last she allowed her thoughts to return to the question her da'
had asked her the night before. She had been reading the Bible she
found. At first, just for something to do, she had opened it up. The
first pages were covered with a fine handwritten script and told a
family history. This had intrigued Kirsty for the longest time. The
names and the dates fascinated her, so now, to take her mind off the
long trudge ahead, she began to recite the record from memory.

"This Bible is presented to Reverend and Mistress Bruce MacAlister, on the occasion of their marriage, by Mistress Beulah MacIntyre, Strathcona House, Glasgow, Scotland, grandmother of the
bride. May the Lord God of Hosts bless it to their use." The next
page had been covered with smears and smudges, but Kirsty had
managed to make out a different handwriting, a bit shaky in places
but readable, except for the date. "Mary Jean MacAlister. Welcome
to our family, my pet. May you grow to love this book as your
mammy and daddy do." The entry following this puzzled Kirsty
even more. "Hamish Cormack, a man of thirty years, was born for
the second time the very same day as Mary Jean MacAlister's first
birth. Hamish is hereby recognized as a member of God's family
and ours. We pray that Hamish, too, will come to love Your Word,
Lord, and Your law. Jean I. MacAlister."

Suddenly Kirsty stopped her recitation. Everything within her
cringed at the word *law*. Not that she or her da' would break laws;
they just didn't heed some of the ones they thought wouldn't hurt
folk. What would the MacAlister think of that philosophy?

At their second meeting, the time Bruce had offered her the houseboat to stay in, he had told her he would like to meet her da'. Again she spoke her thoughts aloud. "I wonder if he ever will?" But he had been so burdened down with the doings at his farm and other important matters, she doubted if he had given the Brodies another thought, even though they were inhabiting his boat.

Now Kirsty brought her mind to the actual printed words of the book itself. It had a margin filled with explanations for some of the strange, hard-to-read words and actions within it. Kirsty had started reading where it had opened itself when she picked it up, and the title of that end section intrigued her! *Revelation*, the same as the name of the boat!

Reading the first few sentences had indeed been a revelation to Kirsty Brodie, and when she came to the words: "Blessed is he that readeth . . . the words of this prophecy . . . ," she wondered if it really could be so. Could that be why a man such as the big highland minister spoke of God as though he spoke of his best friend? She had gone on to read the whole section—plodding through seals and plagues and beasts—with mixed feelings, while outside the weather changed from mild autumn to mild winter and the calendar on the cabin wall showed Christmas to be a short two weeks away.

Sometimes the explanations in the margins helped her to understand, but at other times even those sent her head spinning. Occasionally she found a loose sheet of paper with the words written out in a childish hand, reminding her that in the very brief time she had spoken with Bruce MacAlister, she had learned how this boat had been his family home for quite a spell. She had gathered, too, that no grown woman had ever lived on it until she herself came. She couldn't fathom how folk who had a nice farm to stay on would choose to go round the islands in a bit boat. But then, who was she to talk, when she and her da' never did things the way other folk did them?

When her da' had interrupted her reading yesterday, she had just turned to the last page of the whole book. *Chapter twenty-two*, it said. She had stopped reading then to consider the words,

". . . pure river of the water of life, clear as crystal, proceeding out of the throne of God. . . ."

Her thoughts flew off at a tangent as she called out to the unheeding gulls, "I should've told the minister—I mean Bruce—that my first name is *Crystal*, changed to *Kirsty* because Ma thought *Crystal* too fancy for a railwayman's daughter. Would he have cared, I wonder? Aye, I think he would; he's a caring kind of chap. I should have told him a lot more than my name, but then he might not have been so keen on us staying on his bonny boat." Her steps faltered as she surveyed the next stage of her journey. A scree cliff faced her, high enough that she could not see the top, but not sheer on the sides. She would climb up it to save time the now, when she had nothing much to carry, but coming back she would have a few burdens. A roughly drawn map in the cabin had showed this outcrop plainly. There was a path of sorts zigzagging to the top, but the other side had slid away a bit. Kirsty shuddered as a thought came to mind. What if something happened to her, and she didn't get back to her da', and what if . . . ?

"I'll not think on such things, but I wish I could pray the way the bairn wrote in they notes. What would be the harm? I'll try it! Aye, I will. . . . Dear God! If You are there, help me with all the things I have to do the day. I hate askin', after ignorin' Ye for all they years, but then Your Lordship, I didn't know, till Your man Bruce tellt me, that You forgive folk like me. Forgive me then for anything like that and all the things I've dong wrang that Ye dinna like. Keep Yer eye on my da', too, and I'll not forget it. That's all I have to say the now, as I'll need all my puff." As she reached the edge of the outcrop, the beginning of what must be Aribaig appeared in the distance. She received a fresh spurt of energy, enough to speed up her walk to a half run. Even if she recognized it, she ignored the high-water mark that showed far above her head.

2

The constabulary in the highland township of Aribaig in Invernesshire sported that illustrious title only because one room in the building housed miscreants. In addition to the cell, the room boasted a desk-cum-table and a swivel chair. A notice board almost covered one wall, and on a nail just inside the door, hung a wee bit of a mirror. Constable Neal MacLeod had just finished his morning report and was setting his helmet straight on his head, in front of the mirror, when he heard a knock on the back door. Neal disliked anything interrupting his start on the rounds, so he took his time answering. Who could it be at this hour of the morning anyway? Nobody from the town would be as early as this, and for an emergency summons they wouldn't be wasting time going round the back. He pulled the door wide. Facing him stood the woman who had taken up residence, along with her father, on the Reverend MacAlister's boat. She would have received short shrift from him if it weren't for the letter Bruce had sent him, together with a note giving his permission, which the woman had produced when he rowed out to the *Revelation* to see for himself. Grudgingly he invited her inside now.

"So you see, as my da's wheezin' is gettin' worse, I came for some medicine to make him a poultice and for some paraffin oil and flour and—" She faltered slightly as she caught Neal's glare. The policeman could hardly credit the fact that she had walked in from the cove, where the boat was anchored, and he tried not to show his admiration.

Neal fussed with some papers on his table while he silently pondered on how things had changed in Aribaig this last while.

Official word had reached him that a castle would be built on the east section of the Mains property and that the Cormack Homes had official sanction. Hard feelings had died down after the town meeting in which Bruce MacAlister had talked to the townsfolk, and soon after that the laird, the ClanRanald himself, had started hiring the local tradesmen for the castle's construction. Neal had heard no further complaints.

His attention switched back to the woman who was speaking again, "I'm a bit feart for my da', or I wouldn't be bothering you, and I want to get away back afore long. Can you help me, Constable?"

"Reverend MacAlister asked me to help you, so I will. I canna leave my post for long the day, though. I'll come the morn in the boat and bring what ye canna carry." Noting the young woman's reaction to his words, he added, "Dinna worry, naebuddy else kens you're on the reverend's boat. But does yer faither not need the doctor?"

"He'll not willingly have a doctor since—"

"We have the poor box, ye ken, for the needy."

She tossed her head, and the hood of her cape swung back to reveal a double coil of gleaming black hair. Turning away from him, she responded softly, "We can pay, if we need the doctor. Thank ye, just the same. I want to be on my road back, so if you—"

But Neal felt obliged to mention one more thing, "The sky's gye black, miss. Could ye not go round by the Mains instead of by the shore?"

"As ye've said, nobody else kens we're on the *Revelation*, so till the minister gies the word, we'll not be goin' near the Mains. Anyway it's even further to walk, and I'm no' sure I could find the road."

"At least ye'd not have the tides to worry about. They've been mild so far, but we could still get a bad one this year yet!"

"Could we go the now, then? It's for my da', or I wouldn't bother ye!" Neal shrugged. True she had not bothered him before this, and he had done his best to give warning.

The shopkeeper stared at the strange woman, dressed in men's trews and an old cloak, but he served Kirsty without comment when she produced the ready money.

Neal had accompanied her to the shops in case of any trouble. After that he planned to escort her to the edge of the town, putting off the moment when his neighbors would be asking questions, but even then he would make no comments. Let them draw their own conclusions. Many and varied these would be, he did not doubt, but the truth—that the Reverend MacAlister was protecting a pair of tinkers—would never be suspected. He doubted it his own self.

He had studied the woman as she made her purchases. She handled herself well enough, and although not a young lass, she was a bonny woman for all that. If the minister wanted to do a good turn to the tinker folk and keep it a secret, Neal would never break the confidence. He had kept his promise, remembering, too, how beholden he was to Bruce, since the trouble about the homes and his own Terence's involvement in that. His face darkened as he thought of his son, but he thanked God every day for how that lad's wildness had been nipped in the bud. Terence MacLeod was now in Glasgow, learning the cobbling trade. Quickly he shook off personal regrets as he remembered the waiting woman and picked up one of her bundles. He could spare another ten minutes to escort her to the end of the cobbled street.

A fresh burst of her old fear of water clutched at Kirsty as she faced the long, lonely beach, but nothing appeared to give her fear substance, and a quick glance showed the tide still far out. She settled down to a steady half-trot, deciding she could risk going round rather than trying to climb over the slippery scree cliff. Shifting the heavy burdens from one hand to the other, she tried to hurry her steps. The darkening sky hovered over the water's edge, and Kirsty fervently wished now that she had paid more attention to her da's attempts to teach her about such things as seas and tides. Before bringing her to these parts, Matt had studied up on them, but Kirsty only knew that this particular stretch of water, Loch Haven, merged with the North Atlantic, becoming part of that ocean where it lapped the shores of western Scotland and the isles.

Thinking of her father made Kirsty quicken her pace once more, but her habit of speaking to herself, practiced through many solitary hours, brought forth the lament, "Oh, Da'! I shouldna have left ye alane in thon boat, an' you not well." Her voice slapped against the shale cliff and bounced back to her ears again as she poured out more regrets. "Or better still, if only we'd stayed in Motherwell. Things were no' so bad there, and I could have got a job at the gas works, or if you hadn't had the accident and lost yer foot, or if Ma had only stuck wi' us, but you were hard to thole for a while after that."

A flock of gulls screamed over her head, and Kirsty stopped in her tracks to gaze upward. She had reached the end outcropping of rock, and as the water still seemed quite distant, she stopped for a few minutes to rest. Then she would make a race for it. "Am I just bein' daft? Except for thon black cloud, the place seems gye peacefu'." Watching the gulls as they wheeled to fly inland again, some primitive instinct within Kirsty made her jump to her feet. The sky was no longer peaceful. She snatched up the packages and began to run. At that moment a thunderous roar almost split her eardrums; a mountain of surf crashed onto the cliff point, sweeping everything in its path. In abject terror now, Kirsty forgot all except self-preservation. She dropped the bags and the cans of paraffin and began a frantic scramble up the cliff shelf. Moments later the great wall of water reached to swallow her up as if she were a rag doll. Her scream of terror echoed as her last conscious thought became, *Oh, Da', what'll happen to you now?*

Even in the midst of his raging fever, something caused Matt Brodie to stir from his uneasy sleep. He shouted for Kirsty before he remembered she would be away most of the day. What day, he wondered now, and what had wakened him with such a fright? Matt's awareness returned, and he thought, *Just the usual old rhythm of regrets.* They had been strong enough to have brought him out of the dwam.

The boat rocked under him, and Matt raised himself on one

elbow to look about. In the faint glow of the lone candle, above his head, the endless parade of memories started. He fell back on the pillows. This was no dwam. First to appear, a vision of his mother on her knees, the day he told her he had got started on the railway gang and would be on his own bat from now on. His mother's prayer, that he would come to his senses and finish his time at school, he set out to prove would not be answered. Then he met Nellie and went daft for her, and nothing would do for that proud besom but marriage. They had been far too young, but before his eighteenth birthday they were wed. He had been only twenty when Kirsty was born. He had no regrets on that score, though, and as the years passed he realized that his wee lass was the best thing that had ever happened to him. They had had no more bairns, but Nellie had seemed happy enough, and they had been good years when Kirsty was growing up, until he lost his foot and his job and with them all his self-respect.

The boat swayed again, and he gathered his dulling wits. Inland seas and the tides he had read about, and he knew that every now and then, when the sun and the moon had almost equal pull on the earth, the tides in this region of the North Atlantic could be disastrous. He had picked this bit of coast, not only for its bare and beautiful solitude, but for its sheltered inlets. Stories he had read about Spanish galleons disappearing in the waters hereabouts, supposedly loaded with loot, had also drawn him. The boat shuddered again, and Matt remembered how he had admired the *Revelation* for its grand workmanship.

"Och, this boat could last through a thousand storms, 'tis that sturdy." As if to deny such affirmation the boat heaved in the water, and Matt was promptly thrown out of the bunk and propelled across the cabin floor. Scrambling to his knees, he caught sight of the candle, so carefully stuck into its wall sconce by Kirsty. Now it leaned drunkenly, spilling a stream of hot wax onto the bed covers. The blankets had stayed on the bunk. Before Matt could gather strength to reach to snuff out the flame, the boat gave another lurch, and the candle left its moorings. Immediately the flames licked the melted wax, and within seconds the bedclothes had become a solid sheet of fire.

Matt's thoughts took a strange twist, and he spoke them aloud, "If I mind right what Kirsty tellt me thon day, when she said we'd be goin' to stay on this boat for a while, it was aboot a sign on the rock that aye worried her: 'The wages of sin is death.' The minister man had said to Kirsty that if such was the case, then the opposite must be true as well. It makes sense. The wages of good must be life. If that's true, then I'll claim my wages. I've done some daft things, but I've not been a bad chap. Forgie me God, an' you as well, Mither. I've never denied God. I just didna want to give in!" Smoke engulfed the tiny cabin, and Matt managed enough strength to slide his body under the low bunk, before his overtaxed lungs gave up the struggle.

Meanwhile, Constable MacLeod, along with his son William, raced down the road to the Mains as fast as Geordie McDade's old cab horse would go. Time now to forget the promise of silence and face the realities of folk in danger.

Earlier Neal had been drawn back to the place where the tinker woman had disappeared. His eyes had beheld one of the strangest sights of his lifetime. First, the unusual black clouds hid all traces of the daylight. Yet when he had turned to look back toward Aribaig, everything there appeared normal. Facing the water again, he had gasped at the height of the monstrous wave—at least half a mile wide and one hundred feet high—rushing toward the shore. From his vantage point he could tell it was headed east and would not touch even the edges of the town. But, oh, my, the cliffs and cave inlets would suffer, maybe even the place where the braw new castle was going up. What about the Brodie woman? Helplessly he had watched the wall of water as it reached in and swallowed up the Head, the local name for the outcrop of rocky cliff. If she had not managed to get to the other side of it, she was a goner. He had run to get his son. Reverend Bruce's double request of help for the squatters, but silence about their existence, must be overruled in this emergency. If yon wave hit the cove, only God could help the minister's boat and any living soul on board.

3

At the Mains Farm, Mama and Papa Ward were enjoying a few minutes of leisure together. Taylor the Post had just left, and Mama Liz Ward had masked a fresh pot of tea for herself and her husband before they would read the official document brought this very morning by Taylor.

Jeremy grew impatient with his fussing wife. "Leave the tea and come on. I'm anxious to ken what's all in this fancy letter." He did not need his wife to read the finely printed missive, but with only one hand, and that missing three fingers, he found it difficult to open letters without mangling them up.

Liz finished pouring the tea. "Another minute isn't going to change the contents, Papa, besides we already know it must be good news." Nevertheless she spread the folded papers in front of him as she read aloud, " 'This is to inform you that the property, hitherto known as the Mains Farm, of Aribaig, in the county of Inverness, Scotland, may now be officially described as the Cormack Orphanages of the same location.' " She smiled widely as she raised her eyes to meet Jeremy's.

His eyes reflected a look of deep sadness. "It didna come easy, Mama!" She knew what he meant but wisely refrained from remarks as he continued. " 'Tis God's way of recompense for the loss and of remindin' us that although the devil meant it for evil, when our train smashed into yon gully, the Holy Spirit changed it to good. . . . I know that Gran'pa Bruce MacAlister and Elspeth and Andrew Cormack are rejoicin' in heaven that it turned oot so weel. Onyway, Bruce will be that pleased to see this paper. He was instrumental in getting it sorted oot, but ye ken that, too."

Liz Ward never ceased to wonder at the mixture that was her husband. He had been taught by Elspeth Cormack—who was the daughter of a big Edinburgh lawyer—to read and write and understand many basic legal terms. Yet Jeremy had kept the simplicity of the farm talk and the mannerisms of the two most influential men in his life: Andrew Cormack and the senior Bruce MacAlister.

She broke his ruminative silence, "Yes, I do know. I was at that meeting, too, remember, where he spoke so eloquently to the townsfolk about the need for the homes. But we'll never call this place an orphanage, will we, Papa?"

"That we'll not; it doesna matter what the rest call it. Gran'pa always said that names are secondary. Bruce was indeed eloquent yon day, though. Do you mind we came into the hall just as he was summin' up?"

"I remember, and I can see it all quite plain in my mind! But I've sat about long enough. This is the day I have a talk with the latest members of our family—Eddie and Katie Woods are their names. I'll leave you to your rememberings."

Jeremy sat for a while, picturing the Reverend Bruce MacAlister, along with his stepbrother Hamish Cormack, joint heirs of all that the Mains Farm entailed, taking up the cause of the Cormack Homes. Until the day of the town meeting, the homes had been a thorn in the side of most of the residents of Aribaig. Jeremy could almost hear Bruce now, though he had relied on Hamish for the details of his words.

"There is no doubt whatever in my mind that when the options are placed squarely before them, my friends and lifelong neighbors of this parish will choose the highest good. Up to now, I believe you all have been swayed by a lopsided view of the position. I'll try to place it in front of you without let or prejudice."

Bruce's words had been wonderful, and he had done just that— with God's help, the people of Aribaig had been won over.

Jeremy stirred from his rememberings as a soft noise reached him. He glanced at the clock—time for his Howie's lesson. Howie was extra dear to Jeremy, since he had been the first child to be considered for the homes. As it turned out, the small boy would not speak. But somehow Jeremy knew he was not a mute: Something or someone had frightened the child into silence. One of Jeremy's dearest plans was to hear the boy call him Papa.

"Come away in, Howie. What story will we have the day? Och, I mind, we were just coming to the one about David and Goliath."

Liz glanced in at the peaceful scene and decided that Howie's hands maybe didn't need washing now. She went back to the kitchen, where her sister-in-law, Blodwin, waited along with young Dorrie Henderson. The way those two, as different as chalk from cheese, got on so well together always amazed Liz, but she was grateful for it just the same. A glance at the calendar assured her that this was indeed Friday: baking day for Blodwin, polishing silver and brass day for Dorrie.

"Not long now, ladies, before we have the new wing to spread out in. Your father and brother are excellent workmen, Dorrie!"

"They are that, Mama Liz, but I thank you for mentionin' it."

Blodwin bristled slightly but decided on the line of least resistance. "What does 'not long' mean, then, Liz? We're so cramped as it is!"

Liz also wanted no arguments or discord to spoil this day, so instead of remonstrating with her brother's widow, she merely said, "Next week is what Jake told Papa at their meeting this morning. That is, if the threatening storm doesn't come too close."

For a minute Blodwin looked frightened. Then she forgot the weather and began to gather up the utensils and ingredients for the baking today. Welsh rarebit—it seemed a while since they'd had it, and she'd better keep in practice for the day when she would have a new man to cook for. Her eyes became dreamy as she thought of her secret fiancé, the big handsome police inspector, Thomas MacKinnon. Easter he had said, and she had agreed. Liz didn't yet know and would be shocked, although dear Ian would be dead a year by then. She put some extra vigor into the egg beating as she recalled Thomas and his promise that she and her three children would never have to want for anything again. Thankful as she was for the Cormack Homes as a refuge, that's all it was, a temporary refuge.

Dorrie was staring at Mistress Parker in surprise as the other women beat the life out of the eggs. Usually she did things more

quiet and refined like. Och, well, she'd better get on with the
spoons and things, if she wanted Mama Liz to stay in thon good
mood. Dorrie gave a thought to the storm as she whispered to
herself, "I hope it doesna keep Gideon from comin' to help my Pa
and Jimmy wi' the wainscotin'." Being one of the blacksmith's
sons, learning the trade, Gideon was allowed to go to the jobs
away from the smiddy.

Into this contented scene Constable Neal and his son burst with
their astounding news, shattering contentment and peace for many
days to come. Frantic dogs were barking and children shouting as
the women ran to the door to see what all this commotion could be
about.

Jeremy stared at William MacLeod. His words sounded incredible. Their friendship, strained to almost breaking point during the
feuding about the Cormack Homes, still had them a bit shy with
each other, but that didn't account for Jeremy's astonishment.

"Do you mean to tell me that folk have been living on the *Revelation* all winter, and we didna ken?"

"Aye, that's what I'm saying, Jeremy!"

"Dear Lord! And now ye're sayin' ye think she's been wrecked
into the bargain? The wife did remark to me a while ago about the
funny black cloud in the sky, and Jake mentioned it as well. That
noise like thunder didna last long. . . . We thought it too early in
the year for a thunderstorm. Can we do anything—and what?"

"The water's still terrible rough, and we couldn't even take the
boat out the shed, so we'll need to go in from this side. Some of
your workmen might come, as well, but we don't ken what—"
William's recognition of the workmen was in itself an olive branch.
No one thought of past disagreement as they confronted possible
catastrophe.

A short time later, an astounded group of men with one
woman—Mama Ward herself—could only stand and gape at the
remains of what had been the proud Gospel boat. She was half out
of the water, and the charred mast hung as mute evidence to the
fate of the craft. The mooring ropes drooped idly. Strangest of all,

the outer shell of the boat appeared intact, while the fire had gutted cabin and galley.

Jimmy Henderson voiced the single thought: "Onybody in yon boat is done for."

William MacLeod stared at his father. "What'll we do, Faither?"

Neal pushed his helmet back while he scratched his thinning hairline. "As the lad says, Son, nobody'll still be livin' in that boat. Our duty is clear. We canna just guess; we'll need to go on board and find out what's what." He was at a loss as he stared at Mistress Ward.

She spoke for the first time: "It's all right, Constable. I'm a nurse and have seen many sights. What about the—?"

Neal clapped his hand to his forehead. "The wumman! She wouldn't have had the time to get back here before yon wave struck. Whatever came first, the big wave or the fire? But I did advise her to come roon' the long way. We'll need to muster a search party as well as a boarding party. Och, I wish the Reverend MacAlister was here the now!"

4

For the tenth time within the hour the Reverend Bruce MacAlister plucked his watch from its chain and almost willed the hands to leap ahead. His first hour in the train had been fine, even enjoyable, as he contemplated the true reason for his errand to Aribaig. Then the clacking wheels had begun to intrude on his thoughts, bringing back memories of his many train journeys.

That very first one, with his mother, when he was only four years old, he could barely recall, but he did remember that the circumstances had been sad. Yet his mam had said they might as well enjoy a wee holiday anyway. That memory clouded, to be replaced by the journey from the croft in Aribaig to the university in Glasgow. For the first time in his eighteen years, he traveled alone—no first-class ticket for that epic milestone. Other travelers from the highlands, also bound for the famed halls of learning, shared the wooden-benched carriage; and the odor of damp home-spun mingled with the pungent smells of the great variety of food-stuffs being carried in the rolled up sacks. Bruce's humble circumstances had still allowed him enough money to be able to pay for full room and board at Strathcona House, where the woman who would become his Jean had awaited.

His brows furrowed now into their familiar pattern. How many times after that had he made the journey between Glasgow and Fort William? He lost count. One summer he and Peter Blair, his medical-student friend, had left the train at the Fort and hiked the miles to Aribaig and hence the Mains Farm. Most of the time, though, he had been glad enough to board the McBrayne horse-bus.

A brilliant smile crossed Bruce's face as he thought of Peter. Only today that exasperating fellow, after driving him to Central Station in his newfangled motorcar, had dared to shout as they parted, "Go and win her, then, Bruce, my fine highland lad. 'Faint heart never won—' " The rest of the shouted quotation had faded out as Bruce leaped on to the already-moving train.

Alone in the compartment, he addressed his response to his likeness in the looking glass: "Aye, Peter, I intend doing just that—if she'll have me, that is, and if she's still on the *Revelation*!" He glanced again at his timepiece. Half an hour still to go. Knowing that his mind was deliberately skipping a couple of significant railway journeys, he now, just as deliberately, forced it back. He must face them, too, if he would carry out the plan that had been forming, almost subconsciously, for many weeks.

Bruce continued to speak aloud to his lone reflection in the carriage window: "I'm only forty-six, Lord, and if You spare me even for the threescore years and ten of promise, I've a while to go yet. Now Mary Jean's married and happily settled, waiting to be a mammy herself soon. Hamish is set with the brotherhood, and I've got this year of leave from the Kelvin Kirk in which to decide what I'll do with my own life." He sank back into the corner and closed his eyes, but did not sleep. Suddenly he realized that the once-too-familiar flash of pain the memory of Jean, his dead wife, used to bring no longer followed his thought of her. Unsure whether or not this was a good sign, he allowed his mind to roam to places that in the years since her death, he had shunned.

Their wedding journey to Skye: He could see again the guard's van overflowing with the piles of boxes and trunks loaded there by his old friend Benny Stout—then a humble porter at Glasgow's Central Station—and ably supervised by Betsy Degg—more a companion than maidservant to Granny Mac, Jean's maternal grandmother. Those two had been making sure that "Miss Jean" had everything possible to help her endure the wilderness existence that Betsy was so sure the young MacAlisters were doomed for. Bruce's first parish of Inverechny had proved to be far from primitive, and the manse, although not the mansion Jean had been reared in, had nevertheless been a fine place with many conveniences.

A flash of the old pain did enter as Bruce thought, inevitably, of Jean's accidental death in a bright shining room of the manse.

Resolutely he forced his thoughts back to the first train journey in his married life. Again they had not traveled first class. Their compartment had been shared with a family of five. Bruce shuddered anew as he recalled his own stiffness. His wife, friendly and outgoing, had told the other couple of their newlywed state. He remembered the blush warming his face and neck as five pairs of eye swiveled to stare at him. The man's held a definite lewdness and had remained on him for what seemed an endless time.

To escape the scrutiny he had pinched Jean's arm and pulled her into the corridor. "Jean, will you stop your babbling? You needn't have mentioned that we're just married and—"

Her tinkling laugh had ended abruptly as she had caught sight of his stricken look. She had reached for him, but he had stepped away as she had said "Why, Bruce, my love, 'tis nothing to be ashamed of. I do believe you truly are what Faye described and I always denied."

His anger had flared again. "Discussing us with all and sundry—and our private life! I'll not have it, Jean!"

She had sobered instantly. "I'm sorry, love. From now on I'll be good. It's just that I love you so, and I'm so proud to be your wife."

Slightly mollified, he had lifted his hand to touch her shining red head, but she had quickly grasped it, drawing it round her neck, at the same time stretching up on tiptoes to kiss him.

Horrified, he had pulled away again. "Jean, in a public place. Folk'll see us!"

Her face had closed then. "No, Bruce, I glanced about first. Nobody else is in the corridor. But I'm sorry. I'll try harder to be the circumspect minister's wife, if that's what you want." She had turned away then, and he had caught a glimpse of the hankie as she dabbed her eyes. But he was sure he had heard her whisper, "Stuffed shirt, indeed!"

"Beg your pardon, Reverend?"

Bruce had spoken the last phrase aloud just as the conductor slid open the connecting door.

"We're approaching Fort William, sir. Will you require help with your bags?"

"I'll manage fine, thank you." The man closed the door again, and Bruce stood up. He had one more short journey to take after changing to the local train. That would be hard too, since the memories concerning that length of railway line were more recent and therefore more painful. The new trestle, much stronger than the one that had collapsed last year, hurtling his mother, Elspeth, his stepfather, and his dear Gran'pa Bruce to their death, would have to be crossed. He prayed then that he would be able to practice what he preached and leave it, painful memories and all, with the Lord.

In his headlong rush north, Bruce had neglected to inform Jeremy and the others at the Mains of his coming. Standing uncertainly in the street outside the livery stable, he wondered if he should hire a horse or take the cab. The whole town seemed very quiet, and as he moved to enter the stable a figure appeared beside him.

"Reverend MacAlister, 'tis yersel' then? My, but ye got here quick."

Puzzled, Bruce recognized Taylor the Post and smiled a greeting in return. "Hello, Taylor, I'm afraid nobody at the Mains knows yet that I'm coming, so I'll need to find my own way out there. How are you and the family?" It was the other man's turn to be puzzled, but he merely said, "I'm chust fine, Reverend, and so's the wife and bairns." Taylor's thoughts churned. If the MacAlister didn't yet know about his boat and the other things happening out there at the Mains, Taylor wouldn't be the one telling him. The two men gazed at each other before Taylor withdrew his eyes.

Somehow Bruce discerned that Taylor's words and manners contained more than an apology for past conduct, but he also knew that any acknowledgment of the apology on his own part would need to be discreet. Whatever else the strange behavior meant would have to wait. Bruce raised a hand in farewell and proceeded into the livery stable.

More puzzled than ever, Taylor continued on his way.

Complete amazement dominated the scene in the Mains parlor, although those present were all too polite to say so. Jeremy kept glancing at Bruce while his wife fussed about bed sheets and other immaterial things; he decided that he would learn no more about the reason for this unexpected visit by the minister who called him brother until one or the other began to disclose the true state of affairs.

"You didna ken about the *Revelation* then?"

Startled, Bruce responded with a shouted, "What about the *Revelation*?"

"Och, Bruce, I didna want to be the one to tell you. When I saw you ride into the steadin', I thought you must have discovered it somehow, even if it only happened yesterday. But the boat's been near destroyed by a fire that started durin' a storm, and the man's killt and the wumman's—"

Bruce jumped up, his chair crashing to the floor. "What of the woman?"

Liz Ward had rushed back into the parlor at the sound of the crash and answered now, "She's out on the rock shore somewhere, Bruce. The constable and the other searchers think she's still alive, although she may be lying unconscious somewhere!"

But Bruce no longer listened. Running to the door, he called out over his shoulder, "The rock shore! You're meaning the Head?"

"Bruce, wait a minute! The search party's been out since daybreak. Last night, as well, they searched till the tide came in. The plan was to report here at the noon hour."

Bruce's hand automatically went to his watch pocket. At that very moment shouts rang out and dogs began to bark. He rushed from the room.

Liz and Jeremy Ward stared at each other for some moments before Jeremy said, "We'll find out all about it soon enough, I'm thinkin'!"

His wife had another thought: "Maybe some, but not *all* about it,

Papa. I've a feeling there's a big mystery here. Shall we join them to see what happens now?"

Childish voices reached them as one by one they took up the cry, "They've found the wumman."

"She's deed!"

"She's no deed, but she's awfu' near it."

With none of his inborn good manners evident, Bruce forced his way to the leaders of the group, who now made slow progress across the steading, carefully bearing a hammock. On it lay the frighteningly still figure of a woman—a woman Bruce knew at once to be Kirsty Brodie. With a strangled cry of pain, he stumbled to his knees as the stretcher carriers recognized him and allowed him access. Pressing his ear to the blanket-covered chest, he listened as a voice, more authoritative than any of the others, spoke out: "She's alive, Reverend, but only just. Thon storm must have battered her aboot like a broken doll, but she's not been conscious enough to tell us ony facts." Neal MacLeod's suspicion that this tinker woman was more than a squatter on the MacAlister's houseboat was being confirmed very definitely as he looked deeply into the pain-wracked eyes of his friend.

"Can we bring her in the house now?" Wearing the bewildered look of the totally surprised, Bruce moved aside as the men carried their still burden inside.

Liz Ward took control and directed the bearers into the parlor, the room most often used to hold the sick. Her thought that it had been used far too much recently was echoed by her husband as he stood beside her and watched the men gently place the strange woman on the couch. An old and very ragged pair of men's trews still clung to the thin frame, and Jimmy Henderson could have told of the tattered strips of a waterproof he had watched the policeman tear away from the woman before he bent to examine her for signs of life. Those signs were faint and meager as the nurse in Liz reached for her stethoscope and thermometer. Her experience in the amputee ward of the Glasgow Infirmary had already conveyed to Liz that the strange person was comatose and had a skull depression that could indicate brain damage. She spoke those words softly, but no one understood except Bruce MacAlister, who promptly came out of his own dwam and repeated the phrase.

"Brain damage? Could that mean she'll not be recalling what's happened?"

"Reverend, we don't know enough to say that. I'm not a doctor, but I do know that amnesia comes in many different varieties, from minor memory loss, lasting a few days or weeks, to complete and permanent loss of memory. We could be praying that this is the former."

So intent on the problem as not to notice how he was being reminded to pray, Bruce once more surveyed the room and those crowding round the couch and even bursting through the arched doorway.

Liz saw this at the same time. "Could we have quiet and some privacy in here, if you please?"

Dorrie Henderson, who helped look after the orphans in the homes and who had been staring with wondering eyes at the inert form on the couch, swooped on her charges. The children, having felt the sting of her tongue and even the weight of her hand at times, when they were tardy to obey, rushed from the room. Soon only the Wards and Bruce stood beside the couch, although the constable hovered at the door.

Neal coughed politely before saying, "Reverend Bruce, could I ask you to give me some information about the late occupants of your houseboat? We don't even ken the name of the deceased."

Bruce ran his fingers through his hair as he puzzled over the policeman's question. "Of course, Neal, just give me a minute first."

Jeremy murmured that he would go to fetch hot water and towels while Liz went in search of some clothing for the stranger.

Suddenly Bruce was alone with the person who, he was now ready to admit to himself, had occupied his every waking moment and much of his sleep, too, for the last few months. However, he might just as well have been gazing at an effigy of a crusader, for all the movement he observed.

A dry sob escaped him as he prayed, "Is this my answer then, Lord? Is this one going to die as well?"

He leaned closer to see better. Loosened braids of raven-black hair spread across the pillow. The shapely head he remembered was now marred by an ugly concave gash over the right eyebrow, extending to the ear on that side. Otherwise Kirsty's face was not marked, but her arms where the shirtwaist had been ripped through showed some cruel bruising. Where visible through the torn trews, her legs showed deep gashes and weals that would be excruciatingly painful, were the body able to feel anything. Nothing stirred in the room now as he knelt beside the couch of the woman he had hoped to woo and someday ask to become his wife.

His prayer was brief: "Lord Jesus, who rose again from the dead, I pray for the life and wholeness of Kirsty Brodie. Lord, she needs to know You, to learn how full of grace You are. I, who have known and experienced Your miracles, do now beseech You for one more. Make Kirsty every whit whole, Jesus. I ask it in Your Name, Lord, believing. Thank You, Lord! Amen!"

At that moment Liz reentered the room, carrying the tools and equipment of her healing trade. She spoke with that same authority she had used on her wards many times, "I must ask you to leave now, Reverend. My patient requires attention without spectators. Don't worry, I'll be letting you know when and if she comes round!"

Neal MacLeod awaited Bruce in the kitchen, and Bruce spared a moment to wonder where the gaggle of children and the others had disappeared to. His smile was grim as he tried to answer the lawman's questions. "Their name is *Brodie*, Neal. The father was *Matthew* and the daughter *Kirsty*. The only clue I have to where they lived originally is a story I heard from Kirsty some months ago. I do believe their former home was in Lanarkshire, Motherwell to be exact. But that's all I know. Perhaps the *Revelation* will tell us more."

Neal was shaking his head. "I'm sorry, Bruce, but the *Revelation* will not tell us much. Although the outside doesna look too bad, the inside is burnt and black. If you want, though, we could go and see it the now. There's still time before dark." Bruce glanced at the connecting door leading to the parlor, and Neal followed his gaze.

"She's in the best of hands, and Aloysius is bringing the doctor. Och, I near forgot. Lachie Calder, the undertaker, ye ken, is bringing a helper to the boat. They'll be removing the deceased to the mortuary, pendin' identification. If you can identify it, though, that would save a lot of bother."

-·◦⋙{ 5 }⋘◦·-

The late Matthew Brodie appeared surprisingly unmarked, but the pathos of the leg with the missing foot almost unmanned Bruce. He nodded his affirmative that this must be Brodie, and his voice came muffled as he remarked, "I had thought to see more burns, Neal!"

"Aye . . . , well, I think the body must've slipped under the steel frame of the bunk as the boat heaved in the water, Reverend. 'Tis still smoky in there, and I havna' had a thorough search yet. I can say this, though: There's no' much left of yer braw cabin." Bruce raised a hand to protest, and Neal covered the body again with the sailcloth shroud, leaving the head exposed. Then he walked to the rail.

He failed to hear Bruce's whispered words, "Cabins can be re-placed but not folk. I'll not need to ask for your daughter now, Matt Brodie. I've the feeling you would have approved, though not before I had proved myself." He sighed deeply for the sadness of the seemingly wasted life. "Anyway, Matt, from what Kirsty told me, you were a good father to her, and God in His infinite mercy is far above our human understanding. Dear Jesus, I do commit this man to that mercy, amen!" A sudden shout from Neal brought Bruce's attention to the present situation.

"Och, I thought I heard a boat. Here's Lachie, an' he's brought the smithy. We'll have nae bother gettin' the deceased back to the town in the boat. Big Richie is strong as an ox, and as you ken, when the weather's this fine, rowing's the quickest road tae Aribaig."

The black-clad figures gave only grunted greetings as they

boarded the *Revelation*. Then the smaller man said, "Can we get on wi' it then, Neal? 'Tis dry the now, but as I was just sayin' to Richie here, I can smell snaw in the air. Has the corpse been identified?"

Neal approached Bruce, who still appeared to be in deep thought. "Excuse me, Reverend MacAlister, but if ye'll just repeat who the man is, in front of the witnesses here—that he was your eh, ah, guest on yer boat. The men here will take him back to Aribaig and prepare him for decent burial. The parish has funds for such and—"

Bruce again held up his hand. "I have to say this: Although I never met Matthew Brodie in life, I'm positive, from his daughter's descriptions, that this is indeed he. About the plan for burial, from what I learned of Brodie from his daughter, Kirsty, he would want to be buried at sea, and she, if she were able, would agree to that. She would not agree to a charity burial in the beggar's plot, as it is. I'll take care of all the expenses myself, gentlemen!"

This was becoming too much for Neal to fathom. He turned back to the undertaker, who thought he saw his fee vanishing like mist on a summer's morning. "Maist irregular, Neal. As ye ken, we can only sanction sea burials when the deceased is a sailor, and the family gie's permission. . . . I canna see—"

Bruce turned to the speaker. "Lachie Calder, is it not? Good day to you, sir. With all due respect, may I remind you that the man's daughter is far too ill to sanction anything? As for the irregularity, I, as a minister of the kirk, will take full responsibility for it. I can perform a sea burial as easily as a land one, and I'll make sure you receive your fee. You, too, Richard."

Neal still seemed disturbed. "It's no' right, Reverend. I'm no' sure at all. But anyway we'll need to take him to the mortuary first. Doctor Clarkson might have better news aboot the woman, and we could keep it in the mortuary for a day or two in this cauld weather, richt, Lachie?"

Mollified slightly, but not appeased, the man nodded. "Aye, as long as we've no other deaths. I would need a special form signed, and so will the doctor."

A shout came from the blacksmith, "Never heed a' that. It's started to snaw, an' if we're rowin' hame, I'm leavin' this minute!"

He marched toward the shrouded figure and grasped it as he would a sack of potatoes. Without ceremony he dumped his burden over the side, into the smaller craft. It rocked dangerously for a moment, and Bruce thought ironically that the body would have its sea burial, without any form or ceremony. The boat righted itself, and the two men climbed down the rope ladder and took up their oars.

Bruce and Neal together gazed at the sky for a moment before the lawman commented, "He's right aboot the weather, Bruce. Should we no' leave as well?"

The patient Clydesdales waited where they had been loosely tethered, and after making sure Neal was safely seated on the other horse, Bruce got himself onto Samson's back. Soon they reached the steading. A chaise, with the pony still in the shafts, stood beside the front steps, and Bruce wondered briefly why the animal had not been unhitched and fed.

Neal enlightened him: "The new doctor's aye in a hurry, an' he'll not allow strange hands to touch or feed his horse."

Bruce's thoughts flew at once to the doctor's patient. What would the verdict be?

Dr. Clarkson placed his stethoscope carefully into his Gladstone bag, unwilling to admit yet that this case had him baffled. Liz Ward, trying to follow the Mains Farm tradition for hospitality, had offered tea, but had still not received a spoken answer. She walked behind him from the sickroom, her nurse's training foremost as she waited.

"Concussion! Severe! Exposure, mild enough. She must've been sheltered from the worst o' it. Other injuries, external and minor, look worse than they are!" Disapproval edged his tone as he surveyed the hushed occupants of the kitchen. Bad enough that his plans for his day off had been upset by the urgent call from MacLeod, but to have to drive out to the Mains and tend a tinker woman, with this martinet of a nursing sister knowingly watching his every move, he found hard to thole.

Putting on her best hospital manner, Liz asked, "What do you recommend then, Doctor?"

He almost growled, "Nothing much. Feed her gruel and keep her warmly happed up. Try to keep the room quiet. She'll no doot be cleaner and better fed than she's ever been!"

Liz bristled. Although not approving of this squatter woman herself and still very puzzled as to how she ever became a resident of the MacAlister's boat, Liz nonetheless sided up with her against this prig of a doctor.

Knowing her place, Liz said none of this. "Thank you, Dr. Clarkson. . . . By the way, seeing you're here at the Cormack Homes anyway, could I trouble you to take a look at one of the children? They all seem healthy enough, but I'm worried about—"

"Certainly not, Sister, I mean, Mistress Ward! I've agreed to come here today only because this is official police business. Bring any ailing orphans to my surgery—and see they're clean first! Good day to you!"

Furious, first with herself for asking and then with him for such blatant cheek, Liz stood speechless. Moments later she heard voices in the lobby: Her husband's and the deeper tones of the MacAlister mingled with those of the doctor and the policeman.

Setting her anger aside, she went to join them. Quickly reaching Jeremy's side, she heard Bruce say, "Will you not come back in then, Doctor? I'd like to hear your diagnosis on Miss Brodie, and I'm sure there's a drop of tea or something ready." He glanced at Liz as he said this, but she avoided his eyes.

"No thank ye, Reverend. I've a lot to do the day yet. Being the only doctor and coroner doesn't leave me much time for socializin'. About the tinker woman, she'll mend. She's gye fortunate to have yersel' and the nurse here. She might waken up dizzy and forgettin' things, but that shouldna last long. . . . I'll be goin' then. Are ye comin' wi' me, Constable?"

Neal scrambled up beside him, and seconds later they could hear the clop of horse's hooves as they clattered over the bridge.

Jeremy shivered. "He's telling the truth about not socializin', I'll grant ye that! Come away inside. If he doesna want a cup of tea, some of us do."

Obediently the others followed him indoors. The immense kitchen table that Bruce remembered so well from his own childhood was laden with dishes and food. Young Hannah scuttled back and forth from the scullery area, while another woman, whom Bruce recognized as Mistress Blodwin Parker, stood by his mother's prized possession, the paraffin stove. A delicious smell arose from the variety of pots and pans resting on the top of it, and even as he watched, the woman bent over and opened the oven door.

A rush of cinnamon met Bruce's nostrils now, and he had to turn away again as he realized the reason for the spicy aroma. Rice pudding with all the trimmings. He prayed silently. "O Lord, what is this all about? Give me strength, if you please." The company sat staring in his direction, and Bruce realized someone had asked him a question.

Jeremy nudged his elbow.

"What? Oh, aye. Please be seated, everyone, as I ask the Lord to bless the food and us. Then if you'll excuse me, I'll not join you just yet." Jeremy threw him another look, but he ignored it as he began to say the grace. When the chattering began, slowly at first, but gradually increasing as the chidren and adults settled to filling their plates, he left the room.

Kirsty still lay as the doctor had left her. Dorrie Henderson sat on a stool facing the woman on the couch. She rose now. "Reverend MacAlister, I'm not sure, but I think she opened her eyes for a minute and blinked just now."

"Did she so then, Dorrie? I'll watch for a wee while myself. You go and get your tea."

"I will in a minute. How is Mary Jean—or should I say Mistress Douglass?"

"You were right saying *Mary Jean*, Dorrie. You're her best friend outside of her family, and she loves you dearly. Anyway, she's just fine, and I should be asking you about how you're getting on here at the Cormack Homes. Things have been so hectic since I arrived, with all that's been going on."

"Aye. Don't worry about me, Reverend. I like it fine here. Mistress Ward is strict, but she's fair enough, and I enjoy the bairns. Ye knew we got a new bunch just last week?"

"I knew, but I'm afraid I've forgotten to ask or to meet the newcomers. I'll set that right—maybe the morrow."

A noise from the couch brought them both to attention, and Dorrie touched Bruce's arm as she whispered, "I'll away and help in the kitchen then. Mistress Ward is the great organizer, and Mistress Parker a rare guid cook, but they canna handle the wee ones since the new bairns arrived. Can I talk to you after? I want to ask you something else."

Nodding absently, Bruce hardly heard her. His eyes were riveted on the pale face that had haunted his dreams and many of his waking moments for the past few months. Had she moved her eyes? Yes, he was not mistaken, her eyes did open, and he found himself gazing into their deep-green depths. Was there understanding there or not? For moments he knew there was, and a faint flicker of a smile, before they clouded over and became blank, even vacant.

He knelt beside the bed for the second time that day. Grasping the limp hand, he said, "Oh, Kirsty, I'm that sorry. I should've spoken up the first time I saw you and felt that spark between us. I'm sure you felt it, too. Och, why could I not have said something then? Forgive me, I know you're my love. I want to make up to you for all the horror you've been through, this past week and before that. Come out of it. Come to me. I've such plans. We can be married. I care not what folks say. We can go far away together and explore the world and laugh and sing together and. . . . Oh, what am I saying? God, help me! Help Kirsty—or better yet, help me to help Kirsty."

A peat fell over in the grate, but otherwise no sound could be heard in the room as he lifted his head and, still gently clutching the hand, gazed tenderly but intensely at her face. The lids flickered again, revealing the well-remembered intense green. All at once her lips began to move. The words coming forth were not original or in any way connected to his earnest declaration: "Where am I, and who are you?"

6

At first Bruce wanted to shout for Liz, but he quickly changed his mind, deciding to keep her to himself for a while instead. Kirsty's eyes had clouded over in deep concentration and showed no sign of recognition, although the intelligence he knew to be part of her still shone through.

He risked a question: "Kirsty, can you hear me?"

Nothing changed in the expression, but her lips moved again. Then in a low husky voice, she mouthed the words carefully, "Yer talkin' . . . to . . . me?" He choked on his reply, "I am that!" The puzzled frown darkened her face, but before she could form another question, Bruce continued, "Don't try to speak yet, Kirsty, my dear, and don't try to fathom out what I'm going to say. Just listen, and I'll tell you what I know of this. At least I'll answer your questions one at a time and as simply as possible. You asked where you are the now. Well, you're in a farmhouse in the highland parish of Aribaig that's in the process of being changed into an orphanage."

He stopped for breath, noting the closed eyes, but they opened again at once, and he continued, "Your head was hurt after you were caught out on the cliffs in a bad storm. A doctor has examined you, and he says you'll mend in no time if you stay quiet and rest. As for your other question of who I am, I'm part owner of this farm, and I'm here visiting the now. Farming is not how I make my living. I'm a minister on leave from the kirk. That's all I'll say at present, except to tell you your name is *Kirsty* and mine is *Bruce*. The mistress of this house is your nurse. She is called Mama Ward, and she'll be vexed if she thinks I've upset you. Lie still now, or I'll be in for the harsh side of her tongue."

As he spoke the last sentence he reached to keep Kirsty from trying to get up. Moving was beyond her capabilities, and her eyes flashed from an almost frantic appeal for help before she subsided once more and closed them.

Bruce breathed a quiet prayer. "Oh dear Lord, what will I do now?"

"For what my opinion is worth, Reverend, I think you should go and take some sustenance." The voice came from behind him. "Then you should rest yourself for a while. You've been a long time out your bed, and you've been through a lot since then. We've settled the young ones for the night, and Blodwin and Dorrie have your room all ready, under strict instructions from my husband. He knows you very well, I find. . . . No, Reverend, not just now. We can discuss it more in the morning."

"Thank you, Liz. Come to think of it, I am tired and a wee bit hungry. First let me tell you that your patient was conscious for a short spell, maybe fifteen minutes altogether. She asked me two questions, which I tried to answer as simply and as briefly as I—"

Liz placed a finger to her lips in a gesture to silence him; then signaling with her eyes, she motioned him to the corner farthest from the couch. "We've always contended that comatose patients hear and understand every word. Keep that in mind, Reverend, when you discuss her condition. The questions were of a sensible nature then?"

"Not completely sensible. She doesn't know where she is or who I am. She doesn't seem to remember the storm or anything before today. Her vocabulary is very limited, I might add."

"I wish you had called me in when she came round. But never mind that now. She'll start to come out of it soon, and I'll be able to discover if she has true amnesia or if it's only a temporary lapse of memory due to the concussion. Please do as I ask, or we'll have two patients to tend."

With a final lingering glance at the still figure on the couch, Bruce acquiesced meekly. Yes, Kirsty was in excellent hands, and he could do no more tonight. In the morning he would reassess the whole situation.

But the next morning brought further complications. Taylor the Post arrived at his usual hour, but today a complete stranger followed him into the steading. Taylor scolded the other man, "You wait outside until I tell the reverend you're here and whit you want. He micht no' wish to speak to ye at all. Ye've an awful cheek as it is to follow me fae toon." The other man merely smiled, but he did stop as instructed.

Taylor explained to Bruce, ending, "I only said he could come when he told me he would make up his ain story from what Richie MacKenzie—the blacksmith, ye ken—had tellt him. I thought it would be best if he got the rights of it from yer ain sel'!"

"Very wise, Taylor, and I appreciate it. How these reporter fellows hear about such matters so fast is a mystery to me. . . . You're right, though, it will be better if we tell him the true story as far as we know it. Bring him in. A cup of tea might be the very thing for us all."

"Afore he comes in, here's a note from Neal. Maybe you should read it first."

Bruce read the few lines quickly and frowned. "I'll give you a reply to take, although I'm not sure I know myself how to proceed. Miss Brodie seems to be recovering, but she has lost her memory, at least for the now. The lack of other family members seems to place me in the position of making this decision about her late father. Lord, help me. Never mind a note then, Taylor. Tell Neal I'll be in to town later today. Ask him if he can arrange for Reverend Welch to be there. I'll also need to have a further talk with the doctor. Now let's face the reporter. You did say he's from the *Inverness Courier*?"

"Thanks for the tea, Reverend MacAlister. I remember you fine; I was a cub reporter at the time. But when I heard your name in connection with this story, I took the liberty of searching the archives from twenty years ago. You were involved in a miracle then, were you not?"

Bruce groaned. Would he never hear the end of that?

"Some called it a miracle, yes."

"May I ask what you called it then?"

"It did appear to be a miraculous event, to be sure, and I do believe in miracles, but I don't approve of reporters who make them sound like circus acts. What did you want to know today, Mr. Jackson?"

"Is it true that you let out your houseboat to a tinker and his daughter? They say they were using it for contraband purposes, and when they heard you were on your way back, they tried to burn it down. But the man got himself trapped in the smoke, and now she's—"

Bruce erupted in anger. "Rubbish! In the first place, my guests on the houseboat are not tinkers, and second, nobody knew I was on my way home. The fire was an accident brought on by the freak storm and—"

"Beggin' your pardon, Reverend, I'm sure, but folk are saying the woman—"

Bruce was shouting now. "Folk are saying! Folk are saying! You newspapermen are all alike—printing sensationalism and melodrama from hearsay, with no thought that it's people's lives you're tampering with or that your words might cause matters to erupt and go into a chain of events that sorely affects those lives!" His raised voice had brought Jeremy and Liz rushing into the kitchen, and through the doorway he could see an almost frantic Dorrie trying to keep a bunch of frightened children in order. Suddenly his anger subsided.

The reporter, although far from finished, wore a satisfied smile. "My, my! Reverend, I've found in my experience, that when folks I'm talkin' to get that riled up, it must be because I've hit on the truth or some other sensitive area. . . ." He held up a hand as Bruce once more started to speak. "Oh, it's all right, I'm leaving. I think I've heard all I need for my story."

Belated wisdom came to Bruce as he heard Liz say to the departing reporter, "You'll not print from rumors or the reverend's reactions. He's been under a lot of strain and not had enough sleep. . . . I—" She stopped as her husband shook his head at her.

When the man had gone, Jeremy broke out, "We'll need to pray that he'll forget or that the Lord will blind his eyes and ears for a bit. Sometimes I think they don't need to ask a thing. Their own imaginations can do it all."

A loud groan from Bruce brought everyone's attention to him. His hand covered a deeply furrowed brow as he chastised himself, "All I've done is give him grist for the mill of his word machine. Whatever he writes about me after this, I'll only have myself to blame. You're right, Jeremy, we'll pray that only the truth will prevail in that newspaper." Bruce's face cleared. "We cannot make a better of it, the day. How is our patient, Liz?"

"Blodwin is with her. She's awake but still very dazed. She wants to feed herself, but she's not able to hold the spoon. I think she's forgotten how to eat properly as well as a few other things. I hope I'm wrong, but she seems to have reverted to the ways and manners of a child of about four years old."

These words proved only too true, but as the hours—then the days—passed, small signs of improvement became evident in Kirsty Brodie, although she had no idea she was that person.

Meanwhile Bruce had met Neal and the Reverend Welch. After some discussion, Welch agreed that he could find no fault in the request for a sea burial. Arrangements were made, and he, together with Bruce, performed the short ceremony. A substantial sum of money changed hands. Lachie and his sidekick Richie were delighted with it. The latter could not keep it to himself though and later had no compunction about accepting more from the nice gent from Inverness, a Mr. Jackson. For that, he only had to tell his version of the day they had gone out to the *Revelation* for the body and how the Reverend Bruce MacAlister had been in such a hurry to bury the man at sea.

At the Mains, Bruce began, laboriously at first, to teach Kirsty Brodie about herself and the people and places surrounding her.

One of her first questions concerned clothes. "Kirsty wants trews, the same as yours," she demanded.

A scandalized Liz, entering the room at that moment, rapped out, "Certainly not, the very idea!"

Bruce turned away to hide a sad smile. Motioning to Liz, he propelled her to the corner of the room and asked, "Would you not consider that a good sign? She may be more familiar with men's clothing. After all, that's what she was wearing when they found her."

"That does not make it right. She is confused enough without her getting the idea that we are all alike."

Crimson with embarrassment, Bruce returned to the couch. He tried to explain, "Ladies wear skirts, and gentlemen wear trews. You are a lady, so we will be expecting you to wear a dress or a skirt. Mistress Ward will bring you something."

"What for? Kirsty wants trews, and Kirsty wants tea!" Here was another disconcerting fact. She had quickly learned to string words together, but otherwise her behavior resembled that of a fractious child.

Bruce spoke soothingly now, "Yes, you will get your tea, but first one of the ladies will help you to get dressed. Mama Ward is a nurse, and she thinks you are well enough to try to get up."

Immediately he regretted his words, as Kirsty threw aside the covers and pushed her legs off the bed. The nightgown she wore scarcely reached her knees. He hurried to fetch Liz and Dorrie.

"Help her get dressed, Dorrie. Maybe you can find something of my mother's, as Miss Brodie is about the same height as Mam."

Dorrie pursed her lips. *Miss Brodie* indeed! Dorrie had little patience with the newcomer. A grown woman acting up like a bairn. Dorrie considered it all just a big put-on.

"The maid says the lady that wore they frocks before was your mother. What's a *mother*?" asked Kirsty later.

Bruce stared. Could this be the beginning of what the doctor had begrudgingly explained might happen?

"When true and extensive memory loss occurs, the person reverts to a childlike state. *Retards* would be my word," he had explained when Bruce consulted him, shortly after Matt's burial. To the question of what could be done he had shrugged. "Not much! Just wait, if you've the patience. It could be years. If I had my say, I would put her away. She could be an imbecile for life!"

Noting Bruce's shock at this, he amended it slightly: "If they start askin' intelligent questions, there's a bit hope. It also could be put on, ye ken. She's better tended now than she's been all her life, nae doot? You're gye concerned aboot this woman, are ye not, Reverend?"

"Yes, I intend to marry her!" His reply had been a shout.

This time the doctor's horror could not be hidden, and he rose from his desk. "I've patients, who need me, waiting." The uneasy interview had ended.

Returning his thoughts to the present situation, Bruce decided to keep his answers simple and true. "A mother is the person who cares most about you until you are able to care about yourself and then—"

A screech greeted his words. "No! She wouldna care about me. She hated me for—"

Bruce grasped the flailing hands. Maybe this was the first sign of returning memory? "It's all right, Kirsty. Tell me what you remember about your own mother."

But the blank look had come back, and she merely pushed at his hands. "Kirsty wants her tea! You said if I let them dress me, I could have my tea!"

He sighed and resumed his attempt at filling in her empty spaces. "Dorrie is bringing your tea and mine. Do you remember what I told you yesterday, when you asked me who Dorrie was?"

"Aye, she's a friend of Mary Jean's. Mary Jean is your own lass, who is a wife to a doctor. What's a doctor, and does Mary Jean have a mother?"

"Very good, Kirsty. You remember a lot of things. A doctor is a man who is trained in a special way to help sick people."

"I'm sick. Will he help me?"

"You're not truly sick, Kirsty, and I'm sure Jamie—that's the doctor we're speaking of now—I'm sure he would help you, if he could."

Kirsty behaved with surprising docility next time Bruce saw her. His heart gave a double lurch as he recognized one of his mother's good frocks, but he quickly put that aside as he noted how the style suited the other woman.

She was frowning deeply as she pulled at the ribbons on the waist. "It's all black. Kirsty likes frock, but Kirsty wants red ribbons, maybe tartan."

He stared at her in surprise. Tartan, how did she know about red and tartan ribbons? He asked the question, but the vague look had returned, and she could not understand what he said. He tried something else. "Do you think you can still read, Kirsty?"

Her face brightened. "Aye!"

"I've some books in the attic you might want to try." She leaned her head back on the big chair, and he walked quickly through the kitchen toward the attic steps. Liz gave him a questioning glance, and he told her his errand.

She replied with a doubting, "Start her with your first reader then."

"Do you mean to say, Liz, that she'll need to learn everything over again?"

"Maybe not everything, Bruce. I put her now at the level of a five-year-old, a *fractious* five-year-old, I might add." She had glanced at her sister-in-law as she spoke, and Blodwin nodded agreement. In fact Blodwin thought her own five-year-old behaved much better than this black-haired beauty.

"What's to be done? The doctor isn't much help." Bruce wore his troubled frown, and Liz avoided his gaze.

"I believe we're doing all we can. The one similar case I'm re-calling took a while. I'm afraid it's going to be a long, hard road!"

"Maybe I should send for Peter or Jamie?" Intent on the prob-lem, Bruce failed to note the glance that passed between Jeremy and Liz. If the couple thought Bruce afforded too much fuss to this transient person, they were too polite to say so and tried to be discreet, because Bruce MacAlister—the sensible, the matter-of-fact, well-mannered, good-natured, and kind Christian minister—could turn into a raging ptarmigan when it came to this Kirsty.

Blodwin amazed them all by saying now, "We'll need to do something. It's not good for the little ones to hear her goings on, and it's not good for us or her either. Maybe you should tell your doctor friends about her and see what they advise."

Bruce nodded without comment. Up in the attic he found the kist with the books, and he selected a few. His first reader cer-tainly, but some others as well, including *Pilgrim's Progress*.

Everything seemed fine with the picture books, until they came to a page about trains. Kirsty snatched up the book and threw it violently to the floor. "Kirsty not like trains. Trains hurt Kirsty!"

Again, not sure whether to be sorry or glad, Bruce calmly picked up the dog-eared volume before asking, "What do you know about trains, Kirsty? When did they hurt you?"

This time her mobile face held a thoughtful expression before she answered, "Kirsty not know. Not want train picture. Hurt Kirsty."

Bruce made a decision. With no true experts to guide him, he must just fish in the dark and pray the Lord's wisdom, but he would begin to take some risks. "I think I know why you dislike trains, Kirsty, and I'm going to tell you a true story now. We'll put the books away for the day."

7

"**D**o you know what I mean when I say *family*, Kirsty?" Her frown of deep concentration gave him pause, but he persisted. "Do you then?"

"Kirsty not know!"

"I'm going to tell you the stories of two families. First your family and then my own. Some of it will be sad, and you may want to weep, but that's all right."

Her look became one of keen anticipation, then to his complete amazement, she left her chair and plumped herself down on the rug in front of him. Before he could move, she had pressed her head against his knee. At once he realized that she must either be taking up a position familiar to her as a child, or she could simply be imitating Mellie, the dog, who sometimes had this privilege. Instinctively, he reached a hand to pat the shiny head. What harm could there be in showing some affection?

"Once, maybe thirty years ago—I'm not sure of the exact dates for your family, Kirsty Brodie—you were born. To be born you needed a father and a mother, so we know you had both. You lived in a town called Motherwell, and your father—you used to call him your da'—went to work every day on the railway."

At the word *railway* she jerked her head and twisted round to face him. The deep green of her eyes held such a look of pain that he wondered if he should continue. It lasted only a moment, and she quickly resumed her earlier position.

He continued, "On Fridays your da' would bring home his pay— that's the money you get for your work—and then your whole family would plan how to spend it. After the necessary weekly

54

matters were paid and the savings set aside, you would have your own shilling."

Once again her head jerked round, and he leaned over to catch the whispered words. Incredulously he thought he heard, "Only sixpence"! Could she truly be coming back to herself? Or could the doctor and Dorrie have the rights of it, in saying that she was putting on an act? He shrugged the unworthy thought away.

"Do you like this story, Kirsty?"

The reply took so long he thought she must have dozed off and then, "Kirsty like more story."

"Do you understand now about family?"

She searched the room with her eyes. Her voice sounded distant. "Aye! Da', mother, Kirsty, Bruce, family!"

He laughed shortly. "Not Bruce. I belong to a different family." His mind whirled. His own family and relationships could not be explained so simply.

Yesterday he had taken Kirsty to see the animals. This year's crop of lambs were almost fully grown, and no calves had been born recently. Somehow young David Parker had unearthed a litter of kittens at their most lovable, if most capricious, stage. The playful balls of fur had romped and rolled over in the hay. Kirsty had laughed and reached out for the orange one David held cradled in the crook of his arm. At once a tiny barbed paw had swatted her, piercing the skin, and she quickly reciprocated with a hefty swipe, sending the furry creature flying into the hay. A scuffle ensued as David retrieved the kitten while Bruce led a weeping Kirsty back to the house.

Later Bruce had taken David aside to explain, as well as he could, about Kirsty. The lad seemed to understand, so Bruce had recruited him to introduce some of the other children to Kirsty. One at a time they came forward, and she had met Paige Parker; Hannah, now officially named *Ward*; Howie Ward, the silent one; and then small Susan Parker, who came forward to shyly offer her toy lamb. Kirsty had snatched the toy without so much as a thank-you and had not let it out of her clasp since. She appeared at this moment to be dozing against his knee, but she still clutched the stuffed animal. He moved slightly to ease a cramp.

She glanced up at him, wide awake. "Bruce, family, mother, da'?"

No easy way round this, so Bruce, only too glad that she at least remembered this much, began again, " 'Twould be more than forty-five years ago now that I, Bruce MacAlister, was born in this very steading, in another room ben the house. My mother, Elspeth by name, lived here then, with my father, John MacAlister, and my grandfather—we called him Gran'pa Bruce. The house was much smaller in those days, and we didn't have so many byres and barns outside. I mind when I was a wee lad I had to get up early in the morning and go to help Mam milk the cow and fetch the water and other odd jobs like that."

The head on his knee nodded briskly. Jobs she knew, as she learned them from a slightly sulky Dorrie.

"Well, anyway, a family starts with a father and a mother. Then come the children, usually one at a time. Do you understand a bit better now, Kirsty?" But this time Kirsty had fallen asleep.

Bruce sat on for a few more minutes, savoring this rather pleasant domestic scene. Then he began to pray, "Lord Jesus, only You can help us to help Your child Kirsty. I pray for patience with this task of bringing her memory back, if that is what is needed. If not, then help me bring her at least to the stage of adult maturity that she had before the storm. Lord, You knew my intentions when I left Glasgow. They seem far away now, but I'll not be giving up hope. No matter how long it takes, I feel that this very moment holds a prophecy of how Kirsty and I will be related some day in the future." A shuffle in the doorway announced the entry of Liz and Jeremy, so he added a silent amen. "Bruce, Mama Liz and I have been discussing Kirsty," Jeremy told him. "Och, 'tis all right if she hears this. 'Tis for her benefit. As you know, Blodwin and Dorrie have been teaching Kirsty some simple tasks about the house, and she's been doin' well at them, but we've been thinking maybe she could be with the children a bit more. Sometimes little ones have a clearer way of putting things and. . . . Well, what do you say?"

Bruce glanced at Kirsty, but she had sunk into her almost usual state of apathy. He answered his foster brother, "Could we wait until she's more alert, before putting this to her? I've been covering a lot of strange ground with her this morning, and she seems exhausted!"

Liz gave a loud "hurmf," and Jeremy admonished her mildly, "Now, Liz, 'twas your own self that said we should not upset your patient."

"Yes, I did say that, but it's been a month now and very little sign of improvement."

"I think we must wait a while longer for signs. A wee bit every day is all we can hope for yet. What would the children do to speed this up?"

"Treat her more normally than we adults do. Maybe we have been using the soft treatment too much. Tomorrow, instead of the hour in the kitchen with Blodwin, she can go out to play with the younger children. Susan and Howie and Hannah—supervised by Dorrie of course."

A sound like a shriek came from Kirsty. "Kirsty not go out with Dorrie. Dorrie doesna like Kirsty!" Amazement, immediately replaced by an almost smug look, passed from Liz to her husband. Bruce's tone showed his shock. "Dorrie likes you fine, Kirsty. She's a busy lass and has little time for play. Maybe you should be with Hannah and the young ones. We can go and see what they're doing the now." With another of her quick changes of mood, Kirsty walked meekly behind him as he led the way outside.

Therefore the loud screech, followed by a series of screams, came as all the more of a surprise.

Bruce, busy writing a letter to Peter, describing Kirsty's strange symptoms and behavior and the other happenings at the Mains, rushed for the open door as he heard the uproar. The sight that met his astonished gaze seemed incredible. On the ground, a tangle of legs and arms wrestled madly in a pile of loose hay. More recognizable, Dorrie and Blodwin were unsuccessfully trying to separate the frenzied mass of the three Parker children, the girl Hannah, and one or two smaller children he didn't yet know by name. It dawned on him that they all sat precariously on top of what appeared to him to be a moving bundle of his mother's clothes. Not an empty bundle, but one containing a screaming, fighting ptarmigan, Kirsty Brodie. All this took him a few moments to comprehend.

Dorrie kept yelling as Blodwin sobbed out, "She is a vixen in human flesh. She tried to kill my David. O God, help us all."

Bruce grasped the hysterical woman's arm. "You're not helping one bit, Mistress Parker. It seems to me that the one being killed is not your David but is—"

He reached into the melee of bodies and extricated the largest boy. Standing David on his feet, he said, "You call your brother and sister off, and the others will stop!" The boy hesitated, and Bruce gave him a none-too-gentle shove toward the fight. The two dogs added to the chaos with their barking as David pulled at his brother's shirt, while his mother managed to grasp Susan.

Hannah, seeing the struggle was abating, jumped up and ran for the kitchen door, but Dorrie grasped her by the scruff of the neck as she passed. "You wait and tell us what happened."

While Bruce extricated a bruised and battered Kirsty from the ground, the dogs stopped their noise. She fell limply into his arms. A deep scratch ran across her face, from eye to chin, and Bruce shuddered. What had he done by sending her out to play with these young ruffians, after all she had suffered. Lifting Kirsty up, he walked toward the house, carrying her easily.

"We'll need a full explanation. David Parker, as you are the oldest here, I will hear your report as soon as we have rendered aid to Miss Brodie. It better be good." The bewildered and some very frightened children stood in a huddle round Dorrie now. She still held on to Hannah. "I'll not be waiting for the big investigation. Hannah, you tell me what happened."

Five voices piped up to respond, but Dorrie yelled out, "Shut yer faces the rest of ye. Ye'll get yer turn. Now Hannah."

"We were playin' at 'homes,' and I was Mama Liz, but she wanted to play at real families, wi' Howie as her bairn. He didna like that—"

Blodwin interjected, "You hit her, and she—"

"Naw, I just gave her a shove, and she went daft. Howie ran

away, and the next thing the Parkers were in it, to haud her doon. She's big, and she kicks and bites worse than Susan."

Susan was clinging to her mother's skirts while Blodwin examined young Paige for signs of injury. His crying drowned out all the others. Satisfied her second son would be fine, she turned to David. "Come inside, David, and give me the true story. If no one is badly hurt, I think we should all get back to our jobs. Hannah, I'm sure Dorrie can give you something better to do than fight."

"Hannah told you most of it, except that Howie was not feared. In fact he wanted to be Kirsty's bairn, but Hannah didn't like that. I wasn't playing at all. I was carrying a bundle of hay across for the horses, when it happened. I just wanted to get Susan and Paige out of it before they got hurt."

His mother looked at him fondly, hearing this, but Dorrie objected, "What were they doing then, joining in?"

"The daft woman had Susan's lamb, and Susan wanted it back. She went for it when the woman dropped it to fight Hannah. Paige was helping Susan."

Dorrie nodded and then turned her attention to the two silent waiting children: "Eddie and Katie Woods—what about you?"

The small girl hid behind her brother and waited. Did they not know that Eddie always won the fight in any gang, and he would prove it in this place? But this big woman had nearly pulled his hair out by the roots. He had jumped in then to punch and punch. Katie had just been trying to stop him when she got a clout on her own face.

Eddie would not answer Dorrie, so she used the weapon that worked with the orphans every time: "Nae tea 'til ye tell us."

He thought about that for a while and then decided a lie would serve the now rather than miss the good chuck they always had here. "I ken the wumman is no weel, and I didna want her to get hurted!"

Dorrie's glance betrayed her doubt of this, but things had gone far enough, she thought, and it was about time to resume the Christian atmosphere of this home. Besides, Mama and Papa Ward would be back from Aribaig soon. "Right ye are then. That's enough o' that. This time we'll not punish ye, but if this ever happens again, ye'll all be on bread and water for a whole day."

Blodwin thought better of arguing about this, and a semblance of peace once more descended on the Cormack Homes.

Inside Bruce still held Kirsty. He had used his hankie to wipe her streaming face, and then he had pushed back the unruly braids. They were a fearful weapon for an enemy to use, he thought, as he tenderly unwound the silky strands, all mixed up with mud and grit and bits of hay. She looked so pathetic lying there, yet Bruce had heard enough to know how well she could protect herself. Being outnumbered and still weak had made her the defeated in this brief but violent sortie. He groaned aloud. This could not go on, yet watching her every moment seemed impossible. Unless . . . but no, his honest heart would never allow him to marry her in this state. She would need to be back up to the Kirsty he had known before the storm. What then? A nursing attendant? That would not be well received either by Liz or Dorrie. Maybe he should take her to Glasgow and beg the help of . . . whom? Peter and Agatha had enough to care for with their own girl. Granny Mac was too old to be presented with a problem like this. Mary Jean was deeply involved with her pregnancy, and the baby was due at Easter—a mere six weeks away, he calculated. Cairnglen then? Faye Felicity Singh would be most understanding and would welcome Kirsty without prejudice, but she had a nine-year-old son to care for. Then it came in a flash: The Barnabas Hills! That childless couple's state of wedded bliss was another feather in his cap, since he felt responsible for their meeting and their courting. Deborah Hill had been raised in a doctor's home—a home with many problems. She would know what to do. Yes, that could be his answer.

"Thank You, Jesus!" he whispered as he once more looked down on what had become of the woman he loved and would someday have restored to him. She stirred in his arms. Her brilliant green eyes opened, and she dazzled him afresh with her angelic smile. Obviously all traces of the past hour had been obliterated.

"Tea for Kirsty and Bruce. . . . Family?"

He smiled back. It would be well. Maybe not today, but in the Lord's good time, it would be well.

-·◦◦❖{ **8** }❖◦◦·-

"**Y**ou're bound to have overheard me speaking to Kirsty, and I know you have both guessed my intentions toward her."

The Wards avoided his glance and each other's eyes as Bruce waited for some response. At last Jeremy answered, "Aye, we have that, Bruce, but to tell you the truth I'd hoped to be mistook. Are ye sure?"

"I'm sure, Jeremy, and have been for a long time now. Please try to understand. I feel Kirsty's life has been spared for a reason not yet revealed; but in the meantime, she and I have some more firing to endure. Anyway, I need your help. No, stay, please, Liz, this concerns both of you. I know you have a big responsibility here, with the Cormack Homes and the children, and I need to make other arrangements. My plan is to go to Cairnglen and see Barnie and Deb Hill. I'll be asking them to take Kirsty for a while, until she is more herself. Further than that I'll not say the now."

Liz Ward had not spoken since she and Jeremy had joined Bruce in his own room, at his specific request, for a private talk, but now she walked over to stand beside him. "At the risk of being accused of interfering, I'll just say this much, seeing you asked us in here. Yes, Jeremy and I have been dismayed at the signs of affection you've been showing this . . . , this, ah . . . , woman. Certainly take her to the couple you speak of, then leave her there, until she's well enough to continue in her own way of life. Make a settlement on her, if you feel some responsibility for what happened to the *Revelation*, but do no more than that. What you're planning will never work. Your stations in life are too far apart. She will not fit in either as a minister's wife in your kirk or with your own family. It would be hard enough, even had she been in good health, but a woman of her age, with a child's mind! If she is acting, that proves to me there's something far amiss with her. . . . Why—"

"Be quiet!" Bruce's voice rapped out the command so deliberately that at first Jeremy thought he could not have heard aright, but the harsh words rang out a second time. "Be quiet, woman! You've said quite enough! Who are you to talk to me like that and about the person I love and intend to marry someday? That part is none of your business. I asked for your help, not your bigoted advice."

Jeremy protested, "Bruce, I canna listen to you talkin' to my wife that way any longer. Certainly some of the things Liz said were wrong, but Bruce, I'm shocked at ye. What are things comin' to, I wonder?"

Bruce turned away then immediately turned to face them again. "You're right, Jeremy. I should not speak to your wife or any lady in that manner. My apologies, madam. Now, if you'll excuse me, I have some work to do."

But Liz had fled, and Jeremy walked more slowly toward the open door. Stopping as he reached it, he spoke, more gently this time, "Ye can safely leave yer Kirsty here, Bruce. I'll make sure she's cared for whilst you're away. We've took on another helper, to start the morrow. Her name is Isabella Og. Ye ken the family!"

Bruce merely nodded. He had much praying and seeking to do by himself before he would be leaving for Cairnglen. He saw now how he must take Kirsty away from here as soon as decently possible. He would try to be back for her within the week. Hopefully Deborah would return with him.

Jeremy still lingered. "Are ye mindin' that Rob Heriot and his family are due here, as well, before Easter? Ye've been so busy with eh, ah . . . , Miss Brodie—maybe ye havna noticed the school and the dominie's hoose are near ready. Jake and Jimmy and their crew of workmen are doin' a fine job."

"Aye, I have noticed the buildings' progressing, Jer. In fact I was over to congratulate Jake, earlier this morning. You're doing just fine, Papa Ward, with all you've had to do. I'm sorry if I've been too distracted to pay as much attention to the Cormack Homes as I would like. However, I am more interested than you may think. One of Rob's lassies is wanting to work with the bairns. Wait a wee while, and you'll find all will be well. God has a due season for this, too, you know."

"I do ken, Bruce, and I'll be that glad to pray for you and Kirsty. My wife still clings to her old ideas aboot class, but I could never sanction that, kennin' where I come from mysel'."

"It's all behind you, Jeremy, and I know you and Liz will sort your differences. Maybe you should speak up and tell her what you've told me. She knew of your humble beginnings, and that didn't stop her wanting to marry you." He did not add how the same Liz had been extremely anxious to marry Jeremy, in fact she had almost begged for the privilege. Instead he said, "In some ways your wife reminds me of Mam, Jeremy. Have you noticed that?"

"I have, Bruce—except for one or maybe two big differences." Wishing he had not mentioned it, Bruce continued to speak of his mother. "Jeremy, I've been meaning to ask you—in fact, if matters had gone more as I had planned when I came home this time, we would have had a good blether about it before now. Och, not about business or the homes, that's all settled. No, more about myself. I know my mother set great store in having a minister son, and as such I was happy, and aye, proud to be that. I can honestly say, too, that even if she encouraged me and always wanted that for me, it would not have worked if I had not fully agreed and felt the call on my own." He stopped speaking to glance at this brother by choice, but Jeremy merely nodded.

If Jeremy wondered what would come next, he gave no sign, as he said, "She knew that, too, Bruce."

"What I'm coming to, Jeremy, is that I wonder what she would say the day if she knew how unsettled I'm feeling."

Jeremy could no longer hide his amazement. "What are you meanin', Bruce? You're never goin' to leave the kirk?"

"I just do not know, Jeremy. If I did, it would all be so simple. Instead of a sabbatical, I would leave altogether, yet. . . . Oh, well, I get no peace about the idea of going overseas. I've thought of

China or Africa or even India, but nothing gives me that certainty, that knowing I feel I must have if it's a true calling."

Jeremy could think of nothing to add to this, and the two sat for a few more minutes in comradely silence. Bruce moved first. "My troubles are nothing compared to some others I could name." But he refrained from names, and Jeremy shifted the arm with the hook from his knee.

"Aye, but as Gran'pa Bruce would say—"

" 'We canna make a better o' it!' " They spoke the words in unison, ending in a laugh.

"He would have also told us to hold each other up in prayer the way they always did. I'll need it, because I know some others will be thinking as your wife thinks. Not Mary Jean, I'm sure, but— well, anyway, I'll be back from Cairnglen before the week is out, bringing Deb Hill, I trust. Good night Jeremy!"

"Aye, we'll be seein' ye in the mornin' then, Bruce!"

The railway line between Fort William and Aribaig had only a single track, and Bruce, arriving a half hour before his train was due, sat in the draughty waiting room, hunched up against the cold. He pulled the knitted muffler closer round his neck and gazed about. The northbound could be heard coming over the trestle, and he wondered idly how busy it might be on a Thursday morning. With a fussing and puffing, the three-carriage train stopped, and his wondering was answered as he saw two lone women being helped down by the aged porter. Only vaguely interested, he scarcely gave them a thought, except that they were city ladies by their dress, one in widow's weeds, with a veil hiding her face completely, the other by contrast wearing a bright-red leghorn hat. Losing interest, he remembered that his train would only be going up the line to one more station before it reached the shunt and the turnabout for the return trip.

The porter, finished with his escort job, as the women were now in the capable care of Geordie the cabman, suggested to the minister: "Why do ye no' jump in, Reverend? The train's near empty, and it'll be a lot warmer for ye." Bruce applauded the idea, and moments later he was doing just that. Mallaig, at the end of this line, was a bonny place, and maybe he would bring Kirsty here someday, when things were better. That started his imaginings as he realized he might never be able to take her anywhere in his own country. The beauty of mountain crag and rushy glen would have to take second place to his love. America, of course! Since leaving Glasgow, he had been so preoccupied with events as they happened that his earlier plan to visit the United States had faded. He allowed it to flood his mind now with the wonder of new hope and fresh beginnings. Craig Fairbanks, his newly discovered cousin, had assured him that his home in New Jersey was bonny, too.

"Lord, I'll take this year as a gift from you, and I'm going to stop guessing what folk will say about Kirsty or any of my other vague plans, no matter how many don't see it my way. I'll never allow anything to hurt my poor love. Lord, help me, I wish I were on my way back already. I've still got such a feeling of unease. Thank goodness Jeremy is on my side. What harm can come to her at the Mains?"

9

"**B**ut Maimie, are you sure this is the place? It looks like the folk are all sleeping—or worse yet, dead."

"Don't be daft, Nellie, Matt's letter said Aribaig, and that's what it says on the station sign. The bit in the paper as well says that's the place." The two women would have been surprised to know that the town folk were far from being dead and did not sleep. Eyes peered from behind lace curtains and between half-closed shutters as the strangers were noted. Back doors opened, and small children went scurrying to tell neighbors as curiosity rose and swelled to a climax.

It stopped at Mistress MacLeod, the policeman's wife, as she summed it up to the woman serving in the shop. "They must be here aboot something to do with Reverend MacAlister. That's a' I can think on. An' he's the one that rouses the botherations in the town. I'd better tell my man." But Neal already knew of the visitation, and he also knew that Bruce had departed on the train. He could say and do nothing with the newcomers until they asked for help of some kind. Seemingly they didn't need his assistance.

Geordie McDade had heard enough to form his own conclusions. " 'Tis the Mains Farm you ladies want then?"

They glanced at each other. "Did we not say the Cormack Orphanage?"

Geordie had superior knowledge. "They're wan and the same. What wance wis the Mains is turning into an orphanage. Who is it you want to see?"

But they had said all they were going to say for the time being. As the horse clipped along the road to the Mains, the women kept glancing at the bare landscape and back to each other. Finally the one who did most of the talking asked Geordie, "Are we getting close to the seashore then?"

Geordie gave a snort of a laugh. Pulling a doubtful-looking hankie out of his pocket, he wiped his eyes before replying, "No' us. We're goin' in the wrong direction for that. There's Loch Haven. 'Tis a sea loch, but you can only see it from the hill up there and only on a clear day." This seemed to satisfy, and as he glanced back he caught the other one giving her friend a warning nip. Thinking they might be worth watching, Geordie kept his eye on the ornate mirror at the side of his cab. It had proved useful on other occasions when questionable characters like these graced his vehicle. The women conversed between themselves the rest of the way, and the cabbie pretended not to hear.

As he helped them down outside the farmhouse, to the tune of dogs barking and bairns howling, Geordie managed to say, "Will ye be stayin' then?" The question was prompted by the fact that they only had one small valise between them.

This brought a worried sound from the one behind the veil as her companion answered, "That will not be concerning you, cabbie!"

"Two shillin'," was his prompt response to her cheek.

"Two shillings, that's robbery!" and, "Pay him, Nellie," sent him on his way over the Mains bridge. Thinking the traffic fair thickening about this place, Geordie McDade hurried back to town, passing a large supply wagon, then a moving van with what looked like a whole family hanging from every board, as well as a couple of men on bicycles. The cyclists he did recognize: Taylor the Post and young Gideon MacKenzie, the smith's second son. He'd heard tell, too, that young Gid was sparking one of the nursemaids. Och, the place was turning into a fair Sauchiehall Street.

Jeremy scratched his head in perplexity. Why did Bruce have to go today and leave him to sort out this conundrum? Liz was not helping a bit either. Two strange women sat in Elsepth's parlor. They had not been invited to take off their traveling coats, and he had almost had to push Liz out of the room to fetch a cup of tea.

He repeated their errand for the third time: "You're Mistress

Brodie, and you've come for Kirsty, your daughter, you say?" A
swift glance between the two, and the other one spoke, "She is,
and I'll vouch for that, as I'm her sister. Could we see the poor lass,
do you think?" Jeremy still hesitated. "We've been asked to look
after her until the Reverend MacAlister gets back."

The one calling herself Maimie Dickson fanned her face with a
folded page of newspaper. "You've all been very kind to my niece,
and we thank you, but we can take her home now and save you
any more bother."

Knowing he would be telling a lie if he said it was no bother,
Jeremy still hesitated. Not so Liz, who had returned, reluctantly
bearing a tea tray. "Miss Brodie will be back at any moment. Dorrie
took her for a walk with the other. . . . I mean with the children!
Cream and sugar?"

The one who claimed to be Kirsty's mother nodded that she
would take both but the other one shook her head. "No tea, thank
you. Maybe we could go to meet them."

Jeremy eyed their fancy footwear. "The field's gye mucky, and
she's not been too well. Maybe I should go mysel' and warn her."

The spokeswoman bridled. "Warn her of what? That her mother
and her aunt want to take her home? Has the poor lass not been
through a lot already, what with Matt and his funny ways and now
the accident? The paper said she had no memory of anything." Still
cautious, Jeremy said, "She's not been herself, and that's a fact,
although I never knew her afore, like Bruce. Listen, I think I hear
them coming now." But what he heard was the wagonload of men
and materials, followed immediately by the moving van carrying
the Heriot family. Hearty greetings must be exchanged and directions pointed out to the Heriots. By then the two women had
disappeared, along with Liz Ward. Liz kindly directed them to the
person they sought.

Maimie Dickson pulled her sister up for a whispered word: "This
place is a madhouse. We'll take her the day. I'm thinking yon van
will be going back to the town, and it will be empty. We'll hire it."

Nellie Brodie hissed back, although she was careful no one else
could hear, " 'Tis all costin' too much. Are you sure we'll be gettin'
it back?"

"Aye, I'm sure, and if no' in one way, there's another. Just you do what I say, and it'll be grand, you'll see."

By the time Jeremy remembered the two strangers, they had already reached Aribaig. The afternoon milk run pulled into the station even as they arrived, and if the guard wondered why the youngest woman, who surely seemed sonsy enough to him, should be greeting like a bairn as she was hustled on board, it was none of his business. A man saw a lot of strange sights on this job.

10

Kirsty Brodie felt terrible mixed up. At first the two strange women had been nice to her. The one called Aunty Maimie smelled awful nice and gave her sweeties, but the other one frightened Kirsty. For one thing she still hadn't seen her face because of the heavily veiled bonnet she had on. A cold feeling rose up in Kirsty whenever she heard that one speak, and it got worse as the terrifying sound of iron wheels on steel rails reached her. She cried out in fear and immediately received a slap. After that she shrank into a corner of the carriage, and they left her alone and concentrated on their argument for a while. Very soon no sounds could be heard inside, except for Kirsty's fearful whimpering.

She roused enough to notice the nice one standing, gazing down at her. "Kirsty wants a sweetie!"

Maimie Dickson nodded and reached into her immense bag as the other woman spoke, "Has she no' had enough o' that stuff, Maimie? We don't want her to—"

"Nellie, I ken whit I'm doin'! I'll gie her another half, and then she'll no bother us all the road to Glasgow."

After swallowing the sugared tidbit Kirsty tried to wipe her hands, but her fingers came in contact with her woolly lamb. She cuddled it tight as sleep claimed her, but first she managed to cry out, "Kirsty want Bruce . . . , family!"

Her aunt pushed her down on the seat, while Nellie still whined, "I'm fair worriet about this, Maimie. She's like a big bairn. Who's goin' to watch her when we get hame, and what—"

"Nellie, how many times do I have to tell you what a grand case we have here? Thon minister had Matt buried at sea, without so

70

much as a by-your-leave from the grievin' widow. Kirsty has lost her memory and cannot say us nay when we start to kick up a rumpus. Another thing is the letter from Matt that he sent me about a six month ago. You mind how he wanted me to see if we could buy a wee shop for Kirsty. He said he had found some Spanish gold in a treasure chest on some deserted island. You said he aye had daft notions, and that's a fact, but even if there's nae treasure, the money we've spent on this journey, your new rig out and all, will still be made up to us when we sue thon minister, and there'll be a lot left over for us to split atween us." Nellie had thrown back the net, and her doubts were visible in the deep frown on her face. Red spots, not all rouge, stood out on her plump cheeks, while her hair, the most unlikely shade of blue-black, hung limply down. Seeing Kirsty again, bonnier than ever, had caused the mother to ask herself some questions.

Maimie was still blethering about the profit they would be making: "You'll be the ill-done-to widow and mother of the afflicted. Thon reporter chap done us a favor, right enough, by settin' the stage, and we'll just have to add our own bit to it. Onyway, if Matt did leave the gold where we can get our hands on it first, we'll not have all our eggs in one basket. He said in the letter that finders were keepers and what was his is now yours and Kirsty's. Naebody else kens aboot it, I'm sure."

A snore came from the corner where Kirsty lay, and her mother moaned, "Maimie, ye're jumpin fae one thing to another, an' I canna keep up wi' ye. My worry is what in God's name will I do wi' her while we wait? She's a thirty-year-old babby. I'll not be goin' back to being her nursemaid."

"It's only till we get the money. Don't say anything about that until we see what's goin' to happen. Thon bunch of softies at the farm—"

"Maybe they were softies this time, but thon minister wasna there. He'll have more to say and do, I'm thinking. Mind you, though, we would have a harder fight on our hands wi' him."

Maimie smiled. "If what the papers say is true, we can expect to get plenty siller from him. I've heard tell he's rich. He'll pay, either to get her back or for us to keep our mouths shut about the poor lass and the condition she's in."

Nellie stood up at that. Her red spots became even more vivid as she shouted, "No' that as well, Maimie. I'll no' have it, surely ye—"

"Shut up, Nell. She hasn't been touched, but how will they ken that?" She rubbed her hands together. "Och, aye, if we do this right, we'll be richer than we first thought. Dinna wake her up yet." But Kirsty, in a deep, drugged sleep from the poppy syrup in the sweeties she had swallowed so greedily, would not wake for a long time.

"What do ye suppose Bruce'll have to say when he comes back and finds her no' here? If ye think he was hard on ye when ye suggested the woman wasna good enough for him, just wait 'til he hears this. Ye havena seen onything yet."

Jeremy paced the parlor carpet while he raged, and Liz sat at the table with bent head, twisting her hands together. She gave him no arguments, because she agreed with his every word. Her questions, unspoken as yet, were all of why such an illustrious personage as the Reverend Bruce MacAlister should place so much value on this nobody, this Kirsty Brodie. Certainly she, Mama Liz Ward of the Cormack Homes, had made no effort to stop the determined Miss Dickson—along with the other female accompanying her, who claimed to be the Brodie person's mother—from removing her so-called niece. Liz glanced up at Jeremy, who had ceased pacing and now stood in front of her. He had asked a question.

"What did you say, Papa?"

"I said, 'What will we tell Bruce?' That we didn't even try to stop they women fae kidnapping his Kirsty?"

Her voice trembled as she laughed that off.

"Now you're being ridiculous, Papa. How can you kidnap a grown woman? Anyway one of the strangers was her mother."

"He'll knock that argument to bits in a hurry. If she—Kirsty, I mean—is a grown woman, why does she need her mother and her aunt to take her anywhere?"

Liz became silent and thoughtful before she said, "Jeremy, many times in the past months I've heard you quote the old man every-body admired so much. Although I never met your Gran'pa Bruce, I find myself agreeing with some of his sayings, such as this one: 'When you can't make a better of it, dinna make it worse by wor-rying!' We cannot change this situation now. I'm sorry you feel I didn't try harder to stop the women taking Kirsty away, but I honestly thought it would be best for all concerned. My nephews and niece were being affected by her, as well as the other children for whom we are responsible. Even if Blodwin was becoming fond of her, Dorrie was not. There was much dissension in the camp that you, my dear, were not aware of. For the present we must carry on with the work of the Cormack Homes. Taylor the Post brought a large bundle of letters this morning, including two from Glasgow. Mary Jean and her husband must be getting worried about the reverend, and there's another letter with Dr. Blair's seal on it. Shall I begin to open them for you?"

Jeremy's sigh was deep. She did have the rights of it for the now. They must indeed carry on, but his heart wasn't in it, and what about Bruce?

Bruce's jubilation spilled over! His talk with Raju and Barnie, in their office on the top floor of the Phoenix Photographic Company, had proved once more that good friends were God's special gift. Raju's wife, Faye Felicity, had prepared one of her famous meals, and the five adults and one child partaking of it formed a cheery dinner party. Soon the youngest member, nine-year-old Bruce MacAlister Smith, who had been duly admired when he could not overhear, was ushered off, protesting, to bed. Having received Deborah's quiet yes to his request, Bruce allowed his contentment to show as he joined in the good talk. His mind settled down for the first time in weeks.

"Delicious dinner, Faye. I always did enjoy your curried rice dish, and as for those meat things on a stick, words fail me . . . !"

Both Faye and Raju laughed at this, and Raju said, "Meat on a stick indeed! They're called shish kebabs, and they actually are considered a gourmet dish, maybe not in India, but from—"

"I merely wanted to compliment your wife, not to get a geography or culinary lecture!"

As the laughter subsided Barnie Hill added, "His son's the very same, you know. One day, in his hearing, I happened to wonder aloud where and when the first ink appeared, and the young whippersnapper just happened to have written an essay on the very subject. He bent my lugs for a good fifteen minutes before I could—"

"Serves you right!" But the proud father smiled at his friend.

Barnie responded with, "Och, I learned my lesson. No more casual questions to Master Know-everything Bruce MacAlister Smith—or his father either, for that matter."

"Sorry to break up this most enjoyable evening, but I've been up since before dawn, and I'm suddenly very tired. Now that Deborah's agreed to come to Aribaig with me tomorrow, I believe I'll turn in." Seeing Barnie and his wife exchange glances at his words Bruce asked, "You did agree, did you not?"

"Yes, we did, Bruce, but Deb and I have been talking about it, and we thought maybe we'll take a day or two's holiday. Then we can both meet your Kirsty and everybody else at the homes, before traveling back here together, once we've formed some sort of plan."

"That's an excellent suggestion, Barnie, but can Raju and the business spare you? Besides, I must warn you there are a good many children at the Mains now, and space is rather limited."

Another glance passed between the couple before Barnie said, "Och, the hayloft will do us just fine. We're not fussy. We'll take a quilt, and it'll be like a camp outing."

"You asked if I could spare him," Raju spoke up. "The answer is, it will not be easy, but I think we'll survive for, say, up to a week without him. Although, mind you, we were having a very exciting discussion just before your so-welcome arrival today. I don't know if you've been keeping up with photography news at all, Bruce, so you've not likely heard about a new kind of flashing indoor lighting for studio portraits and such. We've almost decided to put out a considerable investment in such a project. What do you think of that?"

"I think that's grand, but you're correct in that I'm a bit out of date on such things. That's the reason I leave such decisions to you and Barnie. Mistress MacIntyre, of course, keeps me informed, but then I've not been to see her for a while."

Silence greeted this remark, and at last Bruce realized that Faye was looking at him, if not exactly in an accusing way, certainly in one full of pathos.

"What is it? Is something wrong at Strathcona House, and I've not heard?"

"Nothing too wrong, Bruce, but Auntie Mac has been wondering why she's heard nothing from you, since you told her a while ago that you would be off to America soon. Agatha Rose, too, complains—well, not exactly complains, as she thinks the moon rises and sets on you—but she and Peter have been anxious at not hearing. In fact the last I heard, Peter was talking about visiting Aribaig in the near future. Since you've been here, we understand better, but surely a note to Auntie Mac would have eased her mind. We just all wonder why."

"I'm not sure myself, Faye. I didn't write to anyone about Kirsty. Mary Jean, Hamish, nobody's had a letter. I think I'm afraid they'll . . . you'll. . . . Oh, Fayfel, I just wasn't sure if—"

"If your Kirsty Brodie would be acceptable to your friends and your family?" Raju broke in. "You grieve us, Bruce MacAlister. You, who married Faye and me as well as Barnie and Deb here. Doesn't the Scripture say, 'Your family will be my family . . .' and so forth? Do you not recall those early days, in the autumn of 1890, when we started up the Phoenix? How angry you got with Barnie here when he wondered if, with his record, he would be accepted in the business community! You said then that if they didn't accept Barnie they wouldn't have the factory either. What about us? When the Women's Guild in Cairnglen congregation ostracized Faye for marrying me, *you* told them what you thought and no mistake. Now you insult us by presuming we will not honor your decision."

"No, no, Raju, I didn't presume anything of the kind—not about anybody here in this room. Not really about Granny Mac or Mary Jean either. But I'm not so sure about Jamie or even about Hamish. Yes, you may gasp; Hamish brags about being just a common working chap, but where I'm concerned, especially about women, he's a terrible snob. Jamie, though maybe not a snob, will certainly have some heavy reservations about my choice, and that may well affect Mary Jean. I suppose that's the reason I've been loath to say anything. I hope and pray I'm wrong though."

The others in the room shared this hope fervently, but none voiced their own doubts on the matter. Quietly the Hills said their good-nights; Faye excused herself; and Bruce and Raju found themselves alone together. Bruce seemed to have forgotten his earlier remarks about retiring.

They didn't resume the conversation where it had stopped, because Raju had some other news to share with Bruce, "You remember Miss Evelyn Galbraith of the Galbraith dynamite works?"

"Of course I remember her, what about it?"

"She's back and she came round last week to call."

Bruce smiled. "Now there was one who could truly be called a snob. What is she doing, and why is she here?"

"I don't know all that, but she's changed since she's been in prison."

"That's not surprising. Prison is apt to change anyone. I supposed she's glad to be alive. After all, she did kill Shaun O'Mulligan, even if in self-defense."

"The judge didn't believe the self-defense bit entirely, or she might have escaped with no sentence. Anyway, she's very active in the Votes for Women league. She's trying to get Faye signed up for it."

"What has Faye to say about that?"

"She's all for votes for women, and why not? But she's not in favor of demonstrating and marching and things of that nature."

"Well, if they cannot get attention any other way, I suppose they think they must go to extremes."

"True, as long as there's no violence. But we have another visitor to Cairnglen this week."

Bruce covered his mouth. Sleep was catching up to him.

"Yes, Father O'Mulligan himself!"

Bruce sprang awake. "The nonrepentant priest. My, would I like to have a good chin wag with him! Because of the fire and the subsequent killings and because of congregational disapproval on both sides, we never had the proper opportunity before. Have you talked with him?"

"I have. He's here to visit his brother's widow. He's been posted to a mission field that sounds like an outpost on the borders of Mongolia and northern China."

Bruce's brows furrowed. "Imagine that. Now isn't that a coincidence. I've been wondering myself if my own inability to settle down and make a decision could be that I'm to start preparing to go abroad to missions myself. I—"

"No, no, Bruce, if that were the case, you would have no indecision. My opinion is that you have to settle down all right, but with somebody like this Kirsty Brodie you've described. She lights you up like one of the fireworks they used to make here. If the time comes for you to go to the foreign missions field, you will know without a doubt."

"Almost exactly Jeremy's words. So long as I'm not using friends' ideas to justify—"

Raju walked over to his friend. "You would never do that, Bruce. We'll just pray that your Kirsty will be every whit whole very soon. My prayer, too, is that you and she will be as happy as Faye and I—"

"Taking my name in vain, are you? May I join the prayer meeting?" Both men turned glowing faces to Faye as she entered the room. As Raju met her Bruce could not help being aware of the sari of opaque blue silk that Faye wore. When she moved, it gave the impression of ripples on the loch on a sunny morning. Her fragrance, which he recognized as jasmine, gave the illusion of the East, and he could not keep a sigh from escaping his lips. The observant pair noticed it, though, and Faye reached to clasp his shoulder for a moment as her husband began to pray.

"Forgive me, Mistress Henderson, but I was on the train to come down before it crossed my mind that I could've brought Dorrie for a wee holiday. You've had a letter from her recently, I suppose?"

"Aye, Reverend. This very week as a matter of fact. . . . And 'tis awricht, I understaun'. My lass has been tellin' me that you dinna have yer ain troubles to seek."

"She's right, troubles seem to seek me out." Bruce's grin was rueful. "But things are not so bad; I believe a turning point has been reached. Thank you for the tea; your scones are just like my own mother's baking. Now I must be going."

But Mistress Henderson had another matter to bring up. "Reverend, I've a wee question about Dorrie. Dae ye happen to ken this fella she's been writin' aboot?"

"I've been rather preoccupied with private matters since being at the Mains, and I've not been paying enough attention to my other friends. But I can report that all the members of your family seemed well—and happy, too."

Kate Henderson stared at the minister who was so admired by her menfolk—so much so that they had been willing to leave home to work for him and his family, away in that wilderness of the highlands, for the last six months. She decided to he honest with him. "Dorrie's told me all about yer Miss Brodie, Reverend MacAlister. Ma lass, well, she thinks too much is bein' made o' the lady. Naw! Naw! Haud on a minute—," she said as Bruce placed his hat firmly on his head and made for the door. "Hear me oot. I kent a lass oncet who had the same trouble. This one hurted her heed as well, only it was because her ain faither had threw her up and smashed her against the ceilin'. At first she was in a real dwam; then she started to enjoy the new life—even her faither was treatin' her nice. Now she didna ken, so she wasna to blame at all, at all, but she never got her memory back till the auld man deed."

Bruce had heard enough. "Thank you! I happen to know that Miss Brodie is in a true state of amnesia, and I will be calling in some experts, after she's had more time to recuperate from the physical injuries. I've been thinking, could Dorrie's new friend be young Gideon MacKenzie, by any chance?"

"The very one. Dae ye ken the family?"

"Not that well, I'm afraid. Richard, the father, is a hard-working blacksmith who has his own forge. There's another son, too—Hector, I believe—who is also learning the trade. I've never met

Mistress MacKenzie. Now, if you'll excuse me, I'll be off. Have you a message for Jake and Jimmy—and Dorrie, too, of course?"

"Could ye be bothered to take this wee parcel? 'Tis just some socks I've knitted."

A young lad of about twelve years catapulted through the door.

"This's never our David John!" Amazement echoed in Bruce's voice.

The boy moved forward shyly, holding out his hand. "Aye, I'm David John. How do you do, Reverend MacAlister?"

"Well, I never! Time does go on, does it not?" He turned back to the mother. "Of course, I'll be happy to take the parcel, Mistress Henderson. Your family has been such a Godsend to the Cormack Homes."

The door burst open once more, this time to admit a tumbling group of children of all ages, or so it seemed to Bruce. Grabbing the parcel by the string, he made good his exit.

11

Leaving Barnie and Deb standing close together on the platform, with the luggage piled at their feet, Bruce moved toward the exit, meaning to call for Geordie and his hansom cab.

Before he could do so however, a familiar voice hailed him; it was Jeremy. "We've brought the jaunty caur, Reverend Bruce. I can sit on the top wi' Jimmy here, whilest you an' your guests can easy fit inside."

Bruce wore his puzzled frown as the vehicle clipped along the road to the Mains, while Deb and Barnie remarked on the beauty of the scenery. The highlands was enjoying one of its rare clear days, with the sky a washed-out blue and a few white clouds scudding overhead. Compliments for the weather went by completely as Bruce wondered what could be bothering Jeremy. His answer, when Bruce asked him how everything was at the farm, had really been no answer at all.

Explanations came soon enough, when they reached the house, after Jeremy had set the newcomers to follow Jimmy toward the newest building, where Jake was hurriedly adding the finishing touches.

Bruce turned on Jeremy. "What is all this about then, Jeremy? It's not like you to be so, well, inhospitable. Is something wrong? Where are the women? And I want Deborah to meet Kirsty. I—"

"I fear something is indeed wrang, Bruce. Ye see, yer Kirsty isna here the now and—"

They had reached the door of the main house, and Bruce stopped abruptly on the step. "Not here! What are you on about, Jeremy? If she's not here, where is she, and why did you not tell me at once?"

"I didna want to say in front of your visitors, and anyway, we dinna ken where she is the now. Her mother came and took her away. 'Twas on the very day ye left." He stared at a stunned and speechless Bruce for a moment before saying, "Can we not go inside, an' I'll tell ye all I ken masel'?"

An hour later, Bruce, still stunned with the news, went in search of the Hills. Barnie had wanted to find Bruce, but his wife had detained him while they had listened to a garbled version of the missing woman given between Jimmy and Jake. In fact the gathering, waiting for Bruce's next move, could be described as a Cairnglen reunion. Rob Heriot and the three Hendersons, Barnie and Deborah Hill, none of them knowing the full extent of the drama going on within their mutual friend and benefactor, had made use of the time by exchanging news and some opinions regarding the town of Cairnglen. Jimmy and Dorrie had eagerly ripped open their mother's parcel, and Dorrie read aloud the enclosed note while the Hills wondered what could be keeping Bruce.

Finally, absorbing the fact that Kirsty was truly gone and that no one knew where, Bruce had resorted to his mother's parlor. Utilizing the DO NOT DISTURB card that the Ward's kept on the door handle when they wished privacy, he had fallen on his knees to ask the Lord for His peace and His wisdom. When he arose, the frown had faded, and the look of despair had been honed to one of deep sadness. Emerging from the room, he politely declined the offer of tea given by Blodwin Parker. Mama Liz had not yet appeared, and he made his way toward the newest building that formed the combination of schoolroom and the Heriot dwelling.

"So you see, Barnie and Deborah, I've brought you here on a wild-goose chase, and I don't know what to say, except, 'I'm sorry.' Of course you're most welcome to stay on for that wee holiday you spoke of, but I'm afraid I'll not be here myself."

"Where will you be goin' then, Bruce, and what will you do now?"

"What on earth is he up to, Peter, and did you know he had romance on his mind when he left for Aribaig?" Beulah MacIntyre's voice held a slight quiver as she asked the question.

"Only in a very vague sense, Auntie Mac, but this letter from Faye does tell us a bit more. He gave me no details, and he swore me to secrecy at the time, or I would have mentioned it sooner. I'm sure he knew it would not be smooth sailing, and he didn't want to have us all outguessing one another."

Agatha Rose gave one of her rare but always astute contributions to the conversation: "He was right, too, was he not, about us guessing and about it not being smooth sailing?"

"I don't think he would appreciate interference at this stage either, unless he asks for it. Anyway our Deb will know what to do, and she'll get word to me."

Beulah MacIntyre sighed deeply, and almost as one, her visitors raised their eyebrows. Seeing their question, she complained, "I'm tired, Peter! Another of Bruce's exploits just seems to be too much for me the now. You asked how I'm keeping, and I must say I just want to rest—even to go to be with the Lord, to see my Jeannie again and my husband. Now that Jessica's away . . . , why—"

Peter sputtered his derision. "Nonsense, madam. As a physician I declare you to be in perfect health. You're to see the century well in and hold your great-great-grandchild. Wait ten more years at least before you think along those lines. Remember, the memories of Mary Jean's wedding are hung over with the shadow of tragedy. If you slip off now to your reward, much as the highland laddie and Mary Jean will know you'll be safe in heaven, it would still put a damper on their joy in the blessed event."

Suddenly Beulah started to laugh. "You always knew how to get round me, Peter Blair, but you are correct. If the Lord spares me, I'll stay a while yet and stop hankering. Now will you humor an old lady and tell me again the story of my Jean's elopement with Bruce? She was such a canny one about it, was she not?"

Peter's smile was crafty. "Aye, but I suspect her granny knew more about that than she's ever admitted—and Faye Felicity as well."

The couple spent another pleasant hour with the old lady before Peter declared, "Time to go home, Aggie!"

In the motor, which Peter drove himself, for once he forgot to concentrate on the mechanics of driving and returned to the topic that had brought them to visit Strathcona House. "I've a feelin' the hielandman is going to be needing us, but not in Aribaig. We'll be hearing from him soon, I'm sure."

His wife clutched the cushioned perch, wondering if she would ever get used to this contraption. It always seemed to Agatha that the thing could not possibly be under Peter's control without the familiar and visible power of a horse or two. At this moment he was negotiating the turn into Carlton Place, narrowly missing a station cab as it wheeled full tilt in the other direction. She gave a tiny scream, and the cabman's curses blued the air about them as he calmed his rearing steeds. Quickly she glanced at Peter, who seemed scarcely perturbed. Normally he would have yelled a sarcastic response.

Today, the doctor's attention rested on their own driveway as he repeated his last remark about Bruce MacAlister: "As I said, we'll be hearing from the hielandman soon, if not this very day. In fact, I believe he's waiting for us the now."

As Peter cut the engine and applied the brake, his son's voice rang out clearly, "Uncle Bruce is here, Father, Mother, and he's in an awful state!"

"Would ye calm yersel', Bruce, lad, an' give it to me a bit at a time? So I understand ye got back to Aribaig from Cairnglen, with Deb and Barnie. Your—ahem, ah—Kirsty had vanished, but ye've no real reason to believe she's in any great danger? As for bein' kidnapped, that's a strong word and a strong charge, she *is* a woman, after all."

Bruce stared blankly at his friend. The decision to come straight to Peter had sprung from a longing for help in his search for his love, who had been so cruelly snatched away before he had the chance to declare his intentions. Peter's remarks shocked him further, yet he spoke the truth.

His friend kept talking, and Bruce made a gigantic effort to concentrate. "You've been under a great strain, my friend. In fact, you've had quite a year altogether. Now, I'm going to insist you take this potion. Och, 'tis nothing sinful. When you've slept, you can begin at the beginning again, and we'll see what can be done. Mind you, we've only hearsay to go on since you left thon day."

Bruce's instinctive refusal remained unspoken. Once again Peter proved right. Sleep had evaded him for the past two nights, and he had been unable to stomach any food. He placed both hands over his face in such a pathetic gesture of weary submission that Peter had to look away to hide his own emotions.

Peter turned back at once. Here sat his good friend. Since student days at Strathcona House each man's life had held no secrets from the other. Twice Bruce had been instrumental in pulling Peter's family back from the brink of destruction. Dr. Peter Blair would stop at nothing to help the bewildered minister through this present crisis and eventually obtain his heart's desire. Peter's voice faltered with the depth of his feelings as he moved to Bruce and placed a hand on the other man's shaking shoulders. "Dinna worry, Bruce, we'll find her, if she's that important to you. With God's help we'll make her well again!"

The potion had done its work, and Agatha Rose had followed it up with a good hearty breakfast of porridge and a tasty kipper beside a plateful of thickly buttered toast. Knowing Bruce's preference for coffee, she had ordered a big potful of the fragrant brew, and he held up his oversized cup for a refill, at the same time pushing back his empty plate.

"That was an excellent breakfast, Agatha. Just what I needed and no doubt what the doctor ordered as well."

She smiled but refrained from saying she didn't really need her husband's prompting to tell her what a hungry man required at such a time, even one as upset as Bruce. "I'll leave you two, then, and I'll send Douglas in the minute he gets back with Hamish."

Bruce's expressive eyebrows shot up. Of course, Hamish; why had he not thought of his stepbrother himself? He realized why just as Peter echoed the thought.

"I'm surprised you never thought of sending for Hamish, yet I'm not that surprised either, because you never think of yourself as the one needing help."

Bruce's smile was rueful as he let that pass. "I'll admit it the now, Peter!" Silence greeted this before he added, "Am I truly that presumptuous, then, in thinking I don't need folk?"

"A wee bit, maybe. But ye have such a deep faith. I've heard you many's the time saying 'His grace is sufficient for me.' "

"Within the context, it is sufficient, but we do need each other as well. . . . It's—"

"We'll not be needing a sermon the day, Bruce, but we'll want a plan of action. When Hamish arrives, we'll go over all you know about Kirsty Brodie—I mean, before the storm and boat fire. We'll need a place to start and something to go on."

Again the eyebrows shot up as Bruce wondered just how much Peter knew about Hamish and the secret brotherhood.

Peter discerned some of his puzzlement. "Hamish wanted a point of contact. He didna want ye to know he was still concerned about ye, so he told me just enough for me to guess the rest. Dinna worry, although Douglas knows where to go with the message, he doesna know the reason.

"Now, as I was saying, Hamish will need a place to start on. When your Kirsty was in the coma, did she not haver at times? Is there no' a hint of her life before thon wave swept her past life away?"

Bruce shook his head in perplexity. "She's a child again, but scarcely even the child Kirsty. A newborn babe, with the ability to speak and the doubtful ability to form conclusions of maybe a six-year-old. At that her strongest reactions came with the mention of railways and . . . then—" He hesitated, reluctant to run any-body down. "Well, she seemed to hate the mention of her mother."

It was Peter's turn to frown. If only he could have the opinion of the nurse Liz Ward. This usually rational being, Bruce MacAlister, lost his ability to be rational when it came to the mysterious Kirsty. For instance, even if Kirsty's mind had reverted to that of a child, what about the rest of her, her body? Did it still function as a possibly thirty-year-old woman's should?

He could never ask Bruce such a question; instead he said, "What age would she be?"

The smile was fleeting. "You may well ask, but at a guess I'd say twenty-eight or so. Women keep that a closely guarded secret, as you very well know. Mind you, from the short acquaintance I've had with Kirsty the woman, I don't think she would be in that category."

Love is so blind, Peter thought, *and thank God for it*, as he dared his next remark. "She'd be well within child-bearin' age then?" Bruce felt the tell-tale rush of blood to his face.

"I would think so, yes. What are you leading up to, Peter?"

"Nothing specific. Just trying to get a picture of her in my mind. Wait, I think I hear voices. Och, don't you get up, Aggie. The maid can bring Hamish in here."

The stepbrothers gazed at each other for a long moment. The older Hamish recognized Bruce's hidden anguish, and although he only had a garbled version from young Douglas, he had guessed the rest of it and knew it involved a woman. His brusque manner belied his compassion. "What's this then? The minute I leave ye on yer lane, ye get into a bother of some kind."

Bruce bristled but then heaved a deep sigh. " 'Tis the truth, Hamish, and I'm thinking you'll not approve. However I have to risk that and ask for your help."

Neither mentioned the fact that Hamish's help had not been sought sooner.

"Right ye are. Where do we start then?"

The whole story came tumbling out, and no one stopped Bruce as he narrated all he knew of the strange woman who had captured his heart and thoughts.

Not until Douglas gasped did his father pounce. "What's that, Son?"

"I said I know where that place is."

He had their full attention, and Hamish spoke up. "Where *what* place is, Douglas, man?"

"That sign whitewashed on the rock cutting." He faced his father. "Do you mind the time, Father, when we went with Nanny on holidays to the places our names were called after? It was on the railway between Cumbercary and Falkirk. Nanny always made us recite the words, and she'd give us a sweetie. Even Fessie could say it."

At the mention of his handicapped daughter Peter cringed, but then he began to fume. "Recite what? Get to the point, Douglas."

" 'The wages of sin is death'!"

Bruce gasped now. "Och, yes, I remember now. Kirsty mentioned Falkirk that first time we talked—the time I skinned my heel, and she doctored me up. Then again when she was asking me to tell her stories she said what sounded like *Cumbercary*. I had never heard of the place. What do you make of that, Hamish?"

Hamish stood up. "It's what we need to start, Bruce. That and the name *Matt Brodie*."

At the station Hamish had some time to wait, and he sat on a bench to watch the people passing. All those years, when his main purpose in life had been Bruce and Mary Jean, he had paid scant attention to other folk, except where it concerned those two. Now suddenly, a whole new perspective had opened up to him.

His musings halted abruptly as a very young couple, engrossed in a deep argument, crossed his line of vision. He looked again, more intently. Could it be? Yes indeed, it was Garnett Ogilvie! My, oh, my, that did explain a lot.

For a moment Hamish almost forgot his other mission as he rose to follow the couple. They had entered the third-class waiting room, and as unobtrusively as he could, Hamish did the same. Unable to hear every word they spoke, the few he did catch made him gasp in wonder as he whispered to himself, "What for have I met with this pair the now, Lord? Am I to leave the search for Bruce's woman and pay attention here? They're in bad need of something, 'tis plain to see." The Falkirk train would leave in ten minutes, and he rose to go. Bruce's needs were still to be his first concern apparently.

Just then Garnett turned and met his gaze fully. The younger man's face flamed, and he grasped his wife's arm without warning, causing her to gasp with pain. Within moments they had melted into the crowd.

Hamish sought his platform, still mumbling, "No' the day then, Lord, but I've a feelin' we've not seen the last of them. Meanwhile I've this other business to take care of before I strike north to

Aribaig. The *Revelation*'s been ower long neglectit. I'll want to use some of the money from Faither's estate, as they call it, and get her in good condition again. After all you never ken wi' Bruce. He might need the boat one of these days."

"Wheest man, will ye? And keep the lantern doon. We dinna want onybody snoopin' aboot to see what we're up to." Geordie McDade's tone of voice revealed his nervousness as he carefully pulled himself over the side of what remained of the MacAlister's braw boat.

His companion sneered, "Geordie, ye're haverin'. There's nane to see the licht or hear the noise."

"Ye're wrang there, Richie. Ye see the castle up there and they caravans wi' the workers? Well, sound carries ower the watter, and the lichts can be seen for a wheen miles."

"Awricht, we should talk less and get on wi' it then. Whit for could we no' come in the daylicht, I'd like to ken?" Geordie chose to ignore this foolish remark as he pushed aside the canvas sail that had been battened down across the gangway of the *Revelation*. His suspicion that the two fancy women he had driven from the station at Aribaig would come back with helpers to do what he and Richie MacKenzie were just going to do had not happened yet, but he wanted to hurry up just the same. The thought of the gold made his hands itch to hold it, but he was wise enough to know he could never have got this far without help. He had chosen Richie as a partner because the strength in the smithy's brawny arms alone could move the whole boat, if they wanted. Silently they crept down the companionway.

An hour later, with every burnt and blackened floorboard ripped up and pushed aside and no treasure chest filled with gold discovered within the foundation beams or anywhere else, Geordie threw down his hatchet in disgust, while the other man uttered a curse.

Staring at Richie without really seeing him, the cabbie pushed his bonnet back and scratched his head. "We've been tacklin' this the wrang way, Richie, man."

The other bridled and balled his fist, advancing threateningly.

"Naebuddy's better than me at tearing things to bits. I could break this boat in two, if ye want."

"Naw, naw! It's no' that, Richie. I'm thinkin' this Brodie, by whit the MacAlister said about him, wasna daft. Would ye no' think he would have a map or a chart or some such thing?"

Richie's laugh was scornful. " 'Twould be burnt to ashes."

But the two men stood unmoving for a time. Geordie scratched his head again as he pondered, "Richie, your ain work has to do wi' heat and burnin' and meltin' and such like. Whit way is this boat no' a cinder wi' thon fire?"

Richie looked pleased as he answered, "It's a brawly built boat. They oak beams take a lot o' burnin', and the supports for the bunks and things are cast iron an'—"

But Geordie no longer listened. "That's it, Richie, ye're a bleedin' genius! The cast-iron supports, they're hollow, are they no'?"

"Aye, but what—?"

"Never mind the now. Just bring yer hammer and chisel. Here's a joint; it looks a bit weaker than the rest. Give it a guid bash or two, that's richt. Do ye hear that? It sounds hollow, richt enough, but there be something inside."

Richie yelled, " 'Tis the gold! Man, we've found the gold!"

"Wheesht, ye daft gowk, If onybuddy hears ye, they'll want a share, and mind whit we decided—finders keepers."

"A share would suit us just fine, mister!" The shock of hearing the fancy English accent, as much as the words, rendered Geordie speechless. Someone had watched after all and possibly for some time past. Sliding his eyes upward to the figures standing over him, Geordie's dismay grew as he discovered not one, but two watchers, each with a businesslike dueling pistol pointed directly at him.

At the same instant, without warning, Richie, who wasn't champion at the shot-put trials for nothing, heaved the giant hammer. With deadly accuracy, the missile found its target, and the foremost intruder went flying, gun and all, onto the pile of ripped-up boards, while the second adversary leaped to escape. Glancing quickly at his pal, where he lay flat on his back, half under the companionway, the second intruder realized it would be a while before the other man would bother anyone. He held up his arms in surrender.

"I give up, oh, yes, I give up. Spare me, and I'll never say a word about the gold mine you found."

Geordie knew his own limits. "This booty doesna belang to onybody here, mister. 'Tis my duty, as a law-abiding citizen, to report it to the constable in Aribaig. As for you, sir, ye'd better make sure your pal here is still breathin'. 'Twas self-defense. Two local inhabitants will swear to it, if he happens to be a goner."

The man wiped his sweating forehead. "He's no pal of mine, believe me. I'm not a violent man myself. We just happened to be up on the point of the cliff, when we saw the lights and heard the voices. But yes, I better make sure he still breathes. Let me say this one thing first—" He held up a hand as Richie advanced menacingly. "With such a wealth of coin, could you not spare us just one, for a keepsake, you see. What the authorities don't know won't hurt them." The impressive pile of gold lay where Richie had shaken it out of the hollow supports, and Geordie could have wept at the idea of how near they had been to getting away with it.

"Souvenirs, man? Be thankful ye're no' in the watter by now."

Geordie did break down in tears next morning, after the constable, along with the Reverend Welch and some other citizens, had rowed out from the town to claim the bounty for the crown.

He ventured a timid question: "Will there no' be a reward?"

Neal glared at him. "Geordie McDade, I wouldna say that too loud. Come to think on it, what were ye doing on the boat after it had been sealed off? Your story about being out fishin' wi' Richie and hearin' noises does sound a bit fishy to me."

"Richt ye are, Neal. We'll say nay mair aboot it. Least said soonest mendit!"

Neal relented somewhat. "As a matter of fact there will be a reward, but it will go to Reverend MacAlister, as the boat is his property. My goodness, what next for the reverend, I wonder? I'm thinkin' he'll not be pleased at the intruders who left his boat in worse condition than the fire. But I'll not have to face him for a while. He went to Glasgow on a tinker hunt!"

12

The search had indeed begun.

Bruce, chafing at doing nothing to help after Hamish had left to set the wheels in motion, exclaimed, "I'm sure I could help Hamish in some way, Peter. I can't just sit about drinking tea while—"

Peter held up a hand. "No offense, Bruce, but I think you might just get in the road at this stage. Hamish'll get word to you when they trace your Kirsty, and then it'll be your turn."

Unable to sit still for long, Bruce began to prowl about Agatha's parlor like a caged tiger. At last he stopped pacing to gaze out of the window for a time before declaring, "Strathcona House! I'll go and see Granny Mac."

Peter shook his head at that, but it was Agatha who spoke. "We visited her yesterday, Bruce, and I would suggest waiting a bit before you go there. You know, without my saying it, that you're welcome to stay with us as long as you want."

Bruce was gazing at Peter. "Is something wrong with Granny Mac then?"

His friend smiled. "She's a bit weary, Bruce, that's all. Write her a note, and one of the lads will deliver it. Then go the morrow to see her."

"If she's weary, she'll not want to hear my tale of woe—or another one of my exploits, as she calls them—and I'll not be able to hide it. But I'd better not write a note either, or she'll wonder why I didn't call in." All at once he clapped a hand to his head. "Mary Jean and Jamie! What must they be thinking, after all this neglect? Even Hamish, I should have told him more about the boat before he rushed away. Och, Peter, I've been so absorbed in my own troubles, I've neglected everybody."

Again Peter shook his head. "Do you want to be tellin' the story over and over again? Leave it be, man. I suggest you bide here till Hamish brings word. I've a feelin' it'll not be so long, and then you can tell the rest of them all at the same time."

Bruce glared at Peter as if his friend had sprouted horns, but he did give in. "Right you are, Peter. Wise words indeed. No need to bother Mary Jean and Jamie—or Granny Mac either—with all this yet." He turned to Agatha. "Have you seen our Mistress Douglass recently, then, Aggie?"

"Yes, Bruce, we met in Ferguson's last week, and we had a cup of tea together. She's looking well, and it'll not be long now before you are a grandfather. Easter's only a month away." Agatha refrained from adding how Mary Jean worried about her father, who at this moment was busy pulling his hands through his hair.

"No doubt she's thinking I'm the worst of fathers and don't deserve to be a grandfather. She'll not have heard a thing about what's happened at the Mains."

Peter intervened, "The Glasgow papers did carry a bit of the story about thon storm and the fire in your boat, too. I talked to Jamie about the whole business. We doctors use the telephone a lot, you know, and we decided, if nothing else came of it, and until he heard from you yourself, that maybe no more need be said yet."

Bruce's smile held more than a hint of sadness. "Jamie's at the protecting again. But I've not been that considerate, have I? Seeing yon reporter snooping about, and I never even read the story. I should know what they're saying. Show me the paper, Peter, if you please."

"A lot of rubbish, Bruce. I burn the papers. I dinna ken why I bother to buy them . . . It's a waste of—"

Bruce was pacing the floor again. "There's more to it than you're saying, Peter. But till I find Kirsty, I'll not be heeding what the papers report. I believe I'll just walk over to see George Bennett the now. I'll be back soon, Aggie, and I'll accept your kind offer."

*   *   *

Fifteen minutes later Bruce faced an astonished Mistress Oliver. His old friend George Bennett had left his faithful housekeeper in charge, while he, on his doctor's orders, trooped off to the south of France for the remainder of the winter. Belatedly Bruce recalled the pile of unopened letters on his dresser at the Mains, accumulated while he visited Cairnglen.

Mistress Oliver ushered him into her cosy kitchen. "Ye'll take a cup of coffee. I mind how you aye enjoyed it. Here's Benny; he's truly goin' to retire from the railway at last." Benny Stout had risen from his place at the fireside. The expressions on each well-remembered and beloved face almost unmanned Bruce, and suddenly he found himself blurting out the whole story, holding nothing back of his feelings for Kirsty Brodie. The fire's embers glowed on, and Mistress Oliver even neglected to light the lamps as they listened. Benny began to pray, his gnarled hand rested lightly on Bruce's head. The silver threads shining through Bruce's hair did not escape Mistress Oliver, and she made no attempt to hold back her tears as she nodded in full agreement with Benny's prayer.

"Dear Lord Jesus! We ken 'tis the cruel hand of our soul's enemy that is the robber here—the one who is determined to destroy our peace and to steal and even to kill all that is good. Well, we'll not put up with that! In the Name of Jesus, we rebuke you, Satan. Take your hands off this woman who means so much to our brother Bruce, who is himself one of Your anointed. I'll say it again: In Jesus' Name we demand that you, Satan, leave our sister Brodie this verra minute. . . . Amen."

Mistress Oliver sobbed, and Bruce made no attempt to hide his own emotion. The other two smiled at him fondly, and the brisk lady began to pour the coffee.

"That's that then. In a wee while you'll know what to do next. Drink up your coffee, and here's a wee bit of shortbread to go wi' it."

Sipping the fragrant drink, Bruce marveled anew at these true believers. What had just been prayed they accepted as already having been accomplished. Suddenly he knew it, too, and peace flooded his being as a new thought came directly to his mind. He gulped down the still-scalding liquid and stood. "Thank you both for showing me, and indeed I do know what I'm to do now."

Peter rubbed his hands together gleefully. "That's more like the hieland laddie I knew. Motherwell, you say, and the railway cottages. Yes, what is it, Aggie?" His wife had caught his sleeve, and he bent to listen as she whispered something. "Och, aye, ye're right. I forgot about that. Oh, well, I'm sorry, Bruce, but I canna go with ye mysel'. I'm not the only driver in the family, though. Douglas, Stirling!" His roar echoed through the house, and soon his two sons stood awaiting to hear what he wanted. As it happened, Douglas had an early class at the university. But Stirling was free, so in a very short time he and Reverend Bruce MacAlister sat enthroned in the front seat of Peter's prized possession, chugging along the road to Motherwell.

Stirling Blair was ecstatic: "I can't get over it, Father letting us take the motor. The most I ever got to drive it was a wee shot when we went to Burntisland last summer, and then he watched my every move. It's all thanks to you, Uncle Bruce!"

Bruce gazed fondly at Peter's son. The lad had carried such a terrible grudge against him for years, but now recognized the minister as a friend. He patted the hand gripping the steering apparatus. "You handle the contraption very well, Stirling, but can we not dispense with the *Uncle*? You're a grown man now, and I'd be pleased if you just call me Bruce."

The vehicle swerved dangerously and then righted itself as the driver took in this statement. Fully concentrating on the road, the younger man's voice came through gruffly as he answered, "Right you are, Bruce. Tell me what we'll do once we get to Motherwell."

13

"Wake up, then, Kirsty, lass. I've a sweetie for you, but first ye'll have to get up and put on this nice new frock I bought for you."

Kirsty Brodie opened one eye, slowly at first, and then suddenly both eyes opened wide as she stared wildly about this strange yet familiar place. She focused on the owner of the voice that had awakened her from the funniest dream. Incredulous at her surroundings, she asked, "Aunt Maimie, is that you? What . . . why—?"

The woman stopped in her action of smoothing out the dress she had been holding up. Surely she hadn't heard right! She tried again, "Get up Kirsty and get yoursel' dressed, and then I'll give ye a sweetie. We're goin' to see thon nice man again. Mind how I told you what to say?"

The woman on the bed listened carefully for the space of thirty seconds, before, with a determined movement, she threw off the covers and literally leaped from the bed. Standing on the drugget rug in front of it and taking time to note the frilly nightgown falling to her ankles, Kirsty reached for her hair. Nothing unusual there, her two plaits hung down as always.

Determined to stay in control of herself, she began slowly to ask the many questions flooding her mind: "What's all this about? What are you talking about, Aunt Maimie? What am I doing in your house, and where's my da'? He'll be needing me. He's on his lane on the boat."

Momentarily stunned by the turn of events, Maimie Dickson tried quickly to recover her senses. "God's strueth, an' ye're back then? Wait a minute, wait now. Ye'll still need to get dressed before ye go rushin' about. Tell me, Kirsty, where do ye think ye are?''

Kirsty stopped on her way to the door, thinking how her aunt could always turn the Doric on and off like a water tap. She walked slowly back to the bedside and sat down heavily. Stretching both hands straight out in front of her, she stared at them dully before saying, "Aye, 'tis so right enough. I'm back, but I don't know where I've been or where I am the now, except it looks like. . . . Is it your house?''

"It is indeed my house, Kirsty. But I'm not sure I can answer your other questions, about where you've been or anything else.''

Kirsty gave out a long shuddering sigh. "Maybe I dinna want to know, but I know I must. First, where is my da'? Is he ben the house?''

Maimie stared again at her niece. Should she tell all, or would that send her back to never-never land or farther? She would put her off for a wee while yet. "I'll get your ma. She just went to the butcher's shop for some sausages for our breakfast. You get dressed now, and then we can—''

Maimie reached for the door handle, but Kirsty again sprang to her feet and flew across the room. She grasped her aunt's arm. "Stop talkin', woman, and tell me: Where's my da'? ''

"He's been dead and buried this two month, and you—''

The scream quickly changed to a wail, and for the space of a minute Maimie thought, *She's away again.* Taking advantage of the cruel distraction she had caused, the older woman wrenched her arm free and dashed through the door. "I hear your ma, Kirsty. You wait now!''

Kirsty paid no heed, even when the key turned in the lock. Her hoarse whisper reached only her own ears, "Two months she said he's been gone, dead, and I didn't even know. Will somebody not tell me where I've been all that time?'' Once again she surveyed her surroundings. Had her da's passing made her demented then? She pushed that thought aside at once, thinking, *Well, I'm not demented the now!* Her next glance caught the basin of water and the soap and towels all laid out for a sponge bath. Then she saw the dress lying on the floor, where her aunt had dropped it. Automatically she began to wash, and soon she was pulling the dress over her head. Kirsty loosened the tight plaits and began to brush out her hair. At least she would be clean and presentable for whatever lay ahead. Finding hairpins, she put her hair up in the old familiar way. Now she could face her ma. Deliberately she pushed back the thoughts crowding her mind, thoughts of a boat called *Revelation* and its owner. A dry sob caught in her throat. She must only consider one thing at a time.

But two words persisted and she found herself saying them softly, "Bruce, family!" Tears of frustration filled her eyes. She dashed them away as her indomitable spirit surfaced. "Whatever am I havering about? If my da' is truly dead, then I've been lollygagging in bed this two months, and it's time I got back to the land of the living. Living! That's it, I'll have to make my own way now, will I not?"

If Nellie Brodie had been angry before, it was nothing compared to the storm that erupted round her sister's ears when she heard the news. "She's what?"

"Aye, she's comin' out of it. I knew we should have proceeded with the plan before this happened. But no, you were that feart. Anyway we can still—"

"Maimie, you're even dafter than I thought. Have you ever seen oor Kirsty wi' her dander up? We'll proceed with nothing. She'll be away, as quick as she can go, but no afore she's gien us the worst side of her tongue, if no' a punch or two into the bargain!"

But Nellie misjudged her daughter. When at last the two women approached the locked room, they could hear no sound whatever from inside. They glanced quickly at each other and Maimie whispered, "She'd never jump out the window, or. . . . Oh, my, I shouldny have left her." Cautiously she turned the key. Holding her breath, she pushed the door inward. Her niece sat demurely on the edge of the bed, its covers neatly in place and Kirsty herself neat and tidy. For a moment Maimie thought she must have slipped back into her child's mind again, but no, the bright-green eyes gazing straight into hers and full of questions belonged to a normal adult woman. Nellie spoke first: "Ye're back to yersel' then, Kirsty?"

The green eyes flayed her from head to toe, but the answer came quietly, "Aye, Ma!"

Flustered, Nellie ran to the bed. "We're that glad, are we no' Maimie? We've been—"

The cool eyes still gazed her down.

"Well, onyway, do ye not mind what's been happenin'?"

"No, Ma, thon calendar on the wall says it's March, and I see some crocuses in the window box, so I seem to have lost a month or two somewhere." Maimie stepped in. "I should just say ye have, but now we'll be makin' it up. Come on. We've got a lot to do the day. . . . First we'll have a bite to eat and a drop tea, then we'll tell ye all aboot it."

During the telling, Nellie Brodie kept stealing glances at her lovely daughter, now seemingly restored to her right mind. Nellie was not deceived by the close and quiet attention Kirsty paid to Maimie. Expressions crossed the mobile face, and once or twice she started to interrupt then subsided again. Could that be whenever Maimie mentioned the minister MacAlister's name? Indeed, aye!

Suddenly the drone of Maimie's voice halted as Kirsty emitted a sharp scream. "No! No! He would never do that!" Nellie had lost track of the tale, and she shot a quick glance at her sister. What had she said about Matt—or maybe thon minister fellow—to make Kirsty's wrath erupt? But the noise abated, and Kirsty subsided once more. She had a lot of thinking to do.

"I tellt ye, Maimie, ye'll get nothin' oot o' her. She's a thrawn besom when she doesn't get her ain way."

"Shut up, Nellie. Doing the washin'll keep her busy till we have a chance to make up a new plan. . . . Now, the night, when you make her cocoa, put in an extra spoonful of the syrup. Then in the mornin', Doctor Hutcheson will be here. He'll send for the wagon, and she'll be admitted. She'll sign the form afore she comes to herself, and by the time the stuff wears off, it'll be too late."

"I'm no' likin' this wan bit, Maimie. She is ma bairn, an' I dinna trust your Doctor Hutcheson. This past week has been quite nice, havin' her here, an' could we not—"

Maimie smashed her fist on the table, causing the dishes to rattle, while one delft plate flew across the room. Ignoring the destruction of her precious property, Maimie spoke through clenched teeth: "Last week is past now, and she's back to bein' the cheeky besom she used to be. She would scratch yer eyes oot, if ye said a wrong word aboot Matt, and now it's that minister MacAlister. She near had a conniption this mornin', when I said that aboot him and Matt."

Nellie said no more, but even if she agreed on some of her sister's words, she had plenty of doubts about the asylum. Instead she asked, "How did ye manage to get her to do the washin', Maimie?"

"I tellt her straight that seein' she's weel enough, she better start to earn her keep. You know how proud she is an'—"

"Aye, I do. She's the same as Matt. But what's to happen after the hoosework's done?"

"She thinks she'll be goin' to look for a job the morrow. She thinks as well that the minister fellow blames her and Matt for burnin' his boat, and she'll be goin' oot tae work to pay him back."

"I still say—"

"Wheesht, Nellie, dae ye want her tae hear ye?"

Kirsty had already heard enough. She stood in the doorway, but they could not tell, from her expression or her next words, how much she knew: "It's raining, Aunt Maimie, so I hung the towels on the pulley. I'm awful tired. I'm goin' for a lie down." With head high, she walked past her mother and on into the room where she had been sleeping for more than a week now, did she but remember. Kirsty felt tired, right enough, and her head buzzed with all the things she had learned this day about herself and her da. She needed more time to think it out. She wanted to think, too, about that other shadow person, the minister. If he did blame her and her da' for the loss of his bonny boat, she would work for the rest of her life to pay him back. But something appeared far wrong about all this; something just didn't add up.

Stretching out on top of the bedspread, Kirsty clasped her hands

behind her head. As she stared at the ceiling a nice memory of
Bruce MacAlister began to stir in her mind. Unable to stay lying
down for long, she rose and started to walk the floor, careful not to
make a noise. She did not trust her mother or her aunt, but for the
moment she felt helpless and weak. Even so maybe she should
leave and get out on her own at once. She could take a live-in job
in service at one of the big houses. Her da' would not like her being
a skivvy for the toffs, but according to her mother and aunt, he had
died and had already been buried at sea. Apparently the two
women blamed the minister for that and actually conducting the
funeral. She stifled a sob. "Oh Da', what happened? Will I ever
know the rights of it?" A light tap on the door brought her head up,
and she called out, "Come in."

"It's me, Kirsty. I've brought you some cocoa and a biscuit.
Maimie's away oot the now, and I wanted to speak to ye. Dinna
forget I'm yer mother." Stony silence greeted her words, and Nellie stopped speaking.

Kirsty opened the door and took the enameled tray. As she
placed the tray on the small table beside the bed, she managed a
weak smile. "Ta! I'll drink it in a minute. I'm not that hungry." But
she didn't drink it after the first trial sip. It was far too sweet, and
even the one wee taste made her feel sick.

Nellie went back to the kitchen, where contrary to what she had
told Kirsty, her sister waited.

"Did she drink it?"

"Aye, I think so."

"Whit dae ye mean ye *think* so? Either she did or she didna. . . .
Anyway we'll wait a while before we go in and then—" She
stopped speaking to gape at the apparition in the doorway.

A raging virago had replaced her calm niece. "What are you two
conniving now? I should have kent no' to trust ye. I'll not be
drinkin' your poison or eatin' anything more that you cook up. In
fact I'll not stay here another minute, but I'll pack my box and go."

Maimie recovered her senses quickly and began to laugh. "Your
box, huh! What box? You've got nothing! Do you hear me? Nothing! Except what your ma and me give ye. If you run the now,
you'll be cuttin' your ain throat, as ye'll not get far. Doctor

Hutcheson says yer off yer head. He would have put you in the asylum last week, if we'd let him. Ye daft gowk, could ye not have stayed the way ye were for another week or two?''

"To end up in the madhouse anyway? No thank ye. I'll be leavin' now."

"Leave then, but take off that frock afore ye go and they shoes. They're mine. Like I tellt ye, nothing belongs to you, and I'll set the polis after you. We'll get ye first for stealin' my belongings, an' then we'll have ye for bein' demented."

Deflated for a moment, Kirsty glanced wildly about. Her mother, noting the hesitation, added, "Do what Maimie tells ye, Kirsty, and we'll all come oot of it rich, set for life. If nothin' else, ye mind thon gold belonged to your da'. He found it, did he not? It was his idea that ye better yersel' wi' it."

Kirsty turned to glare furiously at her mother, her sea-green eyes flashing darkly. "What rubbish are you on about? Did you make this all up or what?''

"Well, Matt wrote in his letter to Maimie, about a six month ago, that he'd found some gold, and he wanted Maimie to help him use it to set you up as a teacher or in a shop."

Belatedly Kirsty recalled her father's last talk with her—the first she had heard of the Spanish gold.

Her mother talked on: "We think yon minister found it and then buried your da' in a hurry at sea to hide his ain misdeeds and—"

"Shut up about the minister, and don't defame my da's character as if he . . . he—" Words failed Kirsty again, and she sank into a chair.

Her aunt took up the berating. "I'll tell you about yer precious da'. He was a good-for-nothing, not even a tinker, because at least they do things like sharpen knives and whatnot. Bad enough that, but he had to go and drag you doon wi' him. His funny ideas, as if the rest of folk owed him a livin', after he lost his foot. What kind of a faither could that be?''

Kirsty was on her feet, towering over the speaker, her eyes murderous. "He was the best of faithers. Don't say another word, or I'll smash yer face in." Horror at her own words made her pause. Astounded, the others sat unmoving as she turned away with a snort of disgust. "My da' didna drag me anywhere. I wanted to go with him. I'll not stay here and listen to another word. If I've no clothes and no money and I've to pay my way, I'll need to borrow what I have on and pay you back when I'm earnin'. I can go in the morning and see if the farmers are hirin' on skivvies the now."

"We don't care how you manage. Go back to the moochin' an' beggin' you an' yer da' used to do, or go to the poorhouse. But you're not leavin' this hoose wi' that frock or they shoes, unless you go at my bidding. You could go in a petticoat to your minister. He might forgie your debt, if you're nice to him. Come to think on it, what did he charge you for rent of yon boat?"

On the last words Kirsty sprang up and rushed out the door, anger and hurt lending her strength. The remark about Bruce had been the last straw.

Her aunt still screamed, "Come back, ye thief! That's my frock and shoes you're stealin'. I'll have the polis efter you."

Still Kirsty kept on running until at last she could go no further. Dusk had fallen, and the drizzle had turned into a downpour, but she hardly noticed. Blinded by a mixture of tears and rain, she stumbled on, caring not for the fine motorcar that passed her on the main street in a great cloud of petrol fumes.

When the rain started, Stirling had stopped the motor to roll up the top, but as the sides were still open to the elements, he went to the boot and rummaged about, emerging with a pair of giant-sized Mackintosh capes. Enveloping himself in one, Bruce the other, they started off again.

"Just two more miles, according to that last milestone, *Unc*—I mean, Bruce!"

"Aye, I noticed that, Stirling. We'll be there in no time."

"What will we do when we get there, Bruce?" Stirling asked.

"I haven't thought that far, lad, but every fair-sized town has its hotel, and if there's a railway station, then it's the Station Hotel. We'll find that and take a room for the night at least. That will be our base."

"A hotel, but we've no luggage. I doubt they'll let us stay without luggage."

"I forgot about that. Well—"

"Wait a minute, maybe a sovereign in the palm of the deskman will get us a room. That's what father does, if he's stuck somewhere."

"I hope it works. The rain's getting worse." This remark needed no answer, so they traveled the last mile in silence.

Finally Stirling spoke, "Look at that poor soul, fair makin' a dash to get home out of the rain, I suppose. I hope she doesn't have far to go, or she'll really be drookit." Bruce followed the pointing finger and joined in the hope. It was an awful night for man or beast to be out in.

So Kirsty and Bruce passed each other like ships in the night.

Kirsty slowed to a walk and began to take note of her surroundings. No one had followed her, and she could take a bit more time. Vague memories stirred at familiar places, and finally they came crashing into her mind, not unlike the deluge on her body. She had run from her aunt's house, on the corner of Hunter Street, where the big Bank of Scotland dominated the rest of the street. Scenes from her past, when her da' would go on about the bank being built too close to the corner, flashed now. He and some of the other workers had wanted the cooperative store to go there, instead of at the other end of Main Street, far away from the houses. Who among the working folk on Hunter Street would need a bank? he asked. The housewives would need the coop store to be closer for walking to on a cold winter's day. Before the accident, her da' spouted on any and every cause, to whomever showed willingness to listen.

Kirsty sobbed, remembering those happier times, as she stumbled across the empty street, not a carriage in sight, nor a body walking either. Only proud eedjits like Kirsty Brodie would be out in such weather. All the shops were shut, too, but maybe Toni's Ice Cream Shop would still be open. She made for it, not knowing what else to do; but Toni's shop was in darkness, the door securely bolted and barred. Sheltering for a minute, she huddled into the small alcove. A fit of shivering shook her frame, not altogether from the cold rain. The new frock, sodden and clinging to her legs and ankles, hampered every movement now. That earlier resolve to try and stick it out with her mother and aunt at least until she earned some money had vanished when they had started to insult both her da' and Bruce MacAlister in the same breath. Add to that Kirsty's very strong suspicion that they were feeding her dope of some kind.

"I'm just like my da'," she whispered to the stone wall beside her cheek, "Rushing away from whatever is flummoxing, the minute my dander gets up, instead of being sensible and waiting for the right time. Oh, well, I've just myself to worry about now, and they'll not come after me in this rain. I'll sit here and rest a wee while, where there's a bit of shelter." As she leaned against the boarded-up doorway, her meager strength suddenly gave way, and Kirsty slithered to the stone step, too exhausted to weep anymore.

14

" 'T is only the traveling salesmen that frequent a hotel such as this, Stirling, except for the off license at the back of the premises, but we'll try it anyway. This is one of the times when I wish I were sporting my ministerial collar. It does open doors in certain places."

Stirling stared at this new concept of his courtesy uncle. Last year Stirling's idea that Bruce was a stuffed-shirt type had vanished completely, after he had personally experienced a healing miracle. Though the minister would take no credit for it, Stirling's mother, always an admirer of the big highland minister, had turned admiration into hero worship.

None of this showed as Stirling answered. "Oh, well, Father always says a sovereign is a good door opener, as well."

They stood on the steps of the Station Hotel. Finding the solid oak door securely locked, Bruce reached for the night bell. "It can't be later than seven o'clock, yet the whole town seems deserted."

"The big steel works, over on the east side of the town; it'll not be deserted!" Stirling remembered lessons from his school geography. "Day and night is the same in there."

Before Bruce could commend Stirling on his superior knowledge, a shutter no more than a foot square slid open to reveal a face behind the solid oak door. No sound came through the thick glass, but the lip movements and the scowl indicated they were less than welcome. Bruce leaned his head on his clasped hands, mimicking sleep. The face cleared, and the shutter slammed, but they heard a bolt being drawn and soon the door swung wide.

"Ye're new, are ye? Stephenson did say a new fella would take over his route."

Bruce winked at the gaping Stirling, who had been ready to deny any knowledge of this Stephenson.

The man was already holding out the register. "Terrible night to be oot! Sign here, and it'll be a pound each, payable in advance, till ye establish yersel's."

Still without having said a word, Bruce produced two sovereigns. He waved away the clerk's search for change as the man continued, "I'll just get the potboy to fetch yer cases."

Stirling leaped to intercept him. "I'll fetch them, thanks just the same!" Stirling dashed to the door to return a few seconds later with a Gladstone bag in each hand. Bruce found it difficult to hide his mirth as he noticed a dripping Mackintosh sleeve sticking out from one of the hastily closed bags. Reaching the room, Bruce collapsed on to the ancient but sturdy horsehair sofa, while Stirling threw himself across the bed. Between shouts of laughter Stirling managed to gasp, "We didn't have to say a word, till he mentioned bags, and I minded Mother. She always puts a bag or two in the boot, as she says, 'Just in case.' "

The unintentional pun sent them off again, but suddenly Bruce sobered. " 'Tis too early for bed, and the shops are shut, or we could go on a buying spree for the things we might be needing if we bide here a day or two. We'll do that the morrow. For the now I'm hungry. What if we dry off a bit and then make a foraging trip to the hostelry below?" He almost choked again at the expression on his young companion's face. "It's all right, Stirling. I've been in a public house before. They often serve food, and I'm sure somebody'll be there to make us a pot of tea or coffee."

The man at the desk barely raised his head as they walked past him and through the green baize door. Following their noses, they entered into an entirely different world.

The hotel had once been a coaching house where the stages would make their first stop from Glasgow, but recent renovations to meet the needs of the ever-expanding coal, iron, and steel industries could clearly be seen. Bruce didn't stop to admire his surroundings but made a beeline through the tobacco-smoke haze toward a buxom lady, standing beside another green door, that he guessed would lead to the culinary center.

Outguessing his need, the woman hissed to the man wiping glasses behind the high countertop, "These gents will want the lounge, Sweenie." To Bruce, she added, "Will ye be wantin' the full meal, or will ye—?"

Bruce held up a hand. "Don't go to a lot of bother, dear lady. A hot pie and some bread and butter will do us fine and maybe a pot of tea."

Candid eyes, used to gauging all manner of men, gave him a close scrutiny before she nodded. "Right ye are. Hot meat pies it is, and what about a nice plate of chips to go with them? The tea will be ready in no time at all." She was leading them into another room as she spoke. There stood a long table with one end already covered by a snowy white cloth. Stirling rubbed his hands, still gleeful.

When the promised repast was set before them, Bruce was stricken with a guilty thought: "All this is too smooth and easy, lad. They think we're some fellow who's supposed to replace this unknown Stephenson on some route. We don't even know what we're supposed to be selling."

Stirling gazed at him for a moment before replying, "We've told no lies, and we're doing no harm. I'd say the Lord has provided this bounty. When you pray, remember to mention the strangers whose place we're taking and pray they'll be held up safe and sound until morning."

During this time Bruce had been gazing in some surprise at the younger man, not knowing whether to smile or scold. He decided on the former. "Yes, I should have known that. You'll make a fine minister yourself someday, Stirling. Meanwhile we do thank You, Lord, for this provision as we pray for safe journey for the missing travelers. Lord, we pray for Kirsty, wherever she is, whatever she's doing. Send your angel to cover her with protective wings, in Jesus' Name. . . . Amen!"

If Constable Harry Livingstone, night patrolman from the main constabulary in the industrial town of Motherwell, had ever heard himself called an angel, he would have dismissed the thought with a laugh of scorn. However, Harry did have three other boasts he did not scorn. First of all his name: Had not his father's cousin's lad been the famous man who had discovered the Zambezi River and the great Victoria Falls, away there in Africa? At the same time, David Livingstone had declared the word of the Lord wherever he went. Never mind what jealous folk might say about David's being more interested in geography than missionary work; his family knew better. Next, Harry proudly held his position in this town. In less than two years he had been responsible for clearing the streets of the so-called night prowlers or corner loungers. Not that he put them in gaol or gave them any such hard punishment, instead he made use of his third reason for pride—his hobby, a boys' club on Hunter Street. To his delight, Harry discovered many of the gentry—some through the goodness of their hearts and others through relief from the threat of their houses and businesses being broken into and vandalized—displayed an eagerness to donate money to his cause.

Why, only last week Sir Thomas Hunter—himself a true descendant of one of the famous doctor brothers of that name—had given them a brand-new billiard table, and the morrow they would be having a wee ceremony for it, although the table had already been given a thorough trial run by himself and young Doctor Tod.

Harry spoke his thought aloud to the empty dripping street: "My biggest worry'll be keepin' the lads from bettin' on the games."

The big policeman swung his lantern in front of the barred gate of the bank in a token gesture. No one could possibly climb over the spiked railings, but he always made sure. Tonight again nothing showed but an empty sweetie poke or two. Harry's next stop would be the Italian ice-cream parlor as they called it nowadays. Auld Toni struggled to keep it going. It seemed the more money folk had to spend, the bigger the demand for fancier things and harder types of drinks. Harry strongly disapproved of alcohol in any form.

"Hello, and what have we here then?" What at first glance appeared to be a bundle of soaking wet clothes had moved slightly, and a pair of clear green eyes sparked at him in the glow from his lamp. "My, ye're a lassie—or no, ye're a full grown wumman." Receiving no response to his exclamation, he went on. "Ran away fae yer man then? Are ye hurt?"

Fear had immobilized Kirsty, but now she moved in a feeble attempt to stand up. The kindly bobby reached a hand to help her, but she cringed away.

"Ye canna stay her, missus. Come wi' me now, and we'll get ye dry an' a drink o' hot tea." He leaned in as he spoke, but the bundle suddenly galvanized into action. With an almost animal cry, she spat at him and slapped his hand away. Taken unawares, the constable stepped back, and the woman, having acquired latent energy from somewhere, seized her chance to break away.

"Ye wee spitfire, ye'll not get far. I'd say ye've not the strength to reach the other side of the road."

Harry had guessed right, and the burst of strength evaporated as Kirsty Brodie collapsed on to the wet pavement, a pavement ironically enough, where she had played peever and stot-the-ball many times as a child.

An hour later, happed up in a blanket and seated in a big, comfortable armchair in front of a roaring fire, Kirsty gazed about in wonder. Mistress Livingstone stood over her, clucking nervously, while her husband, who knew well her bark was worse than her bite, waited for the fussing to end. He had just returned from the doctor's surgery, where Doctor Mike was finishing up his evening shift. Very few patients had ventured out on this wet night, and the surgery would be shutting down soon. The doctor had promised to come in after that.

Carrie Livingstone turned to her husband.

"She'll not tell her name or anything else, so it's hard—"

He walked toward the woman in the chair. "I promise we'll not let ye go back to what ye're feart o', but ye can safely tell us your first name, and then we can talk it oot."

No sound came from the heap of blankets. His wife spoke again, "She drank the tea, but first she asked me if it had sleepin' syrup in it. The very idea!"

"It's all right, Carrie, let me ask her again. Lass, I'm Constable

Livingstone, and this is my missus. I'm not on duty the now, so anything said or done in my private domicile is confidential." He smiled reassuringly. At times he liked to spice his sentences with official-sounding words. "My wife's Christian name is Carrie and mine is Harry. Some folk think that's a joke and make up funny rhymes, but we—"

"Kirsty, Kirsty Brodie!" The voice was so soft that Harry almost missed it.

He turned to Carrie. "That's better then. In a wee while our friend Doctor Tod will be here to help you."

The whisper was louder now, "No, please, I'm just fine, now, Constable. I don't want a doctor."

The couple glanced at each other as Carrie spoke, "Doctor Tod'll not be an official call, eether. He's a friend of oors and comes in whiles for a cup of tea, when he's finished his evenin' surgery. He'll not touch you, if you dinna want him to, but he'll give us an idea—"

"I'm not daft, you know!"

Again a glance was exchanged, and Harry said, "We ken that, Kirsty, and we just want to help ye. Will ye be wantin' to tell us what happened?"

A spasm of pain mixed with such utter dejection crossed the expressive face that Carrie had to turn away. Kirsty's voice began to gain strength as she said, "I'm not sure mysel' what all's happened, but I think I've had a bit of a breakdown, and my memory is playing tricks on me, although some things are comin' back."

A light tap on the door sent Carrie to answer it, but Kirsty, now that she had started, kept talking, not even noticing the dark-haired young man who had joined the group at the fireside.

When she had told all she knew, Mike Tod was the first to speak, "Amnesia, plain and simple. She's had amnesia!"

"What's that, Mike, and is it serious?"

"Serious enough, Harry, but mendable. She's comin' out of it now, and I think she'll be right enough in a week or two." To Kirsty he added, "The big wall of water coming at you, that is the last thing you mind then, before waking up in your aunt's bed?"

Kirsty shuddered. "Aye!"

Carrie Livingstone waxed indignant: "The very idea of that Maimie Dickson, throwing ye oot on the street on a night like this."

Honesty made Kirsty reply, "She never threw me out, mistress. I ran." She had omitted to give the reason and the plans she had overheard. Maybe the good folk didn't need to know all that.

Unknowingly Dr. Tod came to her assistance. "After what you've been through, Kirsty, 'tis no wonder you ran away. What you're running from is your own self, your thoughts and your unhappy memories. My advice to you now is this: If my friends agree, I suggest you stay quietly here with them for a day or two at least. By then you'll be better equipped to make decisions for yourself."

Kirsty's protests were quiet but firm. "I canna be beholden, so I must tell you I've no money, and even the frock and shoes dryin' on your pulley belong to my aunt."

Carrie's lips curled, but before she could speak her husband said, "We'll not be botherin' about money the now, Kirsty. Carrie'll find ye something to wear and whatnot. Michael, do you think—" He signaled to the young man. They both disappeared into the other room.

Mike Tod glanced back. "I'll see you in the morning, Kirsty. Sleep tight."

She smiled her first real smile for many weeks.

Carrie dabbed at her eyes, but her voice was brisk: "Come away then. My nightgown'll drown you, but it'll have to do. I've a brick in warmin' the extra bed. The morrow we can talk some mair."

15

Following another of the friendly cook's full-meal breakfasts, which had not varied by one iota in three mornings, and consisted of porridge with cream, ham and eggs, and a pair of kippers, the two seekers continued their search for Kirsty Brodie. By daylight, without the rain, the streets appeared much less sinister. On that first day they had spent time searching for a shop where they would find some of the items they needed.

Today while Stirling made the purchases, Bruce asked about the Brodies as discreetly as he could. "If a body had some news of advantage to share with someone who used to live here, how would he go about finding that person's whereabouts?"

He received some strange looks, and one young fellow called the manager.

"Excuse me, sir, but we've had strangers in asking too many questions just recently, and even if we knew, we could not divulge information about our customers."

As they made their dejected way back to the hotel, on this, their third fruitless day, the town clock struck the hour of noon. Bruce remarked, "I should have left it to Hamish and the brotherhood. We're not getting anywhere, Stirling. It seems we're stirring up a hornet's nest. Folk here are not too pleased when they think we might be insulting a native son."

"You're not ready to give up yet, are you, Bruce?"

"No, we'll stay another night, but if you would make my excuses to our hostess I'll not take her full-meal dinner the day. I've some things to do."

Correctly assuming that Bruce wanted to be alone, Stirling made his way to the dining room. After he had eaten his fill, he returned to the public lounge. Seating himself, he looked round and soon found the person he sought—the odd-job man, Sweenie, who was polishing glasses again. He obviously took great pride in the occupation as he held up a brilliant example for himself to gloat over and his audience to admire. Stirling obliged in this before he began to ask questions.

The old man glanced at him from under bushy white brows. "Matt Brodie? Aye, I kent Matt, whit aboot it?"

"I was hoping you could tell me something about his life here in Motherwell. He worked on the railway, did he not?"

"Aye." Silence followed this, and Stirling, ready to concede that this was all he would get, made to move away. Then the voice continued, "Aye, ye're no' one o' they reporter chaps, are ye?"

Stirling's laugh was genuine. "Not me. Why do you ask?"

"Och, I had one o' them a while ago, askin' about Matt Brodie, and I tellt him what I'll tell you. Matt was a fine ganger on the railway, a grand family man, no' a drinker. Mind you, his wife was a tartar, but he could aye manage her. They had a braw wee lassie. . . . I mind wanct—"

To halt this walk down memory lane, before it got too long-winded, Stirling interrupted, "He had an accident, did he not?"

"Aye, Matt never was the same efter that. I've said it afore, an' I'll say it again: If ever a man should have got the 'compen,' it was Matt Brodie. But they said it was his ain fault, an' he never got a farthin'. Mind you, the lads had a whip round wi' the bonnet, and they collected enough to pay the doctor and the hospital.

"I went to see him the wanct. He was a changed man. He tellt me he wasna goin' to be a bother tae onybuddy. He wasna goin' to lie in bed and rot eether. He tellt me he was for travelin' aboot. I joked wi' him, askin' if he was ettlin' to take the grand tour of Europe wi' his hop and carry one. He laughed a wee bit, but he was nearer to the greetin' when he said, no' exactly, but him and Kirsty would be travelin' as far as they could go on what money he had left. I mind thinkin', *What bonny lassie is willin' to go wi' her faither on such a journey?* Onyway I never heard tell o' him again 'till thon reporter tellt me he deed."

Stirling nodded and rose to leave. Nothing here that he hadn't known before. He placed a shilling on the counter. "Have one on me, Sweenie."

"Thank ye. Oh, there is wan thing mair, lad. His wife has a sister. Maimie Dickson, they ca' her. She still bides here. She's a stuck-up besom, but she might tell ye mair. Her hoose is on Hunter Street. It'll be shuttin' time in a wee while. I can show ye her hoose if ye like."

While he waited for the old boy, Stirling wondered if he should call Bruce. Then he decided not to. What he had just learned only confirmed his earlier suspicion that old Bruce was a bit daft about this female. Surely the minister could do better than chase after someone such as he had just heard described! The MacAlister might be getting old, but he was still a fine-looking man, with his piercing blue eyes and thick hair. The hair did have quite a lot of silver round the ears—but still—

As if Stirling's thinking about him had brought him there, Bruce suddenly appeared in the center of the doorway. His brows were furrowed in the old pattern that both of Stirling's parents had mentioned many times in the past.

Aware that he was staring, the younger man colored and glanced away as Bruce spoke, "Will you start the motor for one last look about the place, Stirling?"

"I'll do better than that, Bruce. Sweenie here has offered to guide us to the home of a Mistress Dickson. She is Miss Brodie's aunt."

Maimie Dickson eyed the two fine gentlemen on her doorstep. One, the tall, older man, seemed familiar; but the handsome young fellow standing a step behind him could have been anyone. Giving no indication of this, she awaited an explanation.

"I'm Bruce MacAlister, and this is my nephew, Stirling Blair."

The woman's face remained stiff and unyielding, although she allowed her brows to rise in question as she awaited further enlightenment.

Bruce became slightly flustered. Then recalling the pathos of Kirsty's state the last time he saw her, he stiffened his resolve. "I do believe you know why we are here, mistress. May we not come inside?" He said the last as a small crowd of urchins had begun to gather round the fence. Also he had noted more than one set of curtains being swished apart in nearby windows.

"State your business, mister. I'm not in the habit of entertaining strange men."

As he recognized a dangerous adversary, Bruce's expression became grim. His mother would have been staggered, had she seen him now. His eyes flashed the familiar blue fire, and his jaw squared to granite in an exact replica of his grandfather Munro on his Edinburgh judge's bench many years ago. Even the voice resembled Hugh Munro's: "We have reason to believe that you are harboring a victim of your kidnapping endeavors—one Kirsty Brodie. Would you prefer it if I call the constable?"

Her laugh held a note of fear. She certainly didn't want any dealings with do-gooder Harry Livingstone or the likes of him. Grudgingly she stepped aside to allow them entry, saying, "Miss Brodie is my niece, as you already know. What do you want her for?"

Bruce gazed about the small lobby. Obviously they were to get no farther. He sought a sign of Kirsty's presence.

The woman spoke again, "Why would I kidnap my own sister's lass? She's not a wee bairn, but a woman soon to be thirty years old and able to look after herself."

"You are very well aware that Kirsty has not been able to care for herself since she was knocked about in a bad storm a while ago. I happen to know how you came to my home in Aribaig, where she was making a good recovery. But never mind all this talk. I wish to see her, to make sure she is well."

A single word, without doubt a curse, exploded from the woman. "If it's any of your business, sir, she's not here. To get you out of my house I'll tell you about it. As you said, Kirsty has not been well, so after Matt's death her mother and me went to fetch her back to civilization from that God-forsaken wilderness. The ungrateful wee besom left us the minute she had her thievin' hands on some of my money as well as a set of nice, new clothes."

For a moment Stirling thought his minister uncle would attack the woman. He tensed, ready to step between them, but Bruce drew back, his tone icy as he demanded, "Where is Kirsty now?"

The woman gave him a closer scrutiny before replying. Maybe she had been on the wrong track with this fellow. Narrowing her eyes, she finally answered, "I don't know, Reverend, and I don't care, now that I'm reminded what she's truly like. You shouldn't care either. She told her mother and me what a big softie you were. Her and Nellie had a good laugh, but me, I thought it a shame, after you being so nice and all, letting them stay on your boat rent free. Then she bragged how she gulled you into thinking her a we'an again—"

"She *was* a bairn again. You're telling lies! Kirsty would never go willingly with you, and she hated her mother!"

"My, but she did have you gulled." Mockery left Maimie Dickson as she saw how she could get her revenge—not only against the niece who outshone her in every way and now had outwitted her in her money-making schemes, but at the upstart Matt Brodie as well. Her lip curled as she continued, "Your precious Kirsty came with us willingly that day, being sick and tired of your bleating ways. She's not staying with me at present, for she is away, seeking legal advice against you, not only because you had her father buried at sea without her sanction or that you stole his Spanish gold, but that when she lay sick and helpless, you took advantage of her and stole her virtue as well."

Bruce's mouth thinned to a line once again.

Stirling, at first amazed at the woman's vocabulary, merely stood and gaped at hearing this final statement. He could only murmur, "Oh, my goodness!" as he watched to see what Bruce would do now.

But Bruce had heard enough. Wheeling to leave the tiny, cramped lobby, his coattail connected with an ornament. It crashed to the floor. The woman screamed at his departing back, "A house wrecker as well, is it?"

Bruce stepped through the door and sped away, with Stirling running to keep up. To the younger man's amazement, his father's friend tried to hide a smile.

At the hotel they prepared for departure in the morning. Few words had passed between them since the altercation with the Dickson woman, but Stirling kept glancing at Bruce quizzically. With the decision made, he would like to leave now instead of waiting until morning. He began to prowl restlessly about the room, stealing another glance at Bruce. That man was deeply engrossed in a small pocket-sized book which he carried with him everywhere. His Bible?

Feeling the lad's eyes upon him, Bruce forced his attention from the book and faced Stirling, keeping his hand on the open page. "You're wondering about my wee Bible, Stirling?"

No use denying it. "Yes, Bruce, I am—and a few other things as well!"

Still keeping his place, Bruce leaned back in the one chair the room boasted. "There's very few in print this size. My friend Barnie Hill—you'll mind Barnie? Och, aye, I nearly forgot, he's your uncle. Well, he had it made for me by a special order through our printing and photographic business."

"Oh, yes, I see. Bruce?" The last word held a question, and Bruce looked up again. Then with a resigned sigh, he placed the Bible carefully on the bedside table.

"You've more questions, lad?"

"I do, and not about your Bible. With all due respect, we rushed here to Motherwell awful keen to find your Kirsty Brodie. Then when you might say we found the trail, suddenly you stop looking and declare we're to go home without trying anymore. I know that woman said some terrible things that made you angry at the time, but now you're sitting here reading your Bible as if, as if—" Words failed the young man. Bruce laughed softly. "Forgive me, Stirling. I can tell you're thinking of parables like the one about the lost coin and about miracles—after all you've had one in your own life, and I don't blame you. But just because we're leaving here doesn't mean I'll be stopping the search. As for that woman's insults, I know she was lying viciously. You see, she had two different stories. One that Kirsty was against her, and the other that Kirsty was on her side. Anyway, I happened to see a toy lamb on the table next to the ornament I knocked over. If Kirsty had connived to cheat us, she would not have bothered with the toy, so when they took her from the Mains she was still a bairn. On the other hand, if she had been still thinking as a five-year-old, she would never have parted with the toy. So you see, while I would have enjoyed making Mistress Dickson retract her statements, a Scripture verse in Psalm 119 came to mind. Verse 165 it is. I'll read it to you. 'Great peace have they which love thy law: and nothing shall offend them.' It's not easy and I have not achieved that great peace bit yet, but I'm praying for it and believing it will happen. Now, having missed the evening meal, I suggest you eat some of these sweeties we bought the day. I'm away to get ready for bed. We can leave at daybreak!"

Stirling reached for the sweets but picked up the Bible instead. He had been a Christian all his life, and he knew from personal experiences that miracles still happened, but maybe he had missed some other good and important stuff hidden in these flimsy pages. Before he had read far, Bruce returned to the room. He walked toward the bed just as a knock sounded on the door.

The deskman stood in the opening, his expression sour. "Is one of ye Reverend MacAlister then?"

Stirling turned to Bruce questioningly.

That amazing fellow advanced to the door, hand outstretched. "I am Bruce MacAlister. What can I do for you?"

"Well, I'm shocked that a man o' the cloth would trick his road into a decent hotel and leave us thinkin' ye were Stephenson's replacement."

"I'm sorry you thought that, but I did not trick you, sir. I signed your register in my usual manner as Bruce MacAlister, and my young friend—"

The clerk was staring beyond them to the bags on the bed. "You're leavin' then, are ye?"

"First thing in the morning! I thank ye for your hospitality, and of course we'll be paying what is due before we go."

"Aye, well, I've had complaints that ye've been quizzin' customers and other folk aboot the town. We dinna need your kind here. The account will be another ten pound each, if ye please." Stirling moved in protest, but Bruce reached into his pocket, while shaking his head at the other man. Only slightly mollified, the indignant clerk left the room.

Stirling exploded, "Daylight robbery, that's what it is. I—"

"Let it be, Stirling. He's right, we didn't tell the whole truth. Now I want to wipe the dust of Motherwell off my feet and off the wheels of your father's motorcar. Before we go, though, can we telephone Peter from thon contraption in the hall?"

The morning dawned bright and clear, and having completed the telephone call, the two climbed into Peter's Daimler. For a while neither spoke as Bruce ruminated on Peter's news. Hamish had discovered that a Mistress Nellie Brodie was housekeeper to a toff in Cumbercary. Recently she had gone away for a while, but she was due back any day. Nobody in Cumbercary had anything new about either Matt or Kirsty.

Bruce deliberately forced his thoughts in a new direction. Peter had said that Mary Jean was doing just fine. Both he and Jamie agreed her confinement day would likely be on Easter Sunday, as predicted.

Reaching the outskirts of the town, Stirling made his way carefully along the rutted track, thinking he should have taken the east-side route to reach the main turnpike. Then his thoughts returned to the reason they were here. Why had Bruce not contacted the police?

He voiced the thought: "Are you sure you shouldn't have told the bobby, Bruce? I don't trust that woman Dickson; she's too sleekit."

"I agree, in part, Stirling, but she did say some things that set me to thinking. As for the police, I do not wish to imply any form of crime has been committed by anyone. Folk keep pointing out to me how Kirsty Brodie is a grown woman, and apparently she is in control of her memory again. If we are to have any future meeting, it will happen. Our God reigns. Meanwhile I've been neglecting my family for a will-o'-the-wisp dream. I mean to correct that."

Bumping along the rutted road made talking difficult, but soon they reached a smoother place, and Bruce continued, "As I told you before, I'll not be giving up, but now I'll do what I should have done at first. Leave it to the experts. We stayed in the hotel under false pretenses and sometime I'll go back and clear my name."

He stared about absently for a few moments, his mind switching to another track. "The woman Dickson is full of venom, but she, too, is a soul loved by God. I do not believe any of what she told us, but I must be wise. For that I'll get in touch with my friend, Police Inspector MacKinnon. You mind of him of course?"

For a moment Stirling looked blank, and Bruce explained further, "Thomas MacKinnon and Gran'pa Bruce became friends years ago. They corresponded a lot, and Gran'pa showed the agnostic Thomas the plan of salvation. Anyway the inspector is chief of police in the county of East Lothian, and he didn't get that position through anything else but ability. He has helped us to solve more than one mystery at the Mains."

They drove on for a while as Stirling absorbed this. Then he broke the silence with, "Is the inspector a married man?"

Bruce smiled wanly.

"Not yet. I'll be performing the pleasant duty of changing that before. . . . Och, Stirling, I'm that mixed up the now. I wouldn't say this at any other time, but lad, I beg your respect for a confidence. Love does blind a body, you know!"

Amazement filled the young man, and he stopped the vehicle to stare hard at Bruce. Could the minister be joking? The profile beside him remained grim. "What do you mean, sir?"

"Exactly what I said, Stirling. When you're in love, your brain gets addled!"

Hiding his astonishment, being most unwilling to pursue that subject, Stirling jumped down to crank the engine again. Even if he didn't speak of it further, his thoughts continued: Surprise filled him that his uncle—he would always think of him as uncle—should be talking that way about love. Even with its serious implications, running about in search of this woman had been a bit of a lark. But imagine an oldster like him being in love! He glanced sideways again, but Bruce had his eyes closed—either asleep or praying. The younger man agreed with his own grandfather Blair, who would say, "A fine figure of a man!" As if on signal, the blue eyes opened, and Bruce dazzled him with a smile.

Slightly flustered, Stirling asked, "What will you do now, Bruce?"

Bruce sighed. "Och, I'll just spend a day or two between Granny Mac's and Mary Jean's. As I mentioned, I've been neglecting them all. Actually, Stirling, my future plans are vague at the moment, although I've still got America in mind. I had hoped . . . but we'll not get into that again. Nothing is settled."

An irrelevant thought came to Stirling: *He reminds me of our football when we let the air out of it gradually. Deflated, right enough, that's the word.*

Suddenly the vehicle under them spluttered to a halt. Stirling pronounced a word that Bruce chose to ignore as the driver proceeded to punch the dashboard with a clenched fist.

"Petrol! I forgot about petrol. Oh, my! Father'll not be pleased. One of his best lectures is not to let the petrol get low."

Bruce thought for a moment. "I'm not that pleased myself, Stirling. But beating your hands to pulp will not help. What's to do?"

"Pumps are few and far between, even on the turnpike. Likely none till Glasgow."

They stared at each other for a moment, then Bruce began to laugh. "At least it's not raining. I suggest we partake of the food Mistress Cartwright packed for us. *She* didn't seem to care about our names, as long as we enjoyed her 'full meals.' After that, if no one comes by to help us, we'll just start to walk. How far are we from the main road?"

They spread the map on the seat between them. Stirling looked sheepish. "This road's not on the map, Bruce. I mind we took it once when Doug and I were on a bicycle tour."

Keeping his comments to himself, Bruce noticed how the so-called road seemed little better than a cart track. He gazed on toward the horizon—not raining, at least not yet, but a bunch of clouds gathering to the east was fast approaching. Shading his eyes, he scanned the area with a circular motion. "There's somebody in a garden over yonder, beside that old house. They'll not have petrol, but we'll need shelter before too long. Hop to it, lad. I'll race you to the dyke."

16

"What my man told ye, lass, is right enough. We'll not be pushin' ye to do anything ye're not ready for. . . . In fact—"

Kirsty turned from the window before replying, "I know that, Carrie, and I thank ye, but what he said about the sweetie factory in Pollokshaws has been on my mind."

"Och, aye, Harry's got that many cousins and other relations, I canna keep count. This wan is Agnew Grant, and his wee sweetie works has a shop attached to it. I'm suggestin' you work in the front shop then—"

Kirsty interrupted her kind benefactress once more: "I'll just be takin' whatever job I can get and do my best at it."

Carrie Livingstone gazed fondly at the woman who had been her constant companion for this past week. *Except that she's a lot bonnier than me she could have been the sister I never had*, she was thinking as they shared the job of washing up the midday dinner dishes.

The wee factory they had been talking about was too far away for Carrie's liking, because Kirsty would not be able to stay on with them, if she got a job there. Besides Agnew had his own boardinghouse where his lassies lodged. She caught herself up: *What way do I think of her as a lassie, when I'm only eight years older than her mysel'?* Placing the last spoon in the drawer, she carefully hung up the towel before removing her apron.

The constable was in the other room. He liked to put his feet up for a spell before going back on the beat. Thinking of her man's big feet reminded Carrie that she should be getting his clean socks ready. That man was so fashy about his feet.

Kirsty stood waiting. All the other housework was done for the now. She would soon follow Carrie into the front room, where they would seat themselves one on each side of the fireplace. She would turn the heel of the sock she was knitting while Carrie would pick out a pair from the mending basket and begin to darn. She glanced out of the tiny scullery window, where a watery sun was struggling through the clouds.

Carrie followed her gaze and came to a decision. "Maybe for a wee change we'll go ootside an' plant the dahlias. My, I can hardly believe 'tis that near Easter. It seems only a day or two ago since we hung up our stockings for Christmas."

Curious, Kirsty stole another glance at her kindly hostess. "You hang up your stockings?"

Carrie blushed in confusion. She hadn't meant to blurt that out. "Och, I ken it sounds daft, but Harry an' me, havin' nae we'ans, have a rare time wi' some o' the lads from the club. We give them a party, and when they a' gang hame, we hang up oor ain stockings. We fill them when the other yin isna lookin'!"

Kirsty smiled as she pictured the happy scenes. If her thoughts held a form of wondrous envy, she kept it to herself.

"Oh, Carrie, you're that kind, I wish—"

"Wheesht, now, no wishin'. I've a notion that someday a fella is comin' for you. Although he'll not compare to my Harry, he'll be just right for you, and you'll be as happy as we are." A rush of tears overflowed the sparkling green eyes, and suddenly they were hugging each other. Carrie, being the same height but quite a bit bigger boned, held the slimmer woman in a massive grip for a moment.

A cough interrupted the sisterly scene, and Harry appeared in the doorway. He lifted a pathetic bare foot. "Can a man get a decent pair of socks before he has to go back to poundin' pavements in the pursuit of law and order?"

His wife punched him playfully as she hurried past him. "Och, you men and your highfalutin pursuits."

"Am I included in that, and is there a spot of tea for a thirsty, weary bone setter?"

Carrie glanced back over her shoulder as she reached the stairs.

"Kirsty'll get ye the tea whilst I get a pair of socks for that puir neglected polisman there!"

But Michael Tod had changed his mind. "It's such a braw day that I've a better idea. Kirsty, have ye ever been on a motor bicycle?"

She stared at him, uncomprehendingly for a moment, while Harry gasped. "Mike Tod, ye wouldna?"

"But I would, if she's willing. My time's my own until evening surgery, and as her attending physician—with your approval of course, Constable Livingstone—I prescribe a wee jaunt in the country for my patient. I know a nice tea shop in Bellshill. The road's a bit bumpy, but we'll borrow one of Carrie's cushions here for the sidecar, and it'll be worth it." He picked up the cushion and aimed it at his friend.

Kirsty began to shake her head, but catching a glimpse of Harry's face, alight with mischief, and getting a taste of the doctor's enthusiasm, she paused. Why not? Somewhere deep down a memory stirred. She must make a start at living once again.

Getting her tall frame folded into the sidecar proved not too difficult. She laughingly told them she wasn't made of glass, and they discarded the idea of the extra cushion. Soon they were bowling along the turnpike. Kirsty felt a tremor of fear along with the exhilarating sensation of speed and the wind on her face. Carrie had been careful to tuck her bountiful hair inside the leather driving helmet she had found under the seat of the sidecar.

"If my da' could see me now!" She was yelling and laughing at the same time, but the sounds ripped from her mouth, and suddenly nothing seemed funny anymore as her mind rocketed her back to the day of the storm. A state of panic took control, turning her earlier exhilaration into utter terror. The noise from the motor was deafening and the fumes from the exhaust overpowering. She screamed for the doctor to stop, but he didn't hear. Frozen to her seat, she could not move to pull on his jacket sleeve, even if she could have safely reached it. He was going faster and faster. Kirsty even lost consciousness for an uncounted number of seconds, until at last he began to slow down, gliding almost gracefully to a stop.

The face he turned to her showed nothing but pleasure. "Was

that not great fun, Kirsty?" He loosened the strap from his leather helmet as he spoke, but quickly his discerning eye caught her consternation, even as it started to diminish. He leaned down to help her through the tiny opening. "You did enjoy yourself, I hope!" Then, "Are you all right?"

Kirsty's legs caved in under her as she tried to stand up, and she would have fallen had he not grabbed her. Rallying quickly, but still leaning on him for support, she answered, "I'll be all right now. I'm just a wee bit shaky yet—"

Mike Tod stood there, pounding his head with a gauntleted hand. "There I go again, for a doctor I am a complete gommerel, forgetting about you being. . . . Och, well, never mind, a good tea will pull you together again. The tea shop is at the bottom of the hill yonder and just down the wynd. I thought we could walk from here, but if you're not up to it, we can still take the bike."

She held up a trembling hand. "Oh, no! No, thanks! I'll walk it."

The tea shop proved to be all he had said it would be, and by the time they started to walk back to the motorbike, Kirsty had begun to feel better. However the thought of reentering that mobile coffin was enough to bring on a fresh attack of the shakes.

Her companion chattered on about his pride and joy, the motorbike, especially made for him by a pal of his father's, who lived in Lancashire. In fact he told her, " 'Tis the only one of its kind with such a good, safe sidecar that you can take off when you don't need it." Kirsty's thoughts now riveted on how she would get safely to the Livingstones, without having to get in the "thing," one of a kind or not. Suddenly her attention left that problem and swung to something else he was saying.

"Excuse me, Doctor—I mean, Mike—but what did you say?"

"Och, Kirsty, you've not been listening to a word, have you?"

She blushed and looked away across the open stretch of field. If he didn't want to repeat what she thought he had said, then she didn't want to hear it anyway. Unseeing, she bent to pluck a bluebell from a cluster growing on the edge of the banking.

Suddenly she felt her hand being grasped tightly. "I think you heard well enough, Miss Kirsty Brodie, at least the important bits. But I'll repeat it anyway. I'm asking you to be my lass. You'll be staying at the Livingstones until I'm satisfied you're completely better and then. . . ." He squeezed the hand as he said the next part all in a rush. "Then, when they pronounce you well, we can get wed. I've never known a lass like you or one whom I was so sure about from the first. . . . Well, you're bonny, and you're quiet, yet with a deep wisdom inside." Receiving no response, he kept on: "I want a wife and family someday, and you—"

At last Kirsty moved. She snatched her hand away, crying out, "No, no, Mike! Stop saying all that. This canna be! You ken nowt aboot me. I'm not sure of much aboot masel'. . . . I—" Her sincere amazement brought out the mixture of Doric and Irish that was her normal twang and spurted tears as she continued to choke out. "Only two weeks ago you didna ken such a bein' as Kirsty Brodie existed, and now—and now you—"

Mike reached for her hand again, this time closing both of his hands over the trembling fingers that still held the flower. "That's just it, Kirsty. Fate has brought us together. 'Tis true we don't know much about each other yet, but I'm satisfied I need no more. This way we can start a new life, just the two of us. . . . Och, I'm not saying we'll be wed the morrow or even in a month's time. All I ask is for you to think on it and don't say no till you have."

They had reached the motorbike. She stopped abruptly and stared askance at it, then back to its owner. Speechless, she wondered what could have happened to the nice, simple outing they had started on so blithely. Even the weather seemed to be against them.

Almost frantically, her eyes darted about, seeking a way of escape. Mike still held her hands, but catching some of her terror and belatedly realizing it did not all stem from his rash proposal, he allowed his grip to loosen. She shook free from his gentle hold and turned to run, but he caught her at once.

"Och, Kirsty, I'm sorry. I'm that inclined to rush things. You're still under an awful strain, and here am I, supposed to be a doctor, adding to your bewilderment, not seeing it. Can you forgive me and try to forget some of the things I've been saying? Most of them, in fact, and we'll go back to taking one day at a time. Now we'd better be getting away home before the rain comes down in earnest." But it had already started. Great drops of water spattered on the bonnet of the sidecar even as he spoke, and he reached to open the small door.

She shied away. "I'll not be goin' back into that thing!"

He looked up in sincere surprise. "How else will we get to Motherwell?"

"I dinna ken, but it'll not be in that."

He sighed heavily as he leaned over to extract a pair of waterproof capes from the box behind his seat. "Put this on anyway, before you get soaked to the skin. Was that not how Harry found you? Maybe you're a water nymph or something!" He fastened the cape for her before draping the second one round his own shoulders, his mind busy all the while about how to get them both out of this predicament and home to Motherwell.

She stood with bowed head, watching the rain as it formed small rivulets on the shiny surface of her cape.

"All right then," the doctor proposed, "if I push the bike, will you sit in it, as long as I promise not to start the motor? You can't walk, that's for certain. It's a long road back!"

Suddenly Kirsty shook herself in much the same way a dog does when its coat is wet, to be rid of the excess water. Her hair flew loose, and she automatically raised a hand to tuck it into the leather helmet, which he had placed back on her head.

He watched her and waited, wondering what would happen next. Then he gasped.

She was smiling, and a moment later she managed a tremulous laugh, "A water nymph, is it? My da' called me that once, but I've aye been feart of the deep water, as well as some other things I could mention. I think I've been feart to grow up. But no, Mike. I canna let you walk pushing that muckle thing with me in it. I'll not be walking, and you'll not either. I've been that foolish, but I've come a long road this very day, and I think I'm comin' back to myself. Help me into your contraption again, but promise me you'll not be goin' quite as quick."

He stared for one long moment before, reassured, he let out a great burst of laughter, lifted her bodily, and placed her very gently into the sidecar. If his thoughts and feelings flew on to the day when he would ask her again, to the next time, when she would say yes, to another day when he would carry her over their very own threshold, belated wisdom made him speak no more. He had got away with his rushed suit this time, but his heart surged with new hope.

Folding the aproned top over her lap, Mike met her full and open gaze. Kirsty's glorious eyes sparkled at him. No pain or fear lay hidden in their green depths now. Could that be a hint of mischief? Did he dare hope she was completely well? Why not? Inwardly he exulted.

She bent to fasten the last snap on the apron, and he could no longer resist dropping a chaste kiss on the hair escaping from the back of the helmet. A sweet fragrance, a mixture of almond essence and lilac, met his nostrils, and he thought, *'Tis not going to be easy, this waiting, but I will, I'll have patience, and I'll win her yet. The prize will be worth it.*

Their return journey was much more sedate as a chastened Mike pushed the motor into the slowest gear. He found out, too, that one could carry on a limited conversation with a passenger when one went this slowly. She didn't catch everything he said, but some words floated out to her as he waved precariously at a field almost completely carpeted with bluebells. "Virginia Bluebells . . . next week . . . take short walk together . . . closer look, gather some. Do . . . see . . . over yonder's a stalled motor . . . petrol . . . two men walking to it . . . petrol tin. They're soaked. Wonder, och, we'll not stop. They're fine, and I want to get you home." The last sentence came through clearly as he faced her again.

Kirsty snuggled down in the blanket he had tucked about her legs, glad she wasn't out there walking in this heavy downpour. *The thing's not so bad when you get used to it, and you're not trying to win a race of some kind.* If she spared a moment and a thought for the two men plodding toward the stopped motorcar, her only emotion was pity that they were getting so wet.

She voiced the thought, but her companion could not hear, "Hope they'll not catch their death of cold!"

17

"Och, Reverend Bruce, it's a wonder ye didna catch yer death, bein' drookit like that and no' gettin' dry claes for hoors efter!" Betsy clucked and fussed over Bruce while Granny Mac hovered in the background. The old lady had just waved good-bye to Peter, who had pronounced, with a knowing grin, that the patient would live to wallow in self-pity for a while yet, unless his womenfolk petted him to death.

Then Peter had grown serious for a moment as he warned Beulah, "Don't allow Mary Jean in to see him. But I suppose we needn't worry, as Jamie'll keep her away. Being so near her time, she mustn't catch a cold the now."

Beulah had replied, "They are both stubborn enough to defy us all, but if we tell Bruce he could hurt her or the bairn, he'll behave. Mary Jean is another matter, but as you said, Jamie'll see to her." They had gazed long at each other before Beulah put the question they had all been asking, "What of his crusade to Motherwell?"

"Except for catching the cold, they've come back the same as they left. Stirling's mother is clucking over him even more than your Betsy is over Bruce. That son of mine is so bad tempered, I'm not saying much about the petrol business or asking questions yet. I'm hoping he'll learn a good lesson from this experience and not let it happen again. Pray that the cold'll not affect his chest. We've no desire for pneumonia to set in or—"

Beulah waved that thought away. "The Lord brought your Stirling through a lot worse than pneumonia, Peter."

"He did, and I'm grateful, even if I have some questions regarding that to put to the hielandman. But we'll wait a while." He ran down the steps and disappeared before Beulah could ask what questions.

Now, as Beulah stood watching Betsy minister to Bruce with hot-water bottles and chicken soup and all the other remedies she thought fitting—whether or not ordered by the doctors—the telephone shrilled from the hallway below. To Beulah's surprise, Mary Jean and Jamie, with Bruce's encouragement, had insisted on the contraption being installed, saying it saved them both from making the journey when she and Mary Jean wanted to talk. She admitted this, but still resented its clamoring intrusions. She liked it best when she could sit opposite them all and watch their faces as they talked.

The new maid, Maggie—she would ever be the new maid—called up the stairs, " 'Tis Dr. Jamie for you, mistress, and he's that excitit!" Amazingly agile for her ninety-odd years, Beulah descended the stairs again to reach the instrument. As she reached the bottom step her prayer became, "Lord Jesus, let it be good news, good news!" But her voice remained steady as she shouted at the mouthpiece, "Hullo, hullo, is it you, Jamie?"

"It is that, Granny Mac. It's started, and it's no false labor this time. All is normal, now, so dinna fret. 'Twill be a while yet, so let Bruce have a good night's rest before you tell him. Then we both know nothing'll keep him from seeing her. Yes, she's a day or two before time, but that's all right as well. I'm away back to her side now. Next time we speak, I'll be a daddy and you, why, you'll be a great-great-granny!"

Beulah replaced the earpiece slowly. It was fine for Jamie to say all was well, and she did believe him. In spite of that her mind flew to Mary Jean's own birth night and the difficult time their Jeannie had had. Sheer strength of will, along with the deepest of love for her baby and her man, had kept the spirit alight in the frail frame that night and for the two more years God had granted her. Beulah glanced up the stairs. No sound reached her, and she prayed that Bruce was resting. Her own resolve to pray the night through already fixed, she bypassed the stairs and the swinging doors leading to the kitchen, where Maggie would be busy preparing the trays for their breakfast. In her private sitting room, she seated herself comfortably in her chair—she and the Lord had long ago reached an agreement that He would make allowance for her aging knees—and picked up her Bible. Of its own accord it opened at Psalm 103. What better way to begin her prayer vigil? She did not need her spectacles for these beloved verses, and she began softly to recite them: "Bless the Lord, O my soul: and all that is within me, bless his holy name. Bless the Lord, O my soul, and forget not all his benefits. . . ."

"It's a boy, Bruce. You have a fine grandson!" The voice, strangely familiar, yet one he could not immediately place, echoed through Bruce's dream. Whatever Betsy had put in his bedtime drink had surely sent him off into some kind of never-never land. He shook himself awake and blinked his eyes at the bearer of such momentous good tidings.

He struggled to sit up as the voice continued, "Yes, you're not dreaming. It's me, Fayfel, and it's all true. A braw lad, as my nephew-in-law would say."

Bruce groaned. "I suppose everybody else gets to see him before I do? This accursed cold! Mary Jean . . . ?"

"Mary Jean is perfect, and so is the boy," another voice added. "What cold? I perceive you are quite well enough to rise from your couch and venture forth."

Bruce needed no sight of the owner of this voice to confirm who it was. "Raju, you old rascal, I've no doubt you have seen my lad before me, as well."

"Not yet, no. My wife here, along with a dozen or so denizens of the maternity ward, have kept me and his many other would-be admirers at bay. Well, are you going to lie there all day? Wife, nurse or not, you may be excused until this grandfather is properly attired for a lady's eyes." Laughing his delight, Bruce pulled the covers aside and stepped from the bed. "You mean I'll get to see them already?"

"Indeed and you will, if you move yourself. Here, Betsy has your clothes all set out for you. From what I hear, if you don't hurry to join the admiration society, Doctor and Mistress Jamie Douglass will surely burst."

On the way Raju ventured the all-important question. "What will they name the boy?"

"They've said nothing to me, but I'm praying not another Bruce."

Faye Felicity Smith stole a glance at her husband as she said, "We do seem to have an abundance of them, do we not?"

No trace of weakness remained as Bruce MacAlister took the hospital steps two at a time.

Peter met him in the corridor. "Well, chieftain—or should I say Grandfather MacAlister?—it's high time you got here. They're waiting for you. The rest of us can sit here and have a blether." He got no argument from the Smiths, and Bruce proceeded in the direction indicated.

Jamie, taking advantage of his position as a doctor with privileges in this hospital, had been present with his wife for these most important moments. "Reverend Bruce MacAlister, meet your grandson, Jason Philip Douglass, and Jason Philip, meet your granddad." Solemnly Bruce leaned over to take the tiny fist. At his touch the baby's eyes flew open, and Bruce was startled by the brilliant gaze that met his own.

"How do you do, Grandson? 'Tis an illustrious name you have there. I'll not ask your parents what made them decide on it, as it is yours already." Mary Jean held up her son. She had requested that the nurses and attendants dispense with swaddling cloths and binders, except for one small napkin to be pinned on. She began to loosen that as she spoke to her father. "Look him over well, Daddy. Ask God to bless every part. We will have the official service later on, but Jamie and I want our dedication service the now. My love, do you have the oil?"

Her husband stepped forward. "I have it, Mary Jean."

They said no more and Bruce held out his cupped hands to receive the anointing oil from the flask as Jamie poured liberally. He extended his hands then to receive the wriggling infant from Mary Jean. His eyes were dry as he carried out his daughter's request. Enfolding the tiny body, his grasp secure, he felt the strongly beating heart, and he spoke the blessing in his own way: "Be stout hearted but tender, loving, kind, and true. Be joyful!"

The tiny head, perfectly proportioned, with none of the usual birth dents or bruises, was covered with bright-red hair. The sight of it almost caused Bruce to falter, but he continued, "Wisdom above knowledge, we pray, Lord Jesus. Humility in its place and understanding above learning. Healthy, strong bones and flesh, internal and external parts functioning, according to Your perfect plan, O Lord. We pray it all in Thy Name, O Christ, and for Thy Kingdom's sake. Amen."

"Whatever will you do now, Bruce, my lad?"

Peter's question brought his friend out of his daydream. In Bruce's old study at the top of the manse, Peter sprawled in the armchair, while Bruce stood gazing intently out of the high, bowed window. His view, on this unusually clear day, took in, to the west and slightly north, the university buildings. To the east and southward, he could just glimpse the Kelvin Museum and the lush gardens surrounding it. Without turning round, he answered Peter, "On a day like this, it's hard to think of leaving such a fair and pleasant field, Peter. I would that I could linger awhile."

Peter spluttered, splashing some of the delicious, freshly brewed coffee, just brought in by Bruce's new secretary. Recovering, Peter placed his cup carefully back on the tray before he rose and walked over to Bruce. "Fair and pleasant fields is it? Man, you're daft! Fine ye ken what's behind the braw facade. Oh, I'll grant you the city fathers keep the Kelvin and the university grounds fair enough, but walk half a mile, and you leave all this beauty behind and find yourself beside a river that, to put it mildly, is far, far from pure and sweet. No, you'll be in the midst of the shipyards and the engine works and the clamor of the riveters and the pounding of the hammers, and—"

"Stop! Stop! Peter, I get your meaning, and I'm well enough aware of all that. It doesn't stop me from enjoying the pearl in the middle of it, and it shouldn't stop you either. Granted, some of this is for show, but think what it would be like without. Anyway, you forget that go another mile, beyond the shipyards again, and you'll find on every hand more braw buildings. To me they display both beauty and taste and. . . . Oh, I know—" He swept the horizon with a hand before swinging round again to face Peter, purpling with the depth of his indignation. "I know, I know, the facade's there, too, but think of the other alternative."

Peter subsided at that. As usual the highland laddie had the rights of it. "I'm more interested in the folk, Bruce, and that's a fact. A body does what he can, but it aye seems inadequate."

Bruce placed a hand on his friend's shoulder. "Yes, I do understand, Peter. We all do our best in our own way and beyond that as the Lord shows us."

Both men contemplated this for a short while, and then the ever-impatient Peter returned to his question, "You're avoiding answering me, my man. What are you going to do now? What happened to the plan to go to America?"

Bruce went back to contemplating the view, without really seeing it. "Well, I'll tell you, Peter, I've still a hankering to go. But my plans, as you call them, included, for a wee while anyway, that I would not be going alone. It all seemed to be fitting in, Hamish having other things to do now than be my shadow. Mind you, I'm not complaining about that. I needed him, and God provided. Then the way my young cousin, Craig Fairbanks, described his home state, he drew a bonny picture of clear streams—crystal rivers he called them—reminding me of the vision in Revelation. But now I don't know."

"Go anyway, Bruce, man. What makes you hesitate? Mary Jean is safely delivered. She and Jamie have their own lives, which I understand include plans to go to Canada when the lad's a year old. Hamish is well occupied in his pursuits, and you must have about two-thirds of your year's leave left. I'd say you're set to go. If you're still worried about Granny Mac, set your mind to rest. She's taken a new lease on life with the lad Jason, and you should be back before the Douglasses are ready to leave."

" 'Tis all the Lord's prerogative, Peter. We cannot dictate the times or circumstances."

"We cannot do that, I'll grant you, but many's the sermon I've heard from you where you said, 'Acknowledge Him in all your ways, and He shall direct your paths.' My interpretation of that for Peter Blair would be I cannot change the Glasgow slums, but I can help the one or two of the folk forced to stay in it every day, who come to see me."

"Why, Peter, as always you amaze me with your grasp of things. You are right. I must pull myself together. In fact this very day I'll go and book passage. Will you come?"

"You don't need me. I just saw Hamish making his way to the back door. Oh, I know he's not going with you, but I'm sure you'll have a lot to talk about without me putting in my oar. Besides Aggie's expecting me home. I'll go out the other door. I've a strong notion to go through the kirk."

18

As Peter disappeared along the corridor leading to the outside and the path to the kirk, Bruce turned back into his study. His friend would ever question, but his kind heart, which Peter tried unsuccessfully to hide most of the time, would overrule in the end. Waiting now for Hamish to join him, Bruce still puzzled about his friend. Very well, he knew that the persistent doctor was far from satisfied with Bruce's answers about what he would be doing now. In fact if Hamish had not been seen arriving, the personal questions would have gone on, including questions about Kirsty. No one, not even Agatha Rose, had bothered him with questions about her.

What indeed was Bruce going to do? He pushed a hand through his hair, feeling the ridges on his brow that accompanied the old, familiar frown. Prayers, searching, planning the future with or without her, nothing he had done or could think of doing brought him the peace he yearned for at the thought of her.

He smoothed his hair and his brow as he at last heard Hamish in the corridor, but his stepbrother was not alone. Could that be MacKinnon's hearty tones as well? He opened the door in surprised welcome.

The inspector spoke first, "There you are then. I'm hoping that with all this fuss of becoming a granddaddy and all, you've not forgot a friend's wedding next week?"

Bruce's smile was a bit sheepish. "Not forgot the wedding, but I confess misplacing the date."

The other man laughed joyously. "Good job I came to remind you then, but Hamish here tells me you might have a wee job for me first. That would be fine, because I'm finding this year of waiting a tedious one. What is it, my friend?"

Bruce had turned back to the window as a fresh rush of emotion swept him.

Hamish broke in, "I only mentioned the fact, not the details. Shall I go and get some fresh coffee?"

"No, leave it, Hamish. I've had enough for the now. Maybe you should both hear this." He proceeded to tell them all that had transpired in Motherwell. Thomas leaned back in the chair so recently vacated by Peter. "The woman Dickson is a liar surely, but never heed about her the now. I know the man in Motherwell—a grand sort he is. Name of Harry Livingstone. Aye, he is related to the great David, as he tells everybody at first introduction, but he's a good polisman for a' that. I wonder if he has the telephone?" Hamish, who had remained standing throughout, now declared, "I'll go and get the secretary to find oot."

Bruce's brow had resumed its frown. "What good will that do, Thomas? I've avoided the law except for you the now, not wanting to admit to any kind of illegality. Besides, I can't help thinking that if Kirsty is in her right mind again, she should have let me know." Thomas stared at him. "Would she now? Are ye not forgetting that she hardly knew you before her memory lapsed? Does she know any of your intentions toward her, in fact, did any of us know that until you told us the now? I'm thinking any decent lass would be waiting for the man to do the courting, if courting it's to be."

Feeling the flush in his cheeks, but not trying to deny anything, Bruce waited as Hamish came back into the room.

"The only telyphones in Motherwell are at the hospital, the Station Hotel, and some of the doctors. What's to do now?"

Thomas scratched his chin and then gave a sigh. "The doctors, you say? Let me think for a minute. The last time I visited Harry, he and his wife were entertaining a young fellow who was going to be setting up a practice in Motherwell. I wonder now, what was it they called him again?" *Pat Tod* or no, 'twas *Michael*. I mind thinking, for a Scot, his name sounded gye Irish. . . . Hamish, go and find out if a Doctor Michael Tod is on the list."

Amazement at this man's incredible memory rendered Bruce

speechless for only a moment. "Thomas, imagine you remembering all that about a mere acquaintance, even a fellow policeman. You're a wonder, that you are!"

"Not such a wonder. As young constables we walked a beat together once, and when he married, he settled for the quiet life, while I had a different ambition. 'Twas at their wedding anniversary a year or two ago that I last saw them."

"It's still amazing how you mind it all. But supposing this doctor has the telephone, what good will that do?"

"I'll give him a message to pass on to Harry. Oh, don't fash yourself. I'll only say I'm coming to pay a visit. They should be invited to my wedding anyway. We'll see what happens after that. 'Tis a long shot that he's heard anything concerning your Kirsty, but not much transpires on or near his beat that Harry doesn't know about."

Hamish came in, looking pleased. "They do so have a Doctor Michael Tod on the list. What's next?"

"What's next, after I talk to this doctor, is another jaunt to Motherwell. I was meaning to spend some time with my intended, but I'm sure she'll agree this should be settled first. The train I think. Motorcars are more bother than they're worth. Someday that will change, I'm sure, but for the now. . . . Come away then, who else is for Motherwell?"

Michael Tod had been out most of the night on a difficult confinement. When he had returned to his rooms, ready to go to sleep for a few hours before beginning his morning rounds, an emergency case had been brought in from the agricultural-implements works and taken that coveted hour. Returning from the house visits, he thought again longingly of his bed, but afternoon surgery should begin in twenty minutes, so that would be out of the question. When he at last got back from the surgery, his exhaustion almost won.

"I wish Harry had the telephone, and I'd tell him and Carrie I'll not come for tea the night. I need sleep more." Thinking of the thing caused it to jangle, it seemed, and he walked slowly to the cubbyhole where his landlady kept it.

"Hullo. . . . Aye, this is Doctor Michael Tod. What is it? A friend of Constable Livingstone, you say. . . . Yes, I have the message. . . . He'll have it the minute I see him." Mike glanced at the grandfather clock that stood in the hallway. He had the most part of an hour before teatime, and he would just have a wee lie down, before going to the Livingstones.

"May I ask why ye're settin' the good chiny oot the night, Carrie, my pet? What may the occasion be?"

Kirsty glanced up from her task of setting the table. The same question had crossed her own mind when Carrie had told her to use the best dishes and cutlery. Carrie spoke crossly to her man. For a sharp-witted polisman, he surely could be glaiket at times.

" 'Tis a month ago the day since Kirsty came to us. That's a good enough occasion, as you call it, for me. I'll just go and make sure the roast is all right." Wondering why she seemed so nervous, Kirsty thought, *She's been making sure the roast and all the other comestibles for the feast are all right for the past hour.* Harry stared at her quizzically. "Are you sure you dinna ken what this is all about, Kirsty, lass?" Thinking she did not know but had her suspicions, Kirsty shook her head.

Just then a pounding at the door drew their attention, and Harry rose. "I'll go. 'Tis likely Mike, maybe he kens. . . ." His shout from the lobby told all and sundry that the visitor was not Mike, but someone else he knew very well.

Carrie had rejoined Kirsty in the front room, and they gazed at each other speechlessly as Harry's words reached them, "Chief Inspector Thomas MacKinnon, you great rogue. You should have tellt us you were comin'. We would have killed the fatted calf and all that. Come away in this minute, come in. . . . Carrie, you'll never guess who's darkenin' our doorstep the night—"

Rushing to meet them, she answered, "With all that yelling and shouting, I don't need to guess. Thomas, 'tis that good to see you. . . . Dinna stand there. Harry, take his coat, and you come away in. I've somebody I want you to meet. Where did you go, lass?" But the front room was empty and a draft coming through the house indicated the back door was wide open. Clucking in annoyance, Carrie ran to shut it before calling up the steps, "Kirsty, where are you? Come down and meet our good friend."

But Kirsty had snatched an old shawl from the hook on the lobby wall before rushing out the back door. She stumbled across the lane, and her feet took her, without hesitation, in the direction of Mike's lodgings. Not stopping to think clearly, she escaped from the person whom she had heard named *Inspector MacKinnon*. Some deep inner knowing had stirred a memory, and the name *MacKinnon* was a strong part of it. While she'd been lying on a bed or maybe a couch, listening to different voices, she had heard the name mentioned. Sometimes it came in a childish accent raised in argument, and other times a soft dreamy sound, discussing a marriage. Another voice, harsh and resounding, had filled her ears with angry noises, and she could even recall some of the words: "It hasn't taken you long to forget my brother, has it, Blodwin Parker?"

The reply had sounded like, "Ian would approve of my being happy and his children getting such a fine man as Inspector MacKinnon for a father."

In her confused state, now almost as much as then, Kirsty had not made head nor tails of it; she only knew that she wanted away from that memory. The strange, unknown Kirsty Brodie must have done something awful bad for a chief inspector to be after her.

Suddenly she stopped running, having reached the house where Mike stayed. Belatedly she wondered what she would say to him, How would he respond to her foolish fears?

"Kirsty, come away in. Excuse the mess, but I've had a rough day, and now I've overslept for evening surgery. Whatever you're here for is a blessing in disguise because—" Mike stopped as he took in her anguished face. "What is it, lass? What's frightened you so much?" Bewildered, she glanced about, and he led her to his only chair.

"Take your time, now. The patients can just wait another wee while. Tell me."

She managed to gasp out the one word, "MacKinnon!"

His heart gave a lurch as the name registered. The message for Harry! He'd forgotten all about it, but the state of the woman became his first concern. He reached for his medical bag. A small dose of soothing syrup was called for.

Kirsty would have none of it. "No, Mike, not that stuff. I'll just sit here whilst you go to surgery. I'm all right now. It's time I started being my own self again, and I'm remembering some things, things I might have remembered afore, if I had let them come in. Give me a pencil and paper and then you go. When you come back, I'll have it all written down."

He stared at her doubtfully, but catching her determined air, he walked toward the sideboard, where he kept his prescription pads.

She went on, "Trust me, Mike. I do believe I'm coming all the way to myself at last. Some of the memories will be hard, but I'm not the sissy ye've all been pampering. If I have done something bad, or my da' did something against the law, then I'll have to face up to it. I ken that now. Maybe I shouldny have run away, but anyway, off ye go now, and dinna worry."

He gave her one more hard glance before nodding. This was indeed a different Kirsty. As he closed the door carefully behind him, his thoughts ran on. Did he want a different Kirsty, one who could be strong and decisive like this? He would have to consider it carefully. What about the Livingstones? What would they think of this change? Oh, my, what would they be thinking at this moment, when Carrie's pet had vanished? He reached his surgery and stepped out to pass the folk waiting in line on the pavement. He would be here for some time.

Noting a lad near the front, he called out, "Eddie Tamsen, will ye run a message for me, for a penny?"

Jeers and catcalls followed this. "I was here afore Eddie Tamsen!" and "Teacher's pet!" and one other, "I'll run yer message for a penny, Doctor, unless it's to—" The rest of the call drowned out as he closed the door on the crowd.

Quickly he scribbled a note as Eddie sniveled, "I hope it's no' faur, Doctor Tod. I'm no' that weel!"

"Only round to the police station. Don't worry, Eddie, just give this to Mistress Livingstone. She'll have a biscuit for you. Come straight in when you come back, and I'll see to you first."

*   *   *

Carrie Livingstone was in a fair tizzy! Here she had three visitors: One, the chief inspector himself, was their friend, but his status in the force still left her in awe; then he had with him a nice-looking minister whom Thomas had introduced as Bruce MacAlister. She knew of this one as well. Hadn't Harry admitted to her a week or so ago how a Reverend MacAlister was going round the town asking about the Brodies? Harry had let on to her that he would do nothing about it, as he thought Kirsty was far from ready to face any such inquiry.

This was different, though, official, with Thomas acting awful grim. The three strangers in her parlor all had that look, and she risked a glance at her own man. His face had set, too, in that stubborn way she knew only too well. What would he do? He would never tell a lie, but again, he might avoid the truth for as long as he could. Just now he allowed Thomas to do all the talking. The minister and his brother also sat silently. Harry signaled for her to bring the tea, and she left them like that.

As she quietly closed the door she could hear the inspector's voice. "Harry, man, I know you well enough to feel sure you're not telling me the whole story. You're too good a policeman not to be aware that Bruce here visited Motherwell a while ago, seeking information about this Matt Brodie and his daughter, Kirsty. When we came in just now, I swear I heard Carrie shouting that very name, and now you act as if I'm here to do you harm. Well, I'm not. The reverend here only wants what is best for this woman and to reassure himself that she is well enough now. Can you not speak up, Harry, and trust us?"

Harry turned his head away. He did trust Thomas, but what about the other two unknown quantities? Carrie had told him about Kirsty's dreams—she would wake up from them in fright and be saying the same phrase every time. Carrie had said it sounded like, "Bruce . . . family." After looking toward the door, hoping his wife would come back with the tea tray, he realized he must stop postponing the inevitable. Making up his mind at last, Harry began to speak.

19

"**I** knew well enough about the two strangers going about the town, asking for the Brodies. It didn't take much to ken they meant no harm. By then my Carrie—and I must say me as weel—were that attached to Kirsty Brodie, after taking the lass in off the streets in an awful state. Maybe you'll say I did wrong in a lot of ways, Thomas, but when you hear the whole story. . . . Anyway we never let on to Kirsty about the reverend here and his amateur sleuthing. He and his young helper were maist visible."

Bruce stirred restlessly. The man's confession could get long-winded, and he had a feeling something was going on elsewhere in the policeman's house. For one thing the wife had not come in with the customary tea.

Thomas awaited further enlightenment. He had distinctly heard somebody shouting the name *Kirsty*, but the fiery minister seemed to have missed that. If any admonishing had to be done, he, Thomas MacKinnon, needed no help in that department, but he would do it in private with his friends.

Ready to break into the talk, Bruce rose from his chair, but Livingstone's next sentence bade him pause. "So, knowing Kirsty still had a lot of mending to do within herself, right or wrong, I kept quiet. When she got back to normal, able to make up her own mind, that would be soon enough to tell her. Carrie enjoyed having the company of one such as Kirsty, and she had schemes that included our young friend, Doctor Michael Tod. I gave objections to that idea, although nobody said anything definite on that score, that I know of."

Bruce could contain himself no longer: "You mean she's been here all this time, then, well enough, and in her right senses?"

Harry looked grieved, "Right enough, Reverend. . . . I—"

But Bruce stood and walked quickly toward the door. "Where is she the now? I cannot stand this. Where is she, man?" He pulled the door wide. "Once I've seen her and heard her side directly, instead of all this hearsay, I'll set my mind at rest and leave her be, if that's what she wants."

Thomas also rose, and he placed a restraining hand on Bruce's arm. "You're quite right, Bruce. It seems to me there's been enough guessing and rushing about with not enough thought. But sit down whilst I summarize. Harry, there are some aspects of this you don't know and haven't cared to find out. 'Tis true no missing-person report has been bulletined for Miss Brodie, because when she was abducted from the Mains Farm, she appeared to have gone willingly, in the care of her mother. I say *abducted*, and then I say *willingly*, for a reason. As a rule they two don't go together. . . . No, no, Bruce, be patient a wee while yet. We have good reason to believe that by now she is in her right senses. But Harry, at the time she left Mains she was suffering from amnesia. We now suspect she had been drugged in the bargain. Wait, all of you, some of us here know the story, in bits and from our own outlook, but—" Both Harry and Bruce made restless movements, and abruptly Thomas reached a conclusion on the matter, "All right. Maybe it's time now that we let Kirsty Brodie speak for herself. Harry, will you give your wife a shout? Tell her never to mind the tea and—"

But Carrie had appeared at the door, her agitation plain to be seen. "She's run away! I thought her safely upstairs, shy as she is an' all; but it seemed awful quiet, so I went up to her room. She's no' in the hoose. Oh, Harry, she's only wearing her slippers and—" The rest was a wail as Harry reached for her and the other three gaped at each other.

Bruce's lips moved in prayer, but before any could dart off, Thomas spoke up: "No more rushing off at a tangent now! She's been away for close to half an hour at a guess, so another minute or two willna make much difference. Carrie, m'dear, could you pull yourself together and tell us all she would be wearing besides the slippers? Harry, you did say Kirsty's in her right mind again? Do you think we'll be searching at random, or will she make for any one place in particular?"

The Livingstones glanced at each other then back to Thomas. They spoke one word together: "Mike's."

Wee Eddie Tamsen had meant to do the doctor's bidding, but his pain had suddenly left him as he felt the penny in his hand grow heavy. If he hurried up, he could buy some sweeties on the way and then run with the letter. He wasn't feart of Constable Livingstone, because he, Eddie, was a member of the boys' club, so he knew well the big man was all bark and no bite, except when you did something awful bad. By the time he reached the Livingstone house, Eddie's five minutes had multiplied to twenty-five; he'd taken the long road, when he saw some of the other lads at the corner. If they saw the sweeties, they would want a share, and they would take too many away. Quickly he pushed the note through the letter box and began to run like a hare back to the surgery. His sore thumb with the big whitlow throbbed worse than ever, and if he went home without getting it lanced, his own mam would have it in for him even more than the doctor or the polis.

Inside the doctor's lodging, Kirsty had already regretted her hasty impulse to rush here. Thinking about it quietly now, without any other body to tell her what to do, she at last returned fully to herself. Since the outing on the motorbike, she had been allowing matters to slide out of her control again, seeing it was the easiest road to take. She'd let Mike and Carrie and the big policeman, who kept looking at her in a funny way, make her plans. She had not agreed with Mike in words, but well she knew his hopes, and she hadn't said no, either, finding it easier just to be agreeable. Speaking aloud to her reflection in the mirror in the door of Mike's wardrobe, she adjured herself, "Kirsty Brodie! You're a big cowardy custard! Your da' would be ashamed of you. Runnin' and runnin', even after the need to escape had passed. Well enough do you know Bruce MacAlister that he would never make the charges against you that Maimie Dickson accused him of. So then why be

so feart from yon inspector? You know your auntie and your
mother well enough, too. Remember how the money was all-
important to Nellie Brodie and how Maimie Dickson would scheme
and plot and even fight for the sake of a shilling?

"As for the folk you've been staying with, they are the kindest,
best folk, next to your da' and Bruce, you have ever kent. Granted
they've been too protective, but you just sat there and let them be.
You know Mike wants to marry you, and you know you never had
any intention of marrying him, but you let him think you might.
No more excuses, Kirsty Brodie, no more hiding behind Carrie's
skirts or anybody else's. You're your own self again. Be bold and
strong like your da' always taught you and brought you up to be.
Stand on your own two feet!"

She had been addressing her reflection in a loud whisper, but as
she said *feet* the floodgates burst. Scalding hot, though soothing
and healing, the tears came. Kirsty turned to find a chair and sat
down heavily, ignoring the water gushing from her eyes. In a
minute she would go back and face the Livingstones and whatever
else awaited. As it was she had done enough to hurt Mike and his
reputation.

A knock sounded on the door, and as it swung all the way open
the room suddenly filled with folk—some she knew and some she
didn't know. But through them and through her tears, hastily
wiped on Carrie's apron, which she still wore round her waist, she
instantly recognized the startling blue gaze of Bruce MacAlister.
Their eyes locked, and the others moved aside while, slowly at first
and then all in a rush, those two flew toward each other, oblivious
to all else. False shyness and all pretense left, and Kirsty Brodie
allowed Bruce MacAlister to gather her into his arms.

Harry placed a hand on his wife's shoulder as she gasped, but
there was no need for words. True love was plain to see, and they
knew it at once. Thomas MacKinnon backed out of the door, bumping into Hamish as he did. That man's astonishment changed to
understanding as he joined the inspector.

The delegation now met a terribly frustrated and dejected doctor
as he entered his home, spent and weary. A moment earlier Mistress Sutherland, his landlady, had briefly and pointedly explained

all that had been happening in his rooms. Resigned, he moved on up the stairs, and Carrie patted his shoulders as he passed her. Between them they had dreamed up a fantasy, but in truth Mike had always known that Kirsty was not for him. Even before she had begun to get better, the faraway look in her wonderful eyes had always been for this other, this unknown who now had a name, *Reverend Bruce MacAlister*.

"So, you've no objections to marrying a grandfather, then, Kirsty?"

She threw him a startled glance before replying, "Not as long as it's yourself. Don't forget you'll be marrying a pauper!"

It was Bruce's turn to be startled. "Oh, I suppose there would be no way for you to know about the gold?"

She waited, determined not to yell out. Gold! She wanted to hear no more of gold.

"The gold your father found and then hid in the *Revelation*. It has been recovered and is now in the sheriff's safe keeping. It's bound for the British Museum, but there is a reward. We all thought it might be for me, but the sheriff ruled it should be your father's and therefore yours now." She gave him one of her piercing looks, and he was glad he had told the whole truth, as she would have surely known otherwise.

"Is that a fact, Reverend? I'm not sure I want any of it, but on the other hand, Da' would be pleased if I went to my wedding decked out in the usual finery and having a set of wedding china of my own."

Ready to protest that he had enough money and china for them both and to spare, Bruce stopped. She needed to have this independence. He sighed with relief again, thankful that the money truly did belong to her.

The couple sat in the corner of the railway carriage, on the way to Glasgow from Motherwell. A telephone call to the Blair house had assured everyone that Kirsty would be most welcome to stay with Agatha Rose, as long as need be. Bruce had not yet told Mary Jean and Jamie, and he had begged Agatha to hold the news from them and from Granny Mac as well. All in good time. Hamish, in his position of chaperon, roamed about outside in the corridor.

Thomas MacKinnon would be close to Aribaig by this time. Before the week was out he would bring his bride-to-be back to Glasgow, and their wedding would take place next Saturday. Bruce glanced again at Kirsty. In profile she looked just as bonny. The Cairnglen folk would fair gloat over her. Feeling his intent gaze, she flushed a deep rose as she turned to him, and her eyes glowed like twin emeralds.

He took her face between his fingers. "I was going to ask you again if you're sure, but I see you are. Do you have any questions?"

"Are you sure your own self, Bruce? Before we get married, in fact before we speak of putting up the banns, will you teach me about your Jesus? I want to know for myself; because if He's what you and Hamish and even the inspector claim He is, then I want that, too. Do you think He would take in one such as me?"

Bruce glanced away hastily. Could he hold any more joy? Gulping, he prayed for wisdom as he began, "He wants you, Kirsty. He loves you, aye, even as you say, and even me. I've said nothing because I knew in my heart this hour would come, but I never dared to think so soon. Yes, my love, I'll teach you, and I'll show you from the Holy Book. I've gathered you've already learned some of it for yourself, but you didn't need to wait. The very day you ask for Him, believing, is the day of your salvation. Let me show you the verse where it says that, and then, oh, I know He's knocking at the door that is Kirsty Brodie's own heart. All she'll have to do is let Him in." The two heads bent close together, and as he glanced through the window, Hamish decided he might as well go back to the club car and join the man there who had invited him to play a game of whist. Somehow Hamish knew this close encounter already had three present, his brother Bruce, his brother's bride-to-be, and the Lord Jesus Christ. Hallelujah!

The train shuffled into the station, and the angels in heaven rejoiced with Hamish at a new name being written down in the Book of Life there, the name of Kirsty Callahan Brodie, soon to be Mrs. MacAlister.

20

But Kirsty Brodie had many more hurdles to overcome before she would bear the name *MacAlister*. The first one would be her meeting with Bruce's daughter, Mary Jean Douglass. *She'll soon be my own stepdaughter, I suppose*, Kirsty mused.

Mistress Douglass and Kirsty gazed long at each other before Mary Jean spoke, "Pleased to meet you, I'm sure, Miss Brodie!"

Kirsty searched frantically with her eyes for Bruce as she responded, "How do you do?" Realizing that Bruce was not going to pluck her out of this one, Kirsty stood her ground. "I'm not sure what to call you yet. What should it be?"

A lot hung on Mary Jean's answer, and the menfolk, very well aware of what was happening, kept up with their own chatter.

"*Mary Jean*'s my name. You may call me by it. And you?"

Kirsty's laugh still sounded uncertain.

"*Kirsty*. My given name is *Crystal*, but my ma aye thought that too fancy for a railwayman's daughter." There, she had done it now, but she was not sorry. If they couldn't take her for herself, it couldn't be helped or changed.

Mary Jean seemed not to hear or heed the description as she caught the name and picked it up for conversation.

Her usual free manners had deserted her, though, and Bruce decided this might be a good chance to intervene. "Kirsty, you never told me your name was *Crystal*! Are there more things I should know about you?" He quickly realized that last had been a mistake.

Jamie bustled over. "You will have opportunities to find out more about each other later. For the now I think we should go in

149

to lunch." The maid appeared, to announce the meal, and the moment passed.

Later Bruce apologized for his daughter, "It's not like her, in one way, and yet in another it is. She takes her time about judgments, and until she makes up her mind, she's inclined to be, well, cool in manners. I mind one time—"

" 'Tis all right, Bruce. I understand. I would likely be the same if a strange woman had ever come after my da'."

But he persisted, "Just the same, it is not my Mary Jean. I wonder if the ever-canny Jamie is at the bottom of this. He's a wee bit of a snob, but he, too, will come round when he realizes your sterling qualities." All at once Bruce's face lightened. "Come here to me. I appreciate all your qualities, and when you look at me like that. . . . Och, what or who can that be now?"

The first of many interruptions took the form of the wedding party from Aribaig. Kirsty had to meet Blodwin Parker and her family all over again. The young ones kept throwing her funny looks for a while, and she blushed, wondering about the strange dreams she still had, in which she would act like a fractious bairn.

Soon wee Susan slipped up to her and placed a small trusting hand in hers. "You're to be our Auntie Kris . . . Kris. . . ."

Her brother helped, "*Kirsty*, Susan, and you're not to be a bother."

Kirsty leaned over to him, saying, "I promise no biting or scratching, now that I'm all better." Three smiles had greeted her words, and she wished it could be this easy with Mary Jean and her man. Anyway another hurdle had been passed.

Spending what the men laughingly called his last free afternoon with Peter, Bruce sat across the table from his friend, grumbling about what he considered unnecessary banishment. He wanted to be with Kirsty; they had been apart long enough.

"A lot of superstitious nonsense, Peter. I'm surprised you sanction such."

"Och, Bruce, you've the rest of your lives and you'll be away to America soon, so don't grudge your friends a bit time. Besides they women are fussing and clucking like a bunch of broody hens, my Aggie not the least of them."

"I suppose that's fair enough but—"

"So you and the missus are truly going to America then?"

"We are, but we're in no hurry."

"No hurry? The last time we mentioned it, you were on your way to book the passage."

Bruce laughed. "A lot has happened since then, Peter—all these weddings, including my own on the morrow."

"But is it not time now?"

"It will be when we get back from Aribaig. With Jeremy not coming to the wedding, I want him and his good woman to meet the real Kirsty."

Peter rubbed his chin thoughtfully. "I told you what happened when our Deb and Barnie stayed with them, up there, did I not?"

"You did, Peter, but I must confess having other things on my mind at the time. I recall good news though. What did happen?"

" 'Tis a delicate subject concerning intimate matters, Bruce. You don't need to know all the medical details. 'Twill be enough to tell you that certain surgical procedures done on a man can be reversed. Father knew of a specialist, a Mr. Warfield from Germany. After Barnie did some talking, with our Deb nagging him, I've no doubt, Jeremy finally agreed to consider it."

Thinking he really had been preoccupied while all this had taken place, Bruce nodded. "Oh, I see. But Jeremy has been no further than Fort William in all this past year since. . . . How—?"

"Just be thankful we got him that far, and Father enticed Mr. Warfield to a game of golf there. Between the two of them, they assured Jeremy that his trouble was indeed of a nature that the specialist could help."

"Praise God! Now more than ever I must go and see them, before we set sail. What about Mistress Ward though? I suspect she would have been willing enough to keep matters as they were. Will she want him a true husband?" Bruce wore his puzzled frown.

Peter tossed that off, "You mean, will she want to be a true wife?"

"I wonder, but that'll be Jeremy's business, and I'm sure the Lord will take a hand."

"The Lord, aye, with some help from our Deb and some more of her nagging. She's that happy herself, she canna bear it when she thinks others are not. You'll be praying, of course?"

"You're right, Peter. Prayer it is, and we'll not interfere further on that score."

Peter scratched his head. "You did it again, getting me on to another subject. Now, speaking about you and your booking passage, I have some advice. You'll not go rushin' off to take the first boat out of Greenock, I hope?"

Giving Peter the benefit of his most questioning frown, Bruce replied, "Oh, I see—no interference in folks' lives, except when it comes to your hieland laddie, is that it?"

Peter searched Bruce's face. The twinkle was there in the depths of his eyes. "I've not got as far as interfering exactly, but I have made some inquiries. You've done nothing yet then?"

"Nothing definite. I had thought of the Cunard Lines of course. . . . Although, wait just a minute, I can tell you have something on your mind. Out with it, man."

"Just what I suspected. There's nothing at all wrong with the Cunard Lines, but some of the others have more to offer in the way of both comfort and safety."

"Is that a fact, Peter? You might as well go on, but maybe I should tell you that, contrary to popular conjecturing, I have read some material about it all. The other day, for instance, I read about a speech made by the president of Cunard. He mentioned that his lines were built for both speed and safety, but that safety came first. It seems to me we can spare another day or two at sea, if the vessel is safer."

Peter answered with a grunt of derision. "What about having all three? This new boat, the *Kaiser Wilhelm der Grosse*, has not only the fastest time but is a floating hotel deluxe in the bargain, with every safety feature."

"But Peter, that's a foreign line. I would rather—"

"Oh, ho! What have we here? A made-in-Scotland-only policy, and from one who preaches that 'brothers the world ower bit' from Burns, as well as God's equality?"

For a moment Bruce's ire flashed, but then he recognized the strategy, and catching the mischievous glint in his friend's eye, he smiled ruefully. "You caught me there, Peter. I confess to those thoughts. If I'm to cross the ocean, I want a bit of Scotland under me, a *solid* bit, if you please. A Clyde-built ship. You can call that what you want."

"I understand. Underneath all the palaver, you're a canny Scot. Anyway, Cunard does have plans to make bigger and better liners than any in the world, but they're not built yet. Will you wait for them then?"

Bruce ran his hands through his hair, leaving a tuft standing straight up. "Not at all. We'll not be waiting. We'll be going soon enough, as I want a few months there before my year's leave is up. We'll not be needing a floating palace either. In fact I do have a smaller ship in mind. 'Tis the SS *Boadicea* of the Blue Star Line. Heggeson, from the kirk, has shares in that. In fact I have all the particulars."

"You've been pullin' my leg! Here you've kent all the time. I should wash my hands of you. Let me see they particulars."

Bruce's smile broadened. That would be the day, when Peter Blair washed his hands of him. He didn't say it. "Well the *Boadicea* has a displacement of seventeen thousand tons. She's a nice, sound ship with a good safety record. One thing bothers me, though. She carries about two thousand steerage passengers."

Peter stared at his friend for a long moment, thinking deeply. No, this would not be the time, on the eve of his wedding, to remind Bruce MacAlister of his own words to Peter a short while ago, about not being able to aid every needy soul. However, before he took ship, Peter would mention how the steerage folk he had such concern about were usually only too glad to put up with the discomfort for a wee while in order to get a better life later on.

All he said now was, "We should go back to the house. They women have had ample time to blether. I'm supposed to talk to you about husbandly responsibilities and suchlike. You might have the decency to appear suitably subdued and not so much like an eager twenty-year-old."

His answer was a friendly punch on the shoulder.

21

On the surface everything appeared to be running smoothly within Strathcona House as once again it echoed with the sound of happy voices. The young Douglasses played host and hostess, after a rigidly opposed Jamie had to be reminded that it was his Christian duty to his father-in-law that he fill this role. Only slightly less rigid, although possibly with different reasons at the root of her unease, his wife still smarted from the talk with Faye Felicity in the summerhouse, earlier in the week.

Faye had newly arrived from Cairnglen, but it did not take her long to discern Mary Jean's unhappiness. She had broken into the almost hysterical chatter to say, "Mary Jean, could we walk to the summerhouse? I've something I want to ask you." The others in the room, Aggie and Deb as well as Granny Mac and a most chatty Alicia MacKinnon, had hardly glanced up from their wedding talk, while Kirsty just sat, taking it all in. Aggie and Granny did exchange knowing looks.

The moment they were seated on the bench, Faye had begun, "What is bothering you, Mary Jean? You're covering up something, I know."

"If you know that much, Fayfel, then you must know why, too. Jamie is against this marriage, and although I'm not agreeing with all he says, like Daddy being unequally yoked and that, I think he's correct in some ways." She peered at Faye quickly, awaiting some response, but that lady had gone quiet and had no intentions of interrupting. Mary Jean's eyes clouded over, appearing troubled and dark as she went on to explain her feelings further, trying her best to be fair. "This woman, och, I'm sorry, Fayfel, but Kirsty

154

Brodie is not good enough for Daddy. I'm willing to admit that in my view no woman ever would be, but that's only part of it. Jamie took it on himself to make some private inquiries about the Brodie family. He got a report yesterday. Oh, Fayfel, what can we do?" She turned impulsively to the woman who had known and been so close to her dead mother and who was such a close friend to the entire family.

Faye patted the dark head, still not speaking, as she sensed more to come.

"There's nothing truly bad about Kirsty in the report. Her parents have been living separate lives for many years, ever since the railway accident that made the father unfit for work. Of course we've known all that before, and it's not the big issue. 'Tis the mother—and her sister, too. They've been in trouble with the law more than once, and the mother, Nellie Brodie, has been . . . been in—"

"Jail!" Absorbed in each other, the two in the summerhouse had failed to hear the third woman's approach. Kirsty stood now on the bottom step, hands on hips, in a stance that could not be mistaken for anything else but bitter defiance.

"I'm that sorry to break in on your private talk, ladies, but I heard my mother's name and—"

Faye Felicity moved toward the newcomer, while Mary Jean turned her face away.

Kirsty continued, "You don't need to worry, Bruce kens all our family secrets. It makes no difference to him, and I thought it to be nobody else's business."

Mary Jean spoke, her voice muffled, "It may make no difference to him the now, but when he's not so . . . well, blinded, he'll realize what it will do to the kirk and his position there."

Faye grasped her arm. "Mary Jean, your father would not be pleased at your saying such things, and you know well enough that, whatever folks' opinions might be, Bruce MacAlister goes his own way. Pay no heed to her, Kirsty, she's just upset because—"

But Kirsty had walked away. Determined to do no more running, at the same time she still recalled how her da' had always warned her to stay with her own kind, the working folk. He had told her that even the best of the so-called upper classes, with the kindest intentions in the world, still could not help their own re- actions. She had wondered at him. This didn't seem to match up with his other teaching, that she could hold up her head, being as good as any other in the land. Kirsty faced a dilemma that many before her could not solve. Living the life she had, it had not occurred to her that she would ever be in this position, but here she found herself having first-hand experience of that very thing.

"I'll not run to Bruce, and I'll not try to escape it. I'll do what he would do his own self, I'll pray. . . . Dear God, help me and show me if I need to explain about my ma to his Mary Jean and her man, and if I do, then how am I to do it?"

Although she heard nothing of the conversation taking place in her summerhouse Beulah MacIntyre easily discerned the under- currents. So when Bruce's intended bride came back through the door of her drawing room, Beulah knew at once that something had happened. She raised a hand to beckon the troubled young woman. "I'll not get up, Kirsty Brodie. My old bones are a bit sore the day. We've had small chance to get acquainted, lass, and for me to welcome you to this mixed up family, but I'm that glad Bruce has found you at last!"

Relief flooded Kirsty even as she wondered if that meant only the recent search or that Bruce should have found a wife such as she many years ago. She smiled at the kindly old woman. What did it matter?

Kirsty's smile did not reflect total gladness, though, as Beulah continued, "Bruce tells me you'll be off to Aribaig again after the wedding."

A bit choked up by the friendly tone, Kirsty could only nod.

"Did he ever tell you the story of his first meeting with my son-in-law, the late Colonel Cameron Irvine?"

Interested in spite of herself and never able to hear enough stories about her beloved, Kirsty at last responded, "Not that I mind of. I've heard bits of stories from Mistress Smith."

"You'll not know then how close he was to thinking himself an outcast, not only from this family, but from decent society in general?"

Shaking her head in disbelief, Kirsty said, "That is hard to understand, Mistress MacIntyre. . . . I don't—"

Beulah interrupted briskly, "You must call me Granny Mac, the same as the rest of my family.

"Yes, it might be hard to believe now, but it happened just the same. Bruce accidentally knocked the colonel out for the count and then ran away, thinking that he had killed the man. He had not, of course, but in her agitation my Jeannie had screamed out that her father was dead. 'Twas just before Bruce's ordination, at the university, and he thought his life as a minister must be over before it even started. My Jean was awful wise for her age, and as soon as she got over the first shock, put it all right, but not before Cameron and Jessica—my daughter and Jean's mother—had verbally stripped from Bruce every attribute that could possibly have made him a likely suitor for their lass. Although I never heard it, I'm sure my Jeannie reminded them that they were not all that innocent of sin themselves."

Kirsty sighed as the rapid speech halted and the speaker caught her breath. What could all this be leading up to? Beulah answered the unspoken question: "What I mean to say is Mary Jean, encouraged by her Jamie—a fine lad, but a wee bit of a snob—has forgotten her own daddy's humble beginnings. 'Tis not your place to remind them, Kirsty Brodie, but it could be mine. Leave it to me, lass. It might take a wee while, but they'll come round. Whatever you do, don't be insulted. I always say life is too short for all the hurts we give and the slights we hold on to. We must forgive and forget, my dear."

At the word *forgive*, Kirsty started. She had some forgiving to do herself and some to ask for. "Excuse me, mistress, I mean *Granny Mac*, but did you ken about my ma?"

"I do, lass, and I'll not be her judge. When Bruce asked my advice about inviting her to the wedding, his only concern was for you. I advised him to do it, and if she comes, so be it, the Lord will help us all. Do you think she will come, and if she does, what will you do?"

"I dinna ken to baith your questions. But Bruce has been teaching me a lot of things, some from his Gran'pa Bruce. We'll just have to wait and see and pray for the help from the Lord, as you said."

Granny Mac pulled her specs up to her nose again. She had been correct. This woman would make a fair and fit match for Bruce MacAlister. She closed her eyes with a sigh of content as Kirsty tiptoed away.

Yes, Bruce had been teaching her many things, but Kirsty was also learning from one other who had accepted her without question: Faye Felicity Smith. Bruce, being the soul of propriety, had refused to go far alone with her until they tied the knot, so Hamish had accompanied them on the visit to Cairnglen. That bonny and prosperous town had welcomed her, although of course that impression came from the folk crowded on the station platform: four couples at the front and a spate of well-wishers pushing forward to shake hands the first chance they got. She and Faye Felicity became instant friends and confidantes. It had been Faye who told her about the old lady at Strathcona House and a few other details regarding Bruce's own family and upbringing and early days as a student. Reluctant to leave the acceptance of Cairnglen, Kirsty had nonetheless faced her new surroundings staunchly enough.

Faye had warned about Bruce's tendencies to get into, or rather his inability to keep out of, other folks' troubles. He also had so many friends who thought it their business to give him advice, Faye warned, for instance, Dr. Peter Blair and his son-in-law, Dr. Jamie Douglass. Kirsty soon learned though that Bruce had a way of soothing them beforehand and going his own way after. If his own way agreed with their advice, everybody would be happy; if not, he still had a grand way of making them all feel pleased enough.

Her thoughts turned back to her ma. Would she be at the wedding?

Nellie Brodie had swithered long before deciding to accept the fancy invitation to her own lassie's wedding. What for would Kirsty want her? After all, she had not been much of a mother, and then this latest caper with Maimie should have put the lid on it. But no, this nice letter from an old lady called MacIntyre, from a fancy address, Strathcona House, in George Street, Glasgow, assured her it must be real. She would just go and see, without saying a word to Maimie.

Outside Strathcona House Nellie paid the cabman his three shillings, glad to see the last of him, with his grumbling about too many carriages—some of them the horseless kind—that lined George Street. Nellie had on her best coat and a new hat that she considered the height of fashion—purple with a big green feather, to match the paisley pattern on her frock. At least Kirsty would not be ashamed of her mother's dress, should she own her. Nellie flourished the card of invitation to the maid at the door and walked with mincing steps on her high-heeled boots to the place indicated. The note had the letters RSVP on it, but Nellie had ignored that, not knowing what it meant.

The clock on the wall, above a spinet in the big room, chimed the hour of one o'clock, softly muted and in unison with the music. Suddenly the tempo changed to a march of triumph, and Nellie craned with the others, to catch a glimpse of her daughter. Blissfully Nellie forgot the last time she had seen her as she gazed on this beauty. Tears sprung to her eyes as she overheard some whispering, "Oh, my, she's that bonny!" and, "George Bennett looks as spruce as ever. That's him givin' the bride away!" Nellie brushed at the veil covering her carefully powdered nose and well-rouged cheeks, giving no thought to the ruination of her careful artistry. Here stood her own lass, as bonny a bride as she'd ever seen. It should have been poor Matt who gave this bride away, even if she was soon to be thirty years old. Staunching the flow, Nellie continued to sob quietly into her hankie.

Bruce turned to greet his bride. All the whisperings and visitations from strange dressmakers, aided and abetted by Faye and Aggie and, he had no doubt, one or both of the MacKinnon women, had resulted in this breathtaking vision in white. He had asked her, and she had fully agreed that she would not cover her face with a veil. Shiny black tresses of hair coiled on top of the shapely head, threaded through with a cloth-of-silver bandeau that ended in a swathe of tulle at the back, all completely escaped his notice as he gazed deep into the twin green pools of her eyes.

False modesty aside, Kirsty gazed back into his. Today nothing but warmth emanated from his blue orbs as they glinted with the intensity of his love. The couple moved together, as though drawn by a magnet, and every woman present sighed, while every man for a moment stood taller. The ceremony proceeded, and soon Reverend Jamieson, flushed with the honor his superior had shown in choosing him to perform this ceremony, pronounced them man and wife.

As she turned to walk triumphantly through the group of friends lined up to form a human aisle of well-wishers, Kirsty's glance at last met her mother's—a mother so changed that had it not been for the bright feather, perched proudly atop the hat, she might never have taken a second look or recognized the woman under it. Kirsty leaned toward her brand-new husband, and Bruce bent his ear. Immediately he stopped to acknowledge Nellie with a bow, while that lady promptly subsided into a fresh burst of tears. Catching sight of Faye, a few steps behind them, Bruce signaled with his eyes, and Faye went to comfort this mother of the bride, who should have had a place of honor at the wedding, but who was only too happy to be there at all.

22

Sweeping the watery horizon with his spyglass, a present from Barnie Hill, Bruce MacAlister marveled anew at the wonder of God in creation. Words of the Psalmist echoed, and he paraphrased, "Who am I that Thou should bother about me?" He stood in the stern of the great ship, and the glory of the sunrise caused him to catch his breath.

Although many others must be abroad in this floating city, the morning sounds came to him muted, where he stood gazing his fill and communing with his God. Among those sleeping below him, or just beginning to stir, was another cause for wonder: his wife, Kirsty. Bruce's heart thrilled at the thought of her. She had stirred and mumbled his name as he slipped out of their bed about an hour ago, but she had not fully awakened as he carefully locked their cabin door behind him.

Bruce pulled the watch from his waistcoat pocket. Another half hour before they would proceed to the immense dining salon to breakfast together. They did everything possible together, except for his early morning walk and talk with the Lord. Kirsty had acknowledged Jesus fully as her Lord and Saviour, but she did not yet understand Bruce's ability to step directly into conversational prayer with the Almighty at any time. This thought caused Bruce no concern, as he believed that to be the work of the Holy Spirit.

One matter did tend to spoil his content this lovely morning. They had watched the parade of folk waiting in long, bedraggled lines to board and go directly below decks to the steerage. Again thinking of Kirsty, his brow cleared. She had quickly learned to

161

quote Gran'pa Bruce, and she had done so as they had watched the human dramas unfolding.

Settling his wandering thoughts, he placed the spyglass back into its case. Time for a quick prayer before going to wake his beloved.

"Psst!"

Bruce turned at the sound, startled but not afraid. Seeing nothing, he began to pray. Mary Jean and her husband, and the baby Jason, now six months old and perfect in Bruce's eyes, but already crawling about and getting into mischief, were uppermost in his mind.

The sound came again, more persistent, and this time the voice seemed familiar. "Psst! Professor!"

Bruce responded, carefully keeping his own voice low, "Whoever you are, show yourself and tell me what you want."

"I cannot, sir! This is a first-class deck, and I'm traveling steerage. If you come closer to the number-six lifeboat and stand with your back to it, I'll tell you more."

Bruce moved cautiously as directed. "Do I know you then?"

"You do, but you'll not need my name the now."

Trying hard to place the voice, Bruce stood beside the lifeboat. The canvas cover hid the speaker completely. Bruce glanced round. "There's nobody here about. Can you not at least move the canvas a wee bit? I dislike talking to an inanimate object, and I want to see who you are."

"No, 'tis too risky. If I'm caught 'twill be a black mark against me, and then we'll not get past Ellis Island for certain."

Bruce digested this. "I think I'm recognizing the voice anyway. You seem to know a lot about America, Garnett. It is Garnett, is it not?" A gasp from under the canvas confirmed his guess as he went on. "Anyway, if you cannot show yourself on this deck, there's nothing to stop me going to yours. I'll don my clerical collar and make a pastoral visit. Then we can talk face-to-face, and you can tell me what the bother is."

"You would do that, Professor?"

"I would indeed. Just tell me where I can find you, and as soon as I've talked it over with my wife at breakfast, I'll be down to see you. You're carrying a heavy burden."

No more sounds came from the lifeboat, and finally Bruce began to suspect that somehow his ex-pupil had slipped out without his seeing. He spoke again anyway, "Did you hear me, Garnett?"

A muffled sound, suspiciously like a broken sob, came through now. "I hear you fine, Professor, and you're right. I *do* have a burden. I wouldn't ask for myself. . . . We're in section B of the steerage, but if you wait till closer to the noon dinner bell, it will be best. Now walk away and stare hard at something toward the east. Even point your spyglass at anything. That will give me time to slip away unseen. Till noon then?"

Feeling a bit daft and even wondering if he had dreamed it all, Bruce nonetheless did as requested. Any stray strollers about this bit of deck followed his intent gaze, and soon he replaced the spyglass and quickly made his way back to the cabin and Kirsty.

Kirsty had not gone back to sleep after Bruce left her in the early morning hours. She knew he needed this time alone, and wisely she did not intrude on it. Lazily she stretched her full length on the sumptuous bed. Never in her life had she tasted such luxury. She was getting used to it, though, and had stopped wondering if it would end as unexpectedly as it had begun.

Her thoughts raced to the cafuffle about the preparations for their journey. From that had come at last the almost grudging approval and acceptance by the young Douglasses. She recalled it almost word for word as she glanced now at the portholes.

The sun would just be slipping up out of the water, and her man would be a while yet. She sat up in the bed and reached for the hairbrush. She would just give it the hundred strokes she had missed last night, when they. . . . Oh, well, some things came first. Pulling the loose hair forward, she started to form the long braids.

To think all that had been less than three months ago. Her man had insisted that her mother must come with them to Aribaig.

They had just returned from their wedding journey—an all-too-short week in the border county of Dumfries and an idyllic few days on the banks of the Solway Firth. They had toured Sweetheart

Abbey. Then on their way back, via the coast, she had received a thorough history lesson regarding the old Druid standing stones between Stranraer and Girvan. Her best memory of that had been when they found themselves alone in a hired two-seater, and Bruce had turned to her, exclaiming, "You're not listening, my love!"

Her reply had been wordless, and he had forgotten the history lesson for a while.

Her mother had been invited to stay at Strathcona House and had still been ensconced there when they returned. Bruce, raring to get to Aribaig, nevertheless had caught the yearning in Nellie Brodie. Casting a pleading glance at his wife, he had addressed his mother-in-law, "Would you be wanting to come to Aribaig with us, Mistress Brodie?"

"Och, I couldna do that, Bruce. Anyway I'll need to be goin' back to my job soon."

Kirsty, amazed by her mother's changed manners and surprised by the humble answer, still could not hide her distress at having the woman with them on what, after all, was still their wedding tour. Bruce insisted though, and she sighed as he answered Nellie, "Of course you can. We'll go and see your employer first, and then you don't need to stay more than a day or so at the Mains. I feel you want to make some amends there." His clear eyes showed nothing but a desire for the best for them all.

Nellie had brightened. "If you're sure it'll be awricht, Kirsty?" Her daughter shrugged why not?

On the day of departure Mary Jean had arrived with baby Jason. Her expression, when she heard of the proposal, showed dismay. "Granny Mac, how can that woman be so brazen as to go with them?"

"Your daddy invited her, Mary Jean, and we'll not interfere. Besides since when were you that interested in—?" Beulah stopped herself as Kirsty entered.

Mary Jean, bred to be honest above all things, rose to the occasion. "Yes, Granny Mac. Kirsty, may I speak to you in private?"

The private talk had been a revelation to the new Mistress MacAlister and had included a confession of snobbery on the part of both the young Douglasses. But Kirsty had not been quite ready to trust her stepdaughter yet. "Oh, I see, you've judged my ma to be even further beyond the pale than me, so you're taking the lesser of two evils."

Mary Jean had gaped at her, beginning to realize the extent of the lessons given by Faye Felicity to Kirsty. She had regained her composure quickly though. "Whatever we've said and done, before knowing you, Kirsty, you are going to have to forgive us, but what you've just said would be a wrong interpretation. Certainly James was upset when he knew of the jail, but when we heard the right story, it all changed. As for me, I wasn't keen on Daddy taking a wife at all. Before he met you, every time I mentioned it to him, his answer always assured me he would never marry. He has, though, and I'm truly glad."

The younger woman had choked, and at last Kirsty took pity. " 'Tis all right, Mary Jean. I do understand, but what's wrong the now?"

"We think your mother should go somewhere else to stay, and I don't think she should be going to Aribaig with you. After all, you are still on your honeymoon."

"I agree with you there, but I'm sure you ken your father well enough. He's that stubborn when he thinks he's doin' the right thing. As he says, though, it will only be for a day or two, and we have the rest of our lives together." A straight look passed between them, and Mary Jean at last lowered her eyes.

"You know, you're beginning to sound like him. Off you go then, but what will she do after? I hope she's not to go to America with you!"

Kirsty's happy laugh rang through the room. "Hardly that. I have some money left from the gold reward. Bruce doesna want it or need it. I'll do for her what my da' had planned for me: set her up in a wee shop—whatever kind she wants. Then we'll all just have to pray Auntie Maimie leaves her be to enjoy it.

"Did you ken your granny is showing Ma the stories about Jesus? She might even be ready for—"

Just then the door opened, and Bruce entered, carrying Jason, followed by the lady under discussion. "This wee chap needs feeding. Mother Nellie here changed him, but we cannot do more." To prove it, Jason Philip let out a roar, and his smiling mother grasped him.

Bruce glanced from one beloved face to the other. His two sweethearts would be good friends after all. As for Nellie, his hopes for her ran high. She had just now asked him if she was a granny or a stepgranny or even a great-granny to Jason Philip. They had enjoyed that joke together, later, when he and she were alone.

Bringing her thoughts to the present, Kirsty caught her breath in wonder. It had worked out just fine, and all seemed well with her world. The cabin door creaked open, and soon after, husband and wife sat facing each other in the spacious dining room.

"Bruce, ye canna mean it? From what I hear the steerage deck is teeming with folk like that. 'Tis just not possible to help them all."

"I know, Kirsty, and I won't try to help them all. But Garnett was a student in my theology class at the university, one of my prize winners and one I had great hopes for. Besides I'll only be going to see what it's about. No harm in that, is there?"

"The way you say it the now, no great harm, but something makes my skin creep when I think of you going down there. Could I not come with ye?"

"Not this first time. Let me find out more about it, and if I find it to be much ado about nothing, I'll settle that. On the other hand—"

She burst in again. "On the other hand, you could be putting yourself into danger. You've been in that before now."

Bruce shook his head at her, but he was smiling as the steward came to refill his coffee cup. "Aye, I have that, and the Lord has brought me through it all. He can do it again. Och, we're being daft. What danger can there be in visiting a needy fellow, especially an old parishioner?"

She reached to pat his hand. "You're too kind for your own good, Bruce MacAlister, but I'm butting my head against a stane dyke to try and change you, even if I wanted to. On you go then and take care of yoursel'!"

23

"**O**ch, Garnett, you're never telling me you have a wife and she's supposed to have only six weeks to go before giving birth? I can scarcely take it all in, lad. You can't be more than twenty years old yourself!"

The younger man sat with head bowed, his hands clasped between his knees. The two sat on a pair of rough packing crates, found in an otherwise unoccupied corner under the metal steps, and they talked in whispers. Even so sailors going up and down kept glancing at them curiously.

"I am twenty-one! I'll be twenty-two next month. I'm sorry, Professor, but I doubt you'll understand."

Bruce stroked his chin thoughtfully. Garnett was wrong; he did understand, at least a glimmer. "You would not say what trouble you had a while ago, and I was so burdened myself at the time. . . . I'm the one to be sorry, Garnett. I'll try not to prejudge again. Now, what is it we can do in all this?"

"Well, I hoped we'd be safely settled in America, with her uncle, when Virginia's time came. We would have been, only—" He turned away.

Bruce wanted the whole story. "*Only* what? If I'm to be of help, I'll need to know it all, lad."

"Only she took awful badly in yon hold. 'Tis like a prison there, and I've got to get her out of it before the bairn comes. My mother is no help, as I fear she'll go mad if she has to stay down there as well. Virginia's young brother, who is supposed to be fetching and carrying for us, is nowhere to be found."

"How did you all manage to be on the *Boadicea*?"

For a moment Garnett looked startled then his face cleared. "We're here by a miracle." His eyes searched Bruce's for reaction to that word, but he found nothing there but curiosity. Garnett went on, "Since yon time I told you I'd be leaving the university I've had the feelin' many's a time of being watched wherever I went. . . . Not in a spiritual way, but in a very human way. Once or twice I played a wee trick, and that's how I discovered that the man following me about was your brother, Mr. Cormack. Well, one day I waited for him, to ask him what he wanted, and he told me he wanted nothing except my own good. Anyway by then he had found out my true situation. I'm not proud of it. We'd had enough trouble in our family without me and Virginia—well, anyway, I'm the one at fault."

Bruce sighed deeply, and his thoughts wandered for a minute. So many folk came to him with similar stories. Some could be helped and some not.

Garnett continued, ". . . And it was all we could do to survive."

"What about her family, Garnett?"

"Virginia's father threw her out the minute he knew, even when she tried to tell him we would be getting married. She's only seventeen the now so. . . . As for my own mother, I'll not say more about her, except that after father's death she called me the man of the house. Now all her dreams of a minister son are shattered."

Bruce knew well what such an ambition could do to a mother, and he thanked God again for the wise men who had surrounded his own mother and tempered her dreams for him.

"I blame mother not at all. 'Tis myself to blame entirely, and I wouldn't bother you now, except that Mr. Cormack told me you would be on this boat as well, and I don't know where else to turn. The women's hold down here is terrible for Virginia, who has never had to rough it before. My mother stays on the bunk and weeps all day and most of the night, and now Virginia says she'll throw herself off the boat before she'll have the bairn in that hades of a place."

"What is she doing at this moment, Garnett? Did you not mention a young brother?"

"I paid an old woman who promised to keep a watch on her, but

I don't know how well I can trust that one. I used the very last of the money Mr. Cormack gave me, after buying our tickets and paying what we owed in Glasgow.

"I mentioned her brother, aye. Young Roger begged and pleaded to come with us to America. He wanted away from his father, he said, and he did have the money for his own fare. I haven't set eyes on him since last night, although mind you he was far sicker than the rest of us. Och, Professor, if only Virginia hadn't—"

Bruce held up an impatient hand. "Never mind the 'if onlys.' It's happening, and we'll have to sort it somehow. We'll need a bit more money, and I've none on me but. . . . Meet me here again in an hour's time. Pray your wife will have a wee while yet. I'll see what we can do. Pray hard that my idea will work and that my own wife—" But Garnett had vanished, and Bruce made his cautious way back to the upper deck alone.

"Bruce MacAlister, you big eedjit, an' I'm a bigger one to even listen. Ye canna mean it! You say a young lass is havin' a bairn in the steerage hold, wi' naebuddy to help her, and ye want us to give up our cabin and. . . . Och, no, 'tis too much."

Bruce scratched his head and gazed for a moment at this woman, his wife. The laughing sweetheart who had shared his every moment since their marriage and most of his thoughts for months before that seemed to have vanished. Trying to be fair, he recalled some of the hardship she herself had been through and made an effort to understand the feelings of fear the thought of losing her newfound security might bring. Just the same, she would need to learn that he lived by another law—Christ's law of love for others, which, when the need arose, might require sacrifice. But this quandary loomed. Something had to be done at once.

He reached for her. "Kirsty, my love, 'tis not too much to ask of you, or I wouldn't ask. Here is this young girl, and the lad, too, needing not only our help but our compassion as well. Aye, they've done wrong, but God's their judge for that, and I've seen Garnett's repentance plain. For all the short while it will be, we can manage. When we've landed and seen this wee family safely with relatives, we'll continue with our own plans. Anyway, I've called the steward. I just told him to bring tea, but when he comes, I'll give him some money and ask him to make the arrangements. If he can somehow get the lass—Virginia's her name—and Garnett's mother to this cabin, you can stay here with them, and I'll just go to the men's hold with Garnett.

"Dinna greet, sweetheart, 'twill be all right, you'll see. Our future is so bright, and don't forget Craig's family is to meet us at New York and will be whisking us off to visit Craig in New Jersey. Until then, God knows. He will not—"

A discreet knock on the cabin door interrupted his budding sermon. Kirsty rushed into the dressing cubicle, while Bruce opened the door. She could hear the murmur of voices and then the door closing again. Splashing her face with cold water, she emerged to find her husband smiling ruefully.

"They say money can buy anything, but this is ridiculous!"

His expression caused her to smile in spite of herself as she responded, "That's because you've never bribed anybody before, have you?"

As he was about to agree, his mind flashed for an instant to one of the worst nights of his own life, the night following his initiation into the ministry. He would be telling lies if he said he had not at least *tried* to bribe someone that once.

"I see you do mean it, Bruce," Kirsty interrupted his thoughts. "And you *are* a big eedjit, but then I must be Mistress Eedjit, beggin' you to be selfish like me for once. Anyway, what's to happen now?"

Before he could speak, a noise outside the cabin answered for him, and she wailed, "Och, Bruce, they're here. . . . Pray the Lord's help for me, because I dinna ken what to do."

Bruce threw the door open, and this time a bedraggled trio of two women and a man stood there. At once a frenzied sailor thrust them through the open door and disappeared. Immediately Kirsty forgot her own disappointment in the face of the trouble and pain confronting her. Bruce quietly pulled the three all the way inside and closed the door. Within a few minutes he and Garnett left again, ushered out by a different Kirsty, all bustle and competence. This birth would wait no longer.

The unwilling midwife's first act, to silence the woman who cried the loudest, she accomplished by turning and slapping her hard. Mistress Ogilvie, Senior, then threw herself into a corner of the cabin, where she curled up in a ball and closed her eyes, being careful not to let go the bundle she had clutched to her bosom. Then Kirsty focused her full attention on the girl now splayed out on top of her bed. Rushing to the cubicle, she grabbed every towel and cloth available and returned not a moment too soon as, with a great shudder followed by a tremendous lunge, Virginia Ogilvie ushered a new life into the world. Matters dimmed in Kirsty's mind as she tended to mother and child.

The brand-new grandmother would take no part, not even when Kirsty offered her the wet, wriggling child to hold. Instead she pushed the babe away, but she had ceased her whimpering, Kirsty gladly noted. Soon the young mother began to pull herself together, and she held out her arms, encouraging Kirsty to relinquish the heartily bawling infant. Although tiny, the babe appeared to be a healthy enough girl child. Less than half an hour later, mother and infant were cleaned up and ready to face whatever life had in store, while the granny sat clutching her bundle, seemingly unheeding.

Kirsty again lost patience. "You could have stayed away, for all the good you are. Will you not even come and look at your grandbairn?" For answer the woman started to whimper again. Kirsty turned back to the new mother. "What will we do now? I don't know where to go to tell the men, and I don't want to leave you with her."

Virginia uttered her first articulate word: "How can I ever thank you and the Professor, Mistress MacAlister?" She blushed and Kirsty smiled. Poor thing, she had been through it, and after all, who was Kirsty to judge without knowing what went before?

"Don't bother about thanks. Just get your strength back. Have you a name for your babby?" The girl glanced at her prostrate mother-in-law. "Garnett's mother's name is Angeline, but I don't think she—"

At her name the woman glanced up. She had begun to regain command of herself. "No, never that!"

It had dawned on Kirsty earlier that the younger woman was not a product of Glasgow. In fact a distinct flavor of the English nobility came through in her talk. Virginia smiled shyly up at Kirsty, an obvious question in her eyes.

But Kirsty shook her head. "Not Kirsty, either, please. 'Tis truly only a bit of a name. I was baptized as *Crystal*."

But the girl's eyes had brightened. "*Crystal Ogilvie*! Maybe, or else *Christina*. Yes, if Garnett agrees, we shall name her *Christina*!"

In the steerage hold, where Garnett had led him, Bruce already regretted his impulsive rush from the cabin. For one thing, he had forgotten to bring his purse of sovereigns, and for another, his quick change into fisherman's jersey and old trews, while he explained the scheme to Kirsty, had been done without proper thought of what would happen after. Security in the steerage hold had tightened for some as yet undisclosed reason, and leaving would be much harder than getting in had been. Besides that, the sights and smells—never mind the sounds—in this place had already turned Bruce's stomach. It all reminded him of his curate days in the Glasgow slums.

"I can't abide this place, Garnett. Can we not go outside, even for a wee while?"

"There's no place to go, Professor. They watch all the time to prevent any sneaking to the higher decks. I got away with it earlier by using up my money, as I told you, but for some reason they've put on extra sailors to watch."

Bruce's laugh sounded bitter. "I forgot to bring money, but if I could just explain to the sailor at the doorway." He walked in that direction as he spoke.

The man on guard gave him short shrift. "Aye, an' I'm the admiral of the fleet in disguise. My mate warned me about some daft passengers on this crossin', an' he was richt. Get back in there, an' wait yer turn wi' the rest. They'll be bringin' yer supper in a wee while."

The very thought of food nearly finished Bruce, but he rallied and tried again: "My wife, Mistress MacAlister. Send somebody to my cabin for her. She will pay you and—"

"As I said afore, mister, actin' daft'll get ye nothin' here. Forget it an' be thankfu' I'm not throwin' ye in the brig. Bribery is a serious offense on board this ship."

It began to dawn on Bruce that he could have landed himself in a real predicament. In desperation he signaled with his eyes to Garnett, but that one only shrugged in complete subjection. For too many months now he had been trying to fight the powers that be, and he knew from harsh experience that, when they had the upper hand, they would not be letting go.

But Bruce MacAlister faced the man at the door again, not giving up so easily. "I'll ask you civilly once more to allow me to pass. I walked in here of my own free will, to pay a visit as a pastor, and I will leave the same way. If you refuse my request, then I have no choice but to—"

"Watch yourself, Professor!"

Bruce saw the belaying pin just before it caught him above the ear. He went down and out like a light. The wielder of the weapon glanced about fiercely, but the other passengers, including Garnett, cringed out of reach.

"Any mair stupid enough to think theirsel's fancy reverends or lordships in here? I can crown as many as say the word."

A slight titter of laughter greeted this, and the bully rejoined his mate at their post.

Garnett rushed to Bruce. "O dear Jesus, what have I done? If they've killed him, it will be all my fault. Oh *mea culpa, mea culpa*, for this whole mess. O God, what will we do now?"

One of the onlookers came forward then. "First, we'll get him up on a bunk. Move yersel' there, Tam, ye lazy brute. Then we'll see if it's bad or no'. Shut yer girnin', Ogilvie. He's no' killt." Bruce was reviving, and when a smelly, wet rag came across his face, he thrust it away with a shudder. "What is this? What's going on here . . . ? Oh, yes, young Garnett. . . . We'd better set up a plan of action on how to get back to our ladies."

The kindly helpers melted into the crowd, and soon the others dispersed as the excitement lessened.

Bruce pulled his hands through his hair, and finding no blood, he continued on to his chin. It felt bristly, and he recalled not shaving this morning in his hurry to keep this appointment with trouble. He sat up straight, bumping his head on the bunk above. What a mess! But if the Lord had allowed him to be caught here in the middle of it, then He must have a good reason.

Bruce muttered a prayer. "Your ways are not our ways, Lord; they are past our finding out. But could You make an exception in this case and let me know what I'm doing here in the bowels of this ship? Pardon the expression, Lord, but it smells the way it's named. I'm feeling more like a Jonah than a David, so what's next? Could You please show me, Lord?"

24

In spite of his bravado, the guard who had struck Bruce with the belaying pin sounded anxious as he confided in his mate, "What if the big fella is whit he says he is, Joe, a minister visitin'? We could get intae bother!"

The other gave him a scathing glance. "Never mind the *we*, Charlie. *You* hit him, no' me. I've warned ye afore aboot yer quick temper. But dinna worry, the minute they gie us the all-clear sign, we'll be back to the usual. We'll gie the young fella the wink, and the minister, if he is that, can go to his—"

"We'll not be back to the usual on this crossin', Joe, my lad, no' when they think the plague's loose again. We can just hope they've made a mistake, and thon fella has only a carbuncle under his oxter."

"Wheesht, Charlie, we're no' even supposed to ken aboot that, let alane say it oot loud. We darena let the passengers in by hear aboot it. Have ye ever been on a boat where the steerage run riot?"

Charlie scratched his head. "Wanct! But in they days condeetions were a lot worse. Folk packed in like sardines, an' they didna even have bunks. Crossin' took longer then as weel. At least these fellas have bunks an' can lie doon separate, an' the women even have—"

" 'Tis still not fit for humans!" The two contemplated this all-too-true statement until the one named Joe spoke up again, this time softly: "I havena done much prayin' since my mither, God rest her, died, but I ken how to, an' I've been at it since we heard the word *pestilence*."

His mate gaped in astonishment, and neither sailor noticed the movement just inside the opening.

Bruce crept cautiously toward the space. Seeing the guards absorbed, he planned to slip past them from behind. His head ached, and he knew he risked another clout, but this time he would be less arrogant if they caught him. The dread word *plague* didn't quite register in his clogged brain at first, but when it did, he stood quite still before glancing about to see if anyone else could have heard. No one paid any attention to him, except Garnett, who still kept his eyes glued to Bruce.

Garnett had his own plan, should the professor be spotted. He, Garnett, would immediately create a diversion to attract attention away from the doorway. Even as he watched, Bruce turned and began to inch his way back between the close, boxlike bunks.

Squeezing between the rows, Bruce finally reached Garnett. Leaning across the small space, he whispered, "When did you last see young—Roger, is it?"

Amazement, followed by a look of pain, crossed Garnett's expressive features. "He must have slipped by the watch, when they were changing last night. As I said before they've just started being so strict the now and—"

"Never mind that, what did you say was the matter with the lad?" Garnett's incredulity grew, but he answered, "He said he had a sore belly, and he was awful seasick. He complained of boils in his oxters as well, and he was burning hot. The night before he had woke up screaming with a nightmare. I couldn't get him to talk sense, but then he rallied round by morning. Why do you ask, Professor? What is it?"

While Garnett described the symptoms, Bruce tried to keep his growing alarm from showing, but his doubt was diminishing. Bubonic plague! Not the most deadly pestilence, surely, but it could be devastating in circumstances such as they found themselves in now.

"I pray I'm wrong, Garnett, but have you any reason to suspect that Roger may have been exposed to some kind of contagion?"

The other gulped and his face blanched. "I don't rightly know, sir. For all he's only a boy, he's been in trouble with the gambling. Ginny's been so worried about him. The night before we had to embark, I had to go out to look for him. I found him in a dirty, smelly old close, sitting in a set with a card game going. He didn't want to leave, but I told him we wouldn't let him on the boat if he didn't. That did it, and he came with me but—"

"Rats!" The exclamation escaped Bruce before he could help it. Several of the men close by glanced up from their various occupations. Ignoring them, Bruce leaned toward Garnett again. "Where did you think he might have gone last night?"

"I had so much else to worry about, with Virginia and mother, and it was costing me money every time I tried to go and see them. Anyway, Roger didn't need to look far for a gambling school. There's one here in this hold. Over there, see! But when I last saw him, he was past even gambling."

Bruce peered along the space between the rows of bunks. Sure enough, a group of men sat in a rough circle on the floor, and he caught the gleam of coins, deducing correctly that a game of pitch and toss was in progress. Bruce approached the group, and immediately the coins disappeared.

"Don't worry, I'll not be cliping. 'Tis about the lad, young Roger; I'm looking for him, and his brother-in-law here says he played with you yesterday."

Blank stares answered this, but eventually one fellow spoke up, "Whit aboot him?"

"Just that he seems to have vanished from the hold. Do you have any notion of where—"

They all melted away except the one who had answered the first time. "The laddie seemed awful badly, an' I tellt him he better ask for the doctor. Last I saw him, he was talkin' to the sailor on watch. No' the wans on the now," he said as Bruce glanced toward them. "Last nicht it was, an' they had only the wan on." Thanking him, Bruce moved toward the doorway again. This time he made no attempt to hide, but addressed the guard who appeared the gentler of the two.

"I know you have a suspected plague case aboard. Please allow me to go to your doctor. I think I can pinpoint the source and—"

Both sailors gaped at him, and his earlier aggressor moved in menacingly, belaying pin held aloft.

His mate pulled on his arm. "Nae mair o' that, Charlie. I've the feelin' this man is who he says he is. Mind you, we never saw him in here afore the day."

"We have hundreds o' them who could say the same. We're supposed to keep them a' in here the now, till we hear the word. You're forgettin'—"

Bruce did not wait for more. As the two faced each other he seized his chance and slipped through the opening behind them. Gaining the metal steps where he and Garnett had huddled together earlier, he scaled them and reached the next level before stopping to get his bearings.

An uneasy silence pervaded the ship, and few people moved about. Wondering how the crew could manage to keep the hundreds of folk in their places without starting a panic, Bruce trod cautiously along the unfamiliar passageway, seeking an officer from whom he could ask directions. Just then one emerged from a nearby hatchway.

"Excuse me, sir, could you direct me to the ship's doctor? I don't seem to be feeling very well."

The man gazed at him strangely before taking a step backward. Pulling a hankie from his uniform pocket, he delicately covered his nose and mouth before answering. His voice came through, muffled, as he pointed in the direction from which he had just come: "Sick bay, through there and to your left. But you shouldn't be—"

Bruce hurried off, and his informant shrugged. He had done his best to stop the fellow.

The place termed "sick bay" proved as silent as the rest of the ship, and the few cots lining the walls appeared empty. A door marked, RESTRICTED TO MEDICAL PERSONNEL stood slightly ajar, and as Bruce approached it he was finally challenged, not by a fairly innocent belaying pin. This time his challenger wielded a wicked, businesslike dueling pistol. Bruce stopped and held up both hands.

" 'Tis all right, officer. I'm looking for a young lad, name of Roger Nelson. His kin are worried about him and—"

The pistol was lowered, and its owner stepped into the light. "Are ye kin to this lad? Not that I know of him, mind you."

"Not exactly, but—"

"I must ask you to leave. This is a restricted area." Defeated, Bruce turned to obey. It had been a wild guess after all, and the lad was more likely to be below decks, sick and alone. His challenger turned away, and Bruce started to leave, but the sound of voices raised in argument made him pause.

"The lad's no' a rat, man! He's a human bein', like you an' me, an' I'll not allow—" The thick highland brogue faded as the inner door closed. Bruce glanced about quickly before stepping over the metal divider. An unexpected rush of tears welled up as the beloved, peaty sound of his native highlands met his ears again. "As I said, I'll not allow ye to—"

A cultured English voice cut into the admonition, saying, "You'll not allow! You'll not allow! I remind you, Angus MacIllvenney, that I'm superior to you and—"

"You're not my superior in this sick bay, Lieutenant Degnan. Get out." The other voice started to plead, "Don't be stubborn, Angus. What is one life, compared to the hundreds on board here? If word gets out, it could start a panic, and if we dispose of this body now, we can avoid that and the worst of the risk—a dignified burial at sea, with only you and me and a couple of sailors to carry the corpse. If we wrap the shroud well about it, who would know?"

"*I* would know, and I'll not hear another word. Let me remind you, sir, the corpse you speak of is still breathin'. There'll be no burial at sea for a live man while I'm here. Not from my sick bay."

Bruce could scarcely believe all he was hearing, but he still made no attempt to interfere. His countryman was doing fine on his own.

The other voice kept urging, "How much longer will he breathe though? With every breath he releases the pestilence. I have orders to rid the ship of the disease before it endangers every life aboard. Even now we shall have to isolate ourselves and every known contact for the remainder of the voyage, but at least—"

"Enough, man, my sacred vow as a healer is to preserve life, not do away with it. I'll not allow it, I say, captain or no captain, and you can go and tell him that."

"Don't shout so loud, Angus. It's not the captain's orders exactly. He just told me, as officer of the watch, to clear the decks of the pestilence and to use my judgment and discretion. This boy has no name. No hue and cry has come for him, so he'll not be missed, and he's going to die anyway."

Bruce had heard enough, and the sailor guarding the door made no attempt now to stop him as he burst into the cabin where the voices had come from. "The boy *has* a name! And kinfolk on board. He is Roger Nelson. I have authority from his sister to—"

"And who the blazes are you?"

"Get out of here afore ye're smitten, man!" The two men had turned toward the eruption of Bruce through the door. He came to an abrupt halt. Then, taking a chance on his Gaelic and his ancestry, he addressed the last speaker, "MacAlister, Bruce, of Aribaig, grandson to the 'Ranald."

The name and title represented royalty to Angus, and he took a step as he held out his hand, but then immediately withdrew it, remembering. "I canna be touched, MacAlister, as I've been handlin' a very catching disease. I'm MacIllvenney, Angus, M.D., earned at St. Andrews in sixty-two." The doctor pointed to a cot on the far side of the cabin. A low moan came from under the heap of blankets. The other officer stepped away, but Bruce and the doctor moved toward the sound.

A hoarse voice struggled to form words. "Mother, I'm sorry! Mother, make this sore head go away!"

With one bound, Bruce was at the bedside. Before the others could stop him, he had gathered the boy into his arms. "There, now, Roger, lad, your mother is not here, but we've something to take away the pain for you." As he spoke he reached for a cloth from the pan of water placed on the low table beside the cot. He tried to ignore the cry of alarm coming from Angus as he squeezed the cloth out and began to pat the fevered brow.

The officer called from the open doorway, in the most correct English, "By Jove, now you've done it! You will have to be quarantined with the doctor. At least none of the rest of us have touched the victim! How the devil did you get in here?"

No one bothered to answer that, but Angus almost echoed the first sentence. "Indeed and Lieutenant Degnan is right, Bruce MacAlister, grandson of the 'Ranald, now you *have* done it, and what the devil am I goin' to do wi' you?"

25

"**W**hat in the name of God *are* we to do with you?" Dr. Angus MacIllvenney repeated his anguished question, and Bruce noted thankfully that he used God's name instead of the devil's this time. The doctor's anguish was quite sincere. His own involvement in the situation could not be helped and came with the job, but now this fine brother highlander had deliberately placed himself in great jeopardy for what Angus thought could be no good reason. He said as much as he moved about the small sick bay, reaching for a variety of bottles and boxes, some of which he discarded with a snort of derision. Others he placed carefully on top of the steel counter he used as his worktable. Receiving no answer from either of his listeners, he glanced in the direction of the doorway, where the lieutenant still hovered.

That man shrugged as he said, "The fat's in the fire, all right, Doctor. My own question is what to report to the captain. Meanwhile neither of you will leave this place."

Angus moved to the cot, and Bruce surrendered his place beside the patient as he answered the officer, "I'll remain here as long as need be. But could you relay a message to my wife? She's in—" The officer shook his head. "No messages, either, until Captain Spencer gives the word. This could be very serious indeed!"

Angus looked up from his work. "As you havena been near enough this lad yoursel', Lieutenant, ye better leave the now. Mind you, this smit is not as catchy as you all seem to think, but still, the rules say—"

The officer left, calling over his shoulder, "The captain will commandeer crew members he can trust, but if any more cases surface, we could be in for a major quarantine."

The two Scots stared at each other before Angus asked Bruce, "Have ye been exposed to it afore this?"

"Bubonic plague? Not to my knowledge, but I did serve a year's curateship in the Gorbals—"

"Say no more. I've been in they cesspools myself. I would venture to say ye've been immunized without knowing it, but we'll take every precaution. Here, read this pamphlet. I made it up mysel' when I was goin' to the India passage and we were exposed at many a port."

Bruce gave the proffered paper a quick scan before saying, "As you suggest, Doctor, I've likely been immunized unbeknownst. May I ask how young Roger here came to be in your care? I happen to know he's a steerage passenger."

"I could ask you the same thing, but aye, I near tripped ower him this mornin' on my way here. He was oot o' bounds, all right, but I think somebody with half a heart helped him to where I would find him. As my understandin' of my job is to help sick folks, I carried him here masel'. He's skin an' bones. Of course he should have been in the steerage, but 'tis a big job keepin' them all in the right holds down there. I'm glad to say the days are past when they would be locked in—or even chained."

Bruce refrained from mentioning his own recent experience. Maybe he had not been locked in, but it had been the next best thing to it. A question seemed timely: "Is there no provision for sick folk in the steerage then?"

The doctor returned his attention to the patient. "There is, aye, but it's gye skimpy. For instance, on this crossin', 'tis two would-be pharmacy assistants workin' their passage." So saying he began to scrub vigorously at his hands. "Well, Roger, m'lad, that's all I can do for you at the moment." The older man glanced quizzically at Bruce from under bushy white brows, and his look reminded Bruce painfully of Gran'pa Bruce. Angus continued, "You, sir, are you a professional man yourself? If I might ask, what profession?"

"I'm a minister, but—"

"Excuse me then, Reverend, but I'm maist puzzled. You come

crashing in here, announcing ye're a grandson of the 'Ranald, my ain laird. Then you grasp hold on this lad, who's not your ain kin, I take it. Ye're not daft, I see, but there is a story ahint all this."

A faint smile crossed Bruce's features, but his mind strayed to Kirsty and what she must be thinking and doing at this moment. How could he get to her or get a message through without harming others?

MacIllvenney still talked, "Mysel', I'm interested in the business of names and ancestry and all that, and I'm curious about yours. Aribaig, you say? Hm! Beg your pardon, but your connection wi' the 'Ranald must be on the spindle side and not on the official records." He paused for breath then began to shake his head in disbelief. "Och, man, ye're never related to the Bruce MacAlister that married our Morag? Morag Campbell, that is. She would've been my auntie, but she—"

At last he had Bruce's full attention. That side of his family tree had not been spoken of much at the Mains, but he did know the facts, and of course Morag Campbell had been his paternal grandmother's maiden name. He also knew she had died at his own father's birth. Before he could respond or conjecture further, the lieutenant appeared in the doorway again, this time his expression full of determined zeal. He had also brought reinforcements.

Long past being worried about what the steward might say concerning the visitors in their cabin, one of them a newborn babe, Kirsty had stormed out on to the bulkhead, only to be stopped by an officer of the watch. She rounded on him in a fury, "What do you mean I canna go down there? My husband has been absent far too long, and I fear something's wrong. I *demand* to know what is happening on this ship."

The man studied his list of passengers before saying, "Reverend and Mistress MacAlister. Yes, well, with all due respect, ma'am, I must ask you to return to your cabin. For reasons I am not at liberty to divulge, no passenger movement is being allowed until we receive orders from the bridge."

"No movement allowed!" she screamed. "No movement allowed? Is this a passenger liner or a prison ship? I'll move about if I want. I'm going to find my husband. Please step aside."

"Sorry, ma'am, orders. Please do not force matters." He stared past her at the open door of the cabin, and belatedly Kirsty recalled that her position lacked conviction for creating a scene.

She subsided, but not without giving the last word. "Orders indeed. When my husband comes back, we'll see who's giving out orders and for what." Only slightly subdued, she made her way back to the cabin, her thoughts in a turmoil. What could be happening? A mere few hours ago she had been reveling in the thought of how at last her life seemed settled into a comfortable mold that had produced deep feelings of joy and happiness that bubbled up from within. She stood for a second, before pushing the door all the way open, aware that her every move was being watched. Surely that good time could not be over already? A sob caught in her throat, but she choked it off. Her faith was too new for her to call on all the inner resources promised by it, but she still held on to the staunch rules of conduct deeply ingrained by her da'. She shuddered. Could he have been right after all? Had her new life been too good to be true? After softly closing the door she stepped over to the partition.

A low murmur greeted her, and she smiled through her fear. Something good did seem to be happening, for those in here at least. Motherhood had worked its own miracle on young Mistress Ogilvie. Kirsty gasped in amazement at the sight meeting her gaze. The elder Ogilvie woman sat on a steamer chair beside the bed. She had baby Christina cradled on her lap, while she softly crooned a Gaelic lullaby as she rocked back and forth. The little one's mother, her pretty face alight, leaned back on the cushions with a smile that could only be described as beatific.

For scarcely a moment Kirsty enjoyed the little scene before shattering it with her words: "This is all very bonny, and I'm pleased you're takin' your right place, Granny Ogilvie, but we canna sit here all night. We must find a road to tell the menfolk, and I'm feart there's something far wrong on this ship, so we'll have to be gye sleekit aboot it."

*   *   *

Two large, brawny sailors flanked the lieutenant as he stood just inside the door of the sick bay, and Bruce glimpsed others of the same caliber in the passageway behind him. He glanced at Dr. MacIllvenney, but that man had scarcely looked up from his task of mercy.

However, mercy was not the errand Lieutenant Degnan had on his mind. He barked an order, and the heavyweights moved slowly forward to obey, although neither got too close to the cot, Bruce noted.

Angus pulled Bruce's arm before hissing through clenched jaws. His words were in the Gaelic: "They're not here for prayer meetin', Reverend. Can you fight?"

Bruce MacAlister, the preacher and purveyor of peace and good-will, nodded affirmatively. "I can fight if I need to."

"Needs be now then and be ready. I see no weapons." The Gaelic for "weapons" came out as *claymores*, but Bruce did not smile as Degnan spoke to the doctor, his voice ringing clear.

"Dr. MacIllvenney, I have a burial party here for the removal of your deceased patient. Please step aside so as they can perform their duty."

Angus turned swiftly and reached into the trolley beside the cot. His hand came forth wielding a scalpel. He held it up threateningly. "There's no deceased patient here, Lieutenant. He might be gye low, but he's not dead, so I must ask you to clear my sick bay at once."

This caused the navvies to surge forward, and the one closest to Bruce lunged with a shout, "He looks deed to me, an' if he's no', he soon will be!" With that he snatched off his seaman's cap and pressed it cruelly down on young Roger's face, covering his mouth and nose completely. A moment later an amazed would-be bruiser lay on the floor with an enraged Bruce MacAlister kneeling astride his chest. But the two Scots were outnumbered and soon over-powered. Angus fought valiantly but could not bring himself to use the scalpel. Belaying pins appeared, and once again Bruce was struck, this time from behind. Before he went down, he noted Angus had reached the cot. As Bruce subsided, the last thing he saw was the doctor's sad face as he slowly shook his head.

Gradually Bruce's senses began to clear, and he sat up, bewildered by his surroundings. Recognizing the sick bay, he gathered his scattered wits together as he heard a moan coming from the other side of the cot, now stripped bare and empty. He staggered to his feet, only to fall to his knees at once as dizziness returned. Determination kept him crawling toward the sound. His fellow highlander lay in what appeared to be a pool of his own life blood, freely spurting from a wound in the doctor's neck. Obviously it was not a fatal wound, as the doctor had managed to pinch two fingers together and hold on grimly. Seeing Bruce, he made another sound. Still unable to speak, he began to signal with his free hand. Bruce got the message and shuddered anew. Angus wished him to sew the two lips of skin together, and Bruce knew he'd better be quick, as a fresh spurt of blood pulsed and flowed over the other man's fingers.

Bruce struggled to his feet again, this time clutching the iron sides of the cot. Without ceremony he rifled through the contents of a tray until, finding a needle at last, he thanked the Lord that it held in readiness a long strand of cat-gut thread. Keeping up his silent prayer for strength and wisdom, he knelt beside Angus MacIllvenney. No time for fancy stitching, even if he knew how, but he did recall seeing his mam pull seams and patches together on his trews and other items. At his first piercing of the soft folds of the skin he felt the fingers, already slippery with their owner's blood, slacken their hold. Angus went limp. Bruce thanked the Lord once more and got on with the gruesome task. Trying not to think of it as flesh, he quickly stitched on until the flow of blood eased and finally stopped. Angus still lay unconscious, enabling Bruce to try to make sense of whatever else must have transpired here after he had jumped on the navvie.

The empty bed told its own sad tale of Roger's fate, and Bruce prayed again, aloud this time: "Dear Jesus, receive the lad, Roger, in your great mercy. He knew not what he did!"

Over in another corner of the cabin a strangely familiar figure sprawled. No blood here, and Bruce rubbed his eyes to clear them as he recognized Lieutenant Degnan. Yet, could it truly be he?

Bruce had said that aloud, too, and was gratified to hear the faint response, "Yes, 'tis me. Like yourself I was belayed in the course of my duty. Mutiny, sir! Pure and simple. By adversaries, who, having escaped, must remain unnamed!" A sound not unlike a croak came from the doctor, who now struggled to sit up. Bruce leaned down to help him. Moments later all three sat staring at one another in the most bizarre of semicircles.

Angus tried to speak, but Bruce admonished him, "Don't try to talk, Doctor, or you'll undo all my handiwork." Angus subsided at that and rested his head on the cabin wall in a motion of despair as he cast his glance round about. The sick bay was a shambles, but worst of all, to him, his fight for the life of a patient had been in vain.

As if reading his thought, Degnan offered, "You did all you could, Doctor. I swear 'twas an expired patient the burial party removed. No blame to be attached to anyone here, nor to the ship's captain, who only knows the deceased has been buried at sea with Christian rites." The last he said with tongue in cheek, avoiding Bruce's eye.

Bruce was far from satisfied. "Roger was not dead when I saw him last. I cannot believe he died that fast, and how can you know so much about it, if you lay here unconscious as I did?" More strangled noises came from the doctor, but Bruce kept his eyes fast on the ship's officer.

"Reverend, my advice to you is this: Take it as truth that the lad had a relapse and expired during a raid on the sick bay by a gang of mutineers. Be content that you and Doctor Mac here both did your best, and leave it there. This is for everyone's benefit and may have—no, most surely will have—averted a full-scale tragedy. When no more cases come forward and the gang attacking us has been placed in the brig, our entry into New York harbor will only have been delayed by one day."

"But how . . . when—?"

"Let me say it again, Reverend MacAlister. Oh, yes, I know who you are. Should the dread word *plague* be mentioned again outside this cabin, then not only would you be deported, but you would not be allowed to rejoin your wife until you were both back in Scotland. As it is, I'm not sure what to do about you. If we try to quarantine you, we risk the rumor's starting up again, but if we trust the doctor's theory, then we may not have to take it any further."

The doctor moved and made a sign, which Bruce interpreted as a need for a drink of water. He rose shakily and searched for a drinking vessel. Finding one, he held it to the other man's lips. Into another container Angus spat out the first mouthful, which consisted of a mixture of mucus and blood as well as the water, before he painfully swallowed a small amount.

Bruce took a second drinking cup, filled it, and held it out to Degnan, who accepted it gladly. Wiping his mouth on his hand, he continued his exhortation: "You cannot bring the lad back, and that's the truth."

Bruce shook his head wonderingly. "I still have many questions. Among them, how many more need be sacrificed?" He turned to Angus, whose eyes had lost their glazed look and now held one of warning.

Lieutenant Degnan made his slow, shaky way to the door. Before reaching it, he turned back and surveyed the two occupants. "If we are agreed, we can now proceed to be more comfortable." He did not wait for a reply but tapped the door with his knuckles. At this prearranged signal, the door flew open. He rapped out a spate of orders, and seconds later a bevy of stewards, armed with mops and pails and other cleaning paraphernalia, entered. Soon the overpowering smell of carbolic reminded Bruce once more that he was in a sick bay. Dr. MacIllvenney now lay on the bunk, so recently occupied by his patient, being carefully tended to by a pair of white-robed orderlies. Bruce's mind buzzed with more questions, including why he, an abject layman at the job, had been allowed to suture the doctor, when so many folk much better equipped waited outside.

His answer to that must wait many months. Angus MacIllvenney, with a permanently damaged voice box, would never speak coherently again. The doctor could only be grateful he still breathed. Mercifully Bruce knew not the extent of his fellow highlander's disfigurement, and he at last gave up on finding anyone to answer his queries.

Suddenly Bruce became aware of a seaman dabbing away at his head wound with something cool and stinging. Sighing he now allowed himself to be washed and patted dry, even shaved, as his thoughts left the present surroundings and a fresh churning began within. What more could he do here in the face of all this? He must get to Kirsty.

Just then the lieutenant reentered, again not alone.

Bruce gasped as he saw who followed. "Garnett! Is it truly so?" A completely transformed Garnett stood before him. This one emanated a newfound dignity as he approached Bruce.

His words amazed the minister even further, "The Lord giveth, and the Lord taketh away, blessed be the Name of the Lord! Amen!"

A lifetime's habit caused Bruce to echo. "Amen!"

26

The SS *Boadicea* moved serenely through the moonlit waters, oblivious to the diversity of the trials and terrors, hopes and dreams, of the thousands of souls cramming her many decks. Most of these souls slept the night hours away, a few in repletion and utter comfort, following an eight-course gala dinner, always scheduled for the evening before sighting the New World. Many others on board slept in sheer exhaustion, despite the miserable discomfort; but their thoughts before sleep included both thankfulness that only one more day and night need be lived through before they would see an end to these awful conditions and fears for tomorrow. The dreaded and much fabled Ellis Island would be the next hurdle before release into liberty and the streets of gold that had been promised them in this land of the brave.

However, not all aboard slept, even if the hour showed midnight and the late bell had chimed. Besides the watch, others roamed the decks, among them Bruce MacAlister and his wife, Kirsty, with arms entwined. Romance was not their main topic as they shared the different experiences each had been through during the last sixteen hours. Even though they had this portion of deck to themselves, Bruce still kept his voice to a low murmur.

"She's a bonny wee thing, right enough, and you say her name is Christina? Her mother—only a lassie herself, mind you—seems happy, and the grandmother is—"

Kirsty burst in with, "Och, the old yin is more than happy, Bruce, my love. She is fair carried away wi' it. I canna even think of a word strong enough to tell you."

His gaze was more than fond as he said, "Would *ecstatic* be close, or *elated*, or even *overjoyed*?"

She glanced at him through the screen of her lashes, wet with tears. "You're laughin' at me, Bruce MacAlister!"

Instantly sobered, her husband halted their walk and drew her into the shadow of a lifeboat.

"Forgive me, sweetheart. Maybe I was laughing, just a wee bit. I'm so glad to have you this close to me again. For a while there I wondered if. . . . But I'm not able to tell you any more of what's happened since we left our bed this morning." He bent to touch her hair with his lips, but she pulled away.

"I thought we'd be having no secrets from each other, Bruce?"

"Kirsty, darling, if it were just my own self, I'd tell you everything; but there will be times when. . . . Well, in my position as a minister and a pastor, certain things told to me in confidence must never be shared, even with you, my heart. Be sure I've told you all I can about what's happened this day." As he spoke he fingered a scrap of paper in his waistcoat pocket, feeling guilty. How she must be puzzled! He was more than a little confused himself.

When Garnett had followed Lieutenant Degnan into the sick bay and made his statement about the Lord's giving and the Lord's taking away, even as Bruce had responded with the word *amen*, he had his questions ready. "Exactly what are you talking about, Garnett? You wouldn't speak so if you knew all that's happened here."

But Garnett's eyes still shone as he interrupted, "Oh, but I do know, Professor, the officer here kindly sought me out in the men's hold on B deck. Then, after taking me to a washhouse, where I got cleaned up and changed into a new rig out, he explained to me about poor Roger. Sad as I am about that, I cannot help rejoicing about the next part; it can only be a miracle of God."

He had halted for breath, and Bruce waited for more. "The officer then took me to your cabin, where I discovered not only that I had a bonny wee daughter, but that my wife and my mother, with the help of Mistress MacAlister, had become the best of friends. Their only disagreement now is about who gets to hold the baby. Thanks to God!" His face beamed as he went on. "We are naming her *Christina*."

Bruce, whose brows had been drawn into a deep frown from the moment the new father had entered the sick bay, erupted into shouting, "No! No! That's all very nice, but I cannot accept it. Something smells rotten about it."

Garnett stared, uncomprehending, then his face cleared. "Och, you mean poor Roger. We're all that sorry about him, but Virginia tells me her brother aye had a weak constitution, and—"

In desperation Bruce had scanned the cabin until he caught the eye of Angus MacIllvenney. That man had managed to sit up on the cot, and now he signaled to Bruce to come closer. Somehow the doctor had acquired a scrap of paper and a bit of lead pencil. He slipped the paper to Bruce, who had read it quickly while Garnett went on garrulously about his newfound happiness.

The note had said, "The laddie died before they took him from the cot. Wrong diagnosis."

Doubting still but allowing his mind to quieten, Bruce had searched his fellow highlander's face with a discerning look, but Angus returned his stare equally, and Bruce had found no guile.

The lieutenant had spoken up then, "You are free to go now, Reverend."

With a final glance round the sick-bay cabin, Bruce, rather meekly for him, had followed Garnett out.

Now he took his wife's hand again and led her toward the rail, without speaking. The moon spread a silver path along the peaceful ripples of the Atlantic.

Avoiding the sight of the water far below, Kirsty asked him one more question: "I suppose you canna tell me the true reason we'll be delayed for a day before docking in New York harbor?"

"You're right, my love, I cannot, and simply because I'm not at all sure myself. Contrary to your great faith in my abilities, I do not know everything, especially not aboard ship."

Suddenly a smile lit her mobile features, and her emerald eyes sparkled in the moonlight. "There's something else you're not too well versed on, Bruce MacAlister."

"Oh, indeed, and what might that be, Mistress MacAlister?"

Suddenly serious, she turned her head away. "That is on the way of a woman when she is going to have a bairn!"

For a full minute silence reigned, and then Bruce placed his hands on her head to gently twist it, so that he could look into her glorious eyes. He managed a hoarse whisper, "Kirsty, do you mean to say? Och, you're never . . . ?" Words failed, and he choked on the depth of this new emotion.

She mistook his quietness. "Bruce, you're not angry, are you?"

"Angry! Oh, my love, no. That's the last thing I could be. I just can't take it in." Then he asked the question every man asks his wife after such an announcement: "Are you sure?"

She laughed in delight. "I'm sure, Bruce. I couldn't wait any longer to tell you, in case you decided to go off on another one of your—what is it Granny Mac calls them?—oh, aye, exploits."

Coming to life, he gave a shout, and although she could not understand the Gaelic word, she easily recognized its ring of triumph as it echoed across the open space far above the ocean.

A step sounded behind them, and Bruce groaned as another voice spoke, "Excuse me, Reverend. Madam. I know it's very late, but Captain Spencer extends his compliments, and he asked me to escort you and your wife to his guest cabin, since you have been so kind as to give up your own cabin to a needy family."

Kirsty clapped her hands, but her predictable husband, though she could not see it clearly in the moonlight, wore the frown she had yet to learn of as he considered the real reason for the favor.

"Convey our thanks to the captain, Lieutenant Degnan, but we'll not be needing a—"

A sharp pain in the area of his shinbone caused him to gasp as his wife spoke up, "Oh, yes, we will be needing it. Thank your captain for us, but first lead us to it. I'm ready to drop from weariness."

Immediately Bruce became all concern for her, and he gave up. Truly, he could not make better of the situation regarding young Roger, and anyway he had to trust Angus MacIllvenney's word, did he not?

"Right you are then, indeed, and lead the way, Lieutenant."

The man stepped out of the shadows and walked a few paces. Bruce had caught Kirsty's arm. "You're that thrawn, Mistress MacAlister, I don't know how I'm going to manage you."

"Aye, Reverend, I am thrawn, and I hope you'll never manage me. I didna ken that was your intention. I see my main job will be keeping you from being a big eedjit, when we reach America. You mind me of a story we had in school about the fella who wanted to fight a windmill. Whit's his name again, oh aye, Kee-ho-tay?"

Bruce reached for her without answering and swung her up into his arms. "Your disrespect for the cloth, madam, is beyond redemption. I'll teach you how much of an eedjit I can be. Just you wait."

The officer glanced back and decided a few more minutes would not matter. He returned to his own thoughts. Some of the things he had learned this day he would never forget. After his ordeal in the sick bay, the captain had granted him leave until they docked, and he began to wonder if somehow he could drag Reverend MacAlister away from his wife, even for an hour, before they reached New York. There was just something about the man— something that Benjamin Degnan admired greatly, a quality of life that the ship's officer had never before known existed. He murmured softly, "I want that. I want it for myself and for Isabel. Somehow I think he'll help me to find it and even tell me how to share it with her."

All at once the moon vanished beneath the waves, and the couple moved slowly toward him. Bemused as Bruce was with his wife and her wonderful news, he did not miss or misinterpret the yearning on the young officer's face.

"Yes, lead on, laddie, and by the way, we're an old married couple, you know. We'd be delighted if you would join us for breakfast in the morning. Och, 'tis nearly morning already!" Kirsty gasped as Bruce crushed her hand in his own, daring her to contradict him or show surprise at his offer.

The other man, with a catch in his own breath, answered that he would indeed be honored to join them. He turned to leave them, but not before he heard what he took to be some strange form of Scottish endearment.

"Eedjit! Eedjit! Big eedjit! But I love you for a' that, Bruce MacAlister."

27

Although Marshall Bradford Fairbanks would never use the term *eedjit* to describe his newly met nephew, the august New York banker with the proudly held name had a few other choice words with similar meanings in mind for his reverend relative. But he held them in check as he addressed the impetuous man: "See here, Bruce, it will do no good for you to go to Ellis Island. The immigration folk have their rules and regulations, and the correct amount of time must pass before—"

The ladies sat silent, and Kirsty wondered what her man's response would be to this. Nothing mild, she would wager.

"I understand all that, Uncle. What I'm having trouble with is the extreme differences. We've heard much of America's being the land of freedom, a place with equal opportunities for all. Why, then, if that's truly the case, were we brought ashore on the pilot boat without touching your Ellis Island, while the *Boadicea* is still anchored at the mouth of the East River, with most of its passengers awaiting disembarkation?"

His great-uncle stroked a beard that would have been luxurious, if allowed to grow. As it was, the style of the beard reflected most of the man's life, being kept well within the bounds of what Marshall—or Uncle Brad, as he had requested they call him—considered common decency. His deeply blue eyes, shockingly reminding Bruce of his own mother's, flashed with anger at Bruce's criticism of his adored country.

The small, squirrellike woman seated next to Kirsty at the breakfast table held her breath. She also knew her man and his unpredictable temper, when crossed.

His reply sounded mild enough though, "You and your lady have been allowed to disembark early because of my recommendations. I vouched for my own sister's grandson, for your state of health, as well as for your financial solvency. The majority of passengers have no such guarantors. But let us not argue, Nephew. We can do naught for the folk still on the ship, and your aunt and I have been so looking forward to a little family jaunt by boat, around our fair city."

Again the room pulsed with unspoken rebuke, and Bruce's good manners surfaced. "Sorry, Uncle, 'tis just that I thought of a possible delay of two or maybe even three days for the Ogilvies. But it's been a week now, and when I inquired this morning from—"

"That's another thing, Bruce. Complaining to our friends about your shipboard acquaintances being held up by Immigration! I would prefer it if you would keep your remarks inside the family."

Before he could think of a response to that, Bruce felt a sharp jab on his ankle. Kirsty, wiser in the ways of such talk, wanted him to be quiet. His aunt, too, a timid little woman who wished to be called Aunt Polly, although her name, Pauline Huntingford Radcliff, also resounded with old colonialism, seemed to warn him with her eyes. Now she came fussing with the coffeepot. She had early discovered Bruce's fondness for the brew and plied him with it constantly. Breakfast in the elegant Fairbanks townhouse was considered informal, especially today, when the multitude of servants were busy preparing for the picnic.

Polly also had a private word for her husband's out-of-place remarks, although she was far too genteel to kick him. "Brad, my dear, what about Cousin Bellingham, could we not—?" Aunt Polly had the disturbing habit of never finishing her sentences, but her husband usually made up for this.

Only slightly mollified, he turned to gaze at his wife as if seeing her for the first time. Then, "Of course, my dear, I should have thought of Bellingham! He and Rebecca will be joining us today." To Bruce and Kirsty he explained, "Your aunt has many cousins, and Bellingham, who has a high position in the Department of Immigration, is one of them. You'll meet him, as well as many other family members, either today on the trip or tomorrow at church service. Now, my dear, I have some telephone business to tend to, so if you all will excuse me. . . . Say we'll be ready to leave one hour from now!" He swept from the room as Bruce reached for his watch and the two women glanced at the grandfather clock in the corner. Aunt Polly hurried after her husband, and Bruce smiled at Kirsty, his smile a cross between the shamefaced and comical.

Just over two hours later a diminutive paddle steamer, which had been chartered for the outing, chugged its way south along New York's East River. The Fairbank's landau had brought the party from bustling but elegant Washington Square through the aptly named Street of Ships, to the waterfront and Pier 17.

Pleased to note that her husband and his outspoken uncle seemed to have forgotten their earlier upset, Kirsty allowed her other fear to surface in her mind—more deep water. For the past week Kirsty had been delighted to tread the solid ground as they had made the round of places to visit.

Now looking out over the gray-blue waters of the East River, toward Brooklyn, she stepped from the pier to the sturdy gangplank of the steamer. This was the closest she wished to be to water, she thought, but today she hid her fear even from Bruce. Clutching the side rails more tightly, she climbed to the deck, trying to close her mind to the murky depths yawning directly beneath her. No one noticed her hesitation, so she stepped as bravely as she could to the enclosed space in the middle of the first deck, which led to some stairs going down inside. There she found a conveniently safe place where she could wait out the trip. She caught a glimpse of Uncle Brad and Bruce as both men seemed to be enjoying the lovely scene and the glorious weather. The old man acted as if he alone were responsible for both the man-made and the natural vistas opening up before their wondering eyes. Kirsty turned her attention to the other folk thronging the deck and passing back and forth across her vision as the man with the megaphone pointed out the landmarks. She had been introduced to all the relations, but she just knew she would never recall all those long, fancy names. Sighing she settled down to what she had been told would be about a thirty-minute voyage and tried not to think of the murky water churning through the busy paddles she could so plainly hear.

Kirsty's fear of water was one of the few things Bruce could become impatient about with her. He even prayed that she would be healed of it. Oh, would that she could.

A shout from the upper deck brought Kirsty out of her daydream, but fear kept her pinned to the seat, which, she thanked God, was firmly attached to the floor of the inner cabin. When Aunt Polly had passed by, she had assured her that she would be happy to wait here. A moment after the cry, the lady herself appeared in the doorway, looking shaken.

Kirsty forced herself to stand, although the deck seemed to be rising and falling alarmingly. "What's wrong, Aunt Polly?"

The little woman smiled tremulously. "Wouldn't you know this is the very moment your liner, the *Boadicea*, is disembarking its immigrant passengers? The reverend thinks he recognizes the little family you befriended and he tried to shout—"

But Kirsty heard no more as, for the moment, concern for that impulsive man of hers overcame her fear, and she ran toward the steps.

The aunt's voice faltered, "Oh, don't fret about it. He's fine, but my husband is fuming about his making a public spectacle—"

But her Scottish relative by marriage heard none of this, as she had reached the top of the stairs. Relief flooded through Kirsty as she saw Bruce and his obviously agitated uncle bearing down on her. Bruce's eyes flashed a warning message that clearly said, "Don't ask!" So she waited as demurely as she could until they joined her.

"I'll leave you to tell your wife, Bruce," Uncle Brad barked. "Fifteen minutes and we will be docking again." Now she would ask him, but before she could open her mouth, Bruce said, "I can't be doing with all this folderol, Kirsty. I was standing here, looking through Uncle's binoculars—by the way, they've got Barnie's spyglass fair beat—well, I had scanned the horizon and was swinging my sights to closer things when I saw the wee immigrant ferryboats, and there, as plain as you please, stood Garnett. He had the baby up and was showing it the statue yonder. But even as

I watched, I saw this big burly sailor grab the lad and almost throw him back. I let out a yell, and Uncle, well, you noticed!"

Kirsty smiled into her hand. That was not all she had noticed. "Aye, I did. But Aunty Polly will sort him. Oh, Bruce—"

Her husband had the binoculars raised once more, but suddenly he removed them and placed the cord round her neck. "Look, my love! Do you see it, Kirsty?"

Kirsty had been seeing the huge statue of the lady all the time he spoke, but she merely nodded to that as she asked her own question, "Bruce, will you settle down now that they're sure to be landed the day?" He turned in alarm at the tone of her voice, but his eyes held a grieved look. "Och, Kirsty, my love, have I been that bad?" Receiving no spoken answer, he clasped her hand tightly as he went on, "You should know me by now, Kirsty. I'll not be at peace till I know they're safe with their own kin. But you'll have noticed my uncle. He's not too pleased that I tried to get Garnett's attention. It seems so many of the folk on this outing the day are of the same ilk as Uncle, and a lot of them are relatives, too. Uncle Brad is ashamed that his Scottish nephew should be on familiar terms with the immigrants. He forgot how all come from immigrant stock themselves, unless they're American Indians or Africans."

A small oasis of silence surrounded them as he spoke that last sentence, and Kirsty groaned inwardly. She glanced round the sea of faces. Her man had surely done it this time. She clutched his sleeve with her free hand as the onlookers began to drift away. "You never answered my question, Bruce. Will you not leave the Ogilvies now and settle down?"

He gazed at her long and hard before saying, "Not yet, my love. I had a talk with the worthy Bellingham Smith while you were hiding in the lounge. He gave me permission to go to Ellis Island to make sure the Ogilvie family are all right. Here's the note with his signature."

She gasped but did not even glance at the piece of paper as she whispered her next question, fearing she already knew the answer.

"Aye, on the way back the day, they'll make a special stop for me. But you don't need to come, sweetheart. I know you hate the water, so you can go back with—"

Suddenly Kirsty erupted, forgetting all the lessons of correct diction from Granny Mac and Faye Felicity Smith as she burst out in the Doric, "You're gawin' naewhere else withoot me, Bruce MacAlister. I just hope your permit admits two! Dinna argue wi' me. I'm comin' even if I have to swim." Realizing what she had just said, Kirsty blanched, but then she continued bravely, "Aye, I mean it! Och, dinna shout again. We're gettin' too much attention as it is."

He ignored that, and grasping her round the waist, striding with her to the rail, he placed her carefully where she could get a good grip on the rail with one hand and his arm with the other, before he spoke with great jubilation, "Take a good look, Kirsty Brodie MacAlister. Lady Liberty as they call her! Next door, if you like, Ellis Island, the place of tears and fears. As our cousin Craig would no doubt say, 'Only in America, I guess.' "

⟨ 28 ⟩

As it turned out, Great-uncle Brad could not bear to allow the MacAlisters to storm the grim fortress of Ellis Island by themselves. After a whispered conclave with Cousin Bellingham, followed by a word with his own spouse, Brad joined Bruce and Kirsty as they made their way down the ramp on to the jetty used by the workers and keepers of the citadel. A good three hours had passed since the sighting of the immigrant boat carrying the Garnett Ogilvie family. The main landing place was deserted, except for the officials seated within the clearly marked customs shed. Uncle Brad had taken charge of the situation, and he brandished Bellingham's letter. After the men in the booth had read it and scrutinized all of them closely, the three were allowed to go through the ten-foot-high, steel-mesh gate. Kirsty clung tightly to Bruce's arm, praying that he would not say or do anything too daft, while his elderly relative prayed in a like manner—only not so politely. As they entered the building, another set of officials met them, but again the letter paved the way. After the great steel doors had been unlocked with a flourish of rattling keys, the visitors found themselves being led along a passage and directed to a closed-in stairway.

Good manners aside, Uncle Brad made a small gesture with his head, indicating that he would go first. Kirsty went next, with Bruce bringing up the rear. It occurred to Kirsty that few if any words had been spoken since they had left the boat. At the top of the stairs, another immense door loomed, but this one, although also heavy and steel lined, proved to be unlocked, so at last they entered the fabled, fateful place forever to be dubbed the registry.

Rather they now stood on the balcony overlooking the great hall. Not knowing what she might have expected, Kirsty leaned dangerously over the ornate, white painted balcony, to gaze fascinated at the scene below.

If anxious humanity could be described in such a way, Kirsty would have used the phrase "fermenting essence." Fear had its own peculiar scent, but although that most certainly was one of the ingredients, she felt other, stronger, sensations emanating upward, to meld with her highly impressionable spirit. Human perspiration mingled with the odor of strange foods and seasonings, some familiar to Kirsty, some not so, but all pungent. Woolen clothes, worn on unwashed bodies, also gave out a faint mixture of the smell of lye soap and disinfectant. But over all other observations, the ruling sensation could only be the strong miasma of excitement. Thrills and chills alternated through Kirsty, reaching to envelope her in their magic.

Her own entry into this country—a country that she was discovering more and more as a place full of great wonders and delights—had brought forth none of these sensations. For the span of a few minutes, while they watched the human dramas below, Kirsty tried to imagine what her own feelings would be if she were standing down in that hall, in the line of those awaiting inspection. The very thought sent a dart of real fear through her. For some reason her father's face floated into her inner vision. *What would he have made of all this*? she wondered.

As the sea of humanity ebbed and flowed endlessly, small, muted sounds did reach Kirsty's ears—the soft whimper of a frightened child or the sound of a cough quickly suppressed—but the absence of any other noise, except for the steady hiss of the gas lamps clamped to the wall behind them, amazed her. Returning her thoughts to their reason for being in this place, she began to take more note of the actual folk lined up at the railings.

Seeing no sign of the Ogilvies, she dragged her eyes from the poignant scene to steal a glance at Bruce. His brows had furrowed into the pattern she had begun to recognize, and his strong, handsome jaw was set in firm lines in a way she had witnessed only once before—that time on the ship, when he had returned to her after his strange disappearance. To her this only added to the magnetic charm of the man. Oh, how she loved him, and she longed to reach up and touch those stern features, just to watch them change for her.

Oh, Da', you would have loved him, too! I ken fine ye would. The thought became a tiny whisper that no one else could hear. Suddenly the silence shattered into a million bits as an ear-splitting scream rent the air. With one accord both Kirsty and Brad moved closer to Bruce, each catching an elbow tightly. The scream turned into a series of shrieks as a life-changing drama unfolded below them. For one dreadful moment before the noise became fainter and at last stopped, Kirsty thought her man would leap over the banister, but he had no such intentions. Instead he turned to his great-uncle, the obvious question on his face.

Brad shrugged, but his expression also displayed concern. "I don't know, Bruce, except that the rules do say—"

Kirsty felt Bruce's arm tense under her clutching fingers; however he quickly relaxed again as she caught his muttered words, "Rules! Rules!" He repeated it over and over again. But Brad was signaling, and Kirsty followed his pointing finger. "Is that not your friend, at the front of the line there?"

It was! All three tensed up now as they watched with bated breath. Garnett Ogilvie stood between the women. Virginia held her baby tightly to her bosom while the older woman still clutched her own shawled bundle. The uniformed officer indicated the papers and booklets being held out by Garnett, gesticulating toward the child in its mother's arms. The watchers above could hear no words, but the implication seemed plain enough. For interminable moments they held their breaths as one, and Kirsty figured out that the passports would mention no baby. Finally the man shrugged as he motioned for the young couple to pass. The watchers breathed again, but as old Mrs. Ogilvie moved to follow her family, the official again held up a detaining hand. This time it was no false alarm. After a short interval, another uniformed officer appeared, this one a woman. Mrs. Ogilvie did not scream as the other unfortunate had as she was led toward the detention area.

Kirsty turned her attention back to Virginia and Garnett. They were being ushered, politely enough, it seemed, through the coveted door of admittance to the land of so many dreams. Kirsty's next concern became what would that man of hers do now? Were they in for another of his exploits?

Bruce's expression remained rigid as his uncle spoke: "That *was* them then?"

"Aye."

"Can we leave it now then, Bruce, and be satisfied we've done all that's possible?" His voice still held a question.

Gently Kirsty put pressure on her husband's arm, and as if returning from a great distance, he threw her a startled glance. "What? Oh, aye. Yes, as you say, Uncle Brad, we've done all we can for the moment. But I cannot leave it yet. I must know why Garnett's mother is being detained and what we can do to help her with whatever comes next."

The sighs were simultaneous, but Kirsty knew that they should have expected no less.

Cousin Bellingham's letter had run its course. Nothing could open the door leading to the detention area and further enlightenment. What it did, though, was smooth the way for them to leave the island on one of the departing supply boats. Bruce suffered the indignity of having a stamp put on his hand, as did Uncle Brad and Kirsty, and soon they were steaming northeast on the busy waterway. A light rain had started to fall, but Bruce could not at first be coaxed into the sheltered area of the deck. There was too much to see, he declared to any who listened. Inevitably one of the things he saw happened to be a ferryboat packed with hopeful new Americans from the *Boadicea* on the very last lap of their journey.

Kirsty, biting hard down on her fears, would hardly allow her husband out of her sight; so she, too, stood against the rail of the launch, albeit with her back to the water, as she listened to this latest tirade.

He was beginning to run down. "Old lady Ogilvie, she'll truly go mad now. Separated from Garnett just when she was coming back into a normal state of living."

Trying not to moan or cry out at the swift movements of the neat little craft as it cut across currents and the wakes of other boats, causing the deck to heave under her feet, Kirsty managed to say, "My love, I'll be the advocate for Dr. Jamie, and even for Gran'pa Bruce, as you've taught me about him, and say, 'We canna make a better o' it Bruce, lad!' or, 'We cannot win them all, Father-in-law!' " She had caught them both to a tee and Bruce, with one of his swift mood swings, turned to her with a shamefaced laugh, surprise and delight pouring from his eyes.

"Och, Kirsty, dear wife, how right you are. Having done all, we must stand. But not out here, you're shivering. Forgive me, love. I've been neglecting you shamefully!" So saying he swept her up, and his years on the *Revelation* stood him in good stead, his sea legs being well equal to the task of carrying her to the sheltered section of the deck. Tenderly he placed her on the bench before he removed his own jacket, and ignoring her protests, he quickly wrapped her in its homespun depths.

Brad, who had been watching them while talking to one of the officers on board, sighed with relief on hearing Bruce's laugh. Pride echoed through his voice as he spoke to the other man, "Yeah! I guess I've been misjudging my great-nephew. He is indeed a true-blue Christian. Concern for others rules his life. I've never met his like before."

The officer leaned closer. "I see what you mean, sir, but will he make it in this country? Well, you know, he could be a sheep among wolves."

"He'll make it. Underneath that aura he has a core of steel. Why, I remember his grandfather Munro, who married my sister Margaret. A hard-as-nails man, but that minister over there, Bruce MacAlister, has that in his background—and in his backbone, too, I might add. One in a million. Sad to say he's only on this side of the Atlantic for a short while and will not be making it his permanent home. But we were speaking about this old woman of his acquaintance, the one not allowed to go through the registry today. What can I tell Bruce about her, so that he can settle his mind? Because he'll sure not be letting it go."

"Tell him she'll be fine. You say she was taken through the middle doorway? Well, as a rule that means only an extra health check. So long as she has guarantors and does not show signs of tuberculosis or another contagious disease, they'll only keep her for one or possibly two days more. We do look after them well, you know, Mr. Fairbanks, sir. They have good food, good clean beds, much better than the steerage on the ships that most of them come over on."

"Good! Good! Now I just have to convince Don Quixote over there. Thank the Lord he has a sensible woman for a wife."

The sensible woman was making the most of her few moments. Nestled close to Bruce on the bench, refusing to listen to any of his great plans—even his plans for the remainder of this day—she whispered another one of his Gran'pa's sayings, or maybe it was Andrew's, "Enjoy the now!" She spoke very softly, at the same time reaching up to do what she'd been longing to do all day, smoothe the furrowed brow. As she had known it would, his jawline immediately relaxed as he caught her fingers in his own.

"Aye, love, you're right again. We will enjoy the now."

In what seemed a short while, they arrived at the Fairbanks' townhouse to be met by an excited Aunt Polly. "The mail's arrived, and oh, my, such a bundle of letters and packets for the MacAlisters. It'll take them until breakfast time to read them all."

29

"For a lady who wisna goin' to have any mair parties, I wonder what we should ca' this, the day?" Betsy Degg clucked fondly as she spoke, counting on her position as keeper of the keys at Strathcona House, where she had been entrusted with the job of housekeeper for many years, to justify the familiarity of her words. Her listeners included Mistress Oliver, also a housekeeper of renown, being the lady who cared for Granny Mac's oldest and dearest friend, Mr. George Bennett.

The so-called party mentioned by Betsy was comprised of George, as well as Dr. Jamie and Mary Jean Douglass and the whole of Dr. Peter Blair's clan. Beulah MacIntyre had called the get-together so as they could all share the news that she and most of the folk invited today had received in the past week or so from the MacAlisters.

The kitchen occupants were every bit as excited as the drawing-room guests. Each one had his or her own particular reason for admiring Reverend Bruce, and they had, without exception, received a communication in some form. Maybe a picture postcard, chosen with the particular recipient in mind, or as in the case of Benny Stout, who had known Bruce from his days at Glasgow University, a packet of newspaper clippings with his letter. Just as the gentry would be discussing the contents of the precious missives, those who served them would be. Every person under this roof of Strathcona House today loved Bruce MacAlister.

In the drawing room the tea things had been cleared away, and from where she sat cosily installed in her favorite winged armchair with one of Betsy's crocheted shawls draped over her shoulders, Beulah MacIntyre signaled to George.

Clearing his throat, the elderly gentleman began to speak: "As you all know, I have spent much time in North America, so some of Bruce's disclosures came as no surprise to me. Visitors going there with the purpose of teaching or preaching and who intend to leave again are allowed to disembark on their word, without having to go through the immigration process described by Bruce in his earlier letters. However, I must admit to being aware of the conditions below decks on the big liners. Like many others I believed it had to be so, and I made no attempt to change anything. But Bruce tells it much better than I: 'So you see, George, remembering all I learned from you and your friend Charles Booth regarding social reform at home, I took myself and my written report to the very top person in New York for the Blue Star Lines. I was most graciously received, and after I related my own experiences in the steerage hold of the *Boadicea*, as I described it, the gentlemen on the board of directors of that line reached a unanimous decision— one I'm sure would have happened soon, in any case. Beginning in the new year they will discontinue the class known as steerage. They will then have three classes only, first, second, and third. The third class will of necessity cost about double that of steerage, but those traveling by it should give heartfelt thanks to God that they won't need to spend ten or eleven days in those black holes.' "

George stopped reading to dab at his eyes, and he caught his hostess doing the same. "As for the rules of immigration, I think I have come to terms with that, although I would wish some of them changed."

A strangled sound came from the direction of the couch, where Peter Blair lay sprawled at his ease. All eyes turned to him, but he could contain his mirth no longer. "Can you not just see it all? The highlandman, no, I do mean the highland chieftain, because he truly is one, at his very best, storming the gates of American Big Business as well as the bureaucracy. I have it in my heart to feel sorry for the chaps who—how does he say it again?—received him most graciously." Silence greeted this, before Stirling, then Douglas, and suddenly the whole room exploded into joyous laughter as the vision grew.

Beulah recovered first, and she directed her clear gaze toward Peter. "What have you then to tell us from your own letter, Dr. Peter?"

Instantly sobered, Peter thought for a moment before replying, "Agatha Rose and I have been thanking God for giving our Bruce his Kirsty. What a fine wife she's turned out to be! He mentioned in his letter to us how he was all for taking his brand of rescue, which we all know is life endangering for him and at the least startling for those he opposes. This time it seems to have been the tenements. *Lower East Side New York* is how he terms it. Apparently, following their steamer excursion and their impromptu visit to Ellis Island, all of which we've heard about already, he still could not settle down. Kirsty had made it plain that she would not be left behind in any of his exploits. . . ."

Peter paused to glance at Beulah, who smiled in complete understanding as he went on, "I'll read what Bruce writes: 'Kirsty knew I did not want to go on the canal, rail, and coach excursion that our relatives had planned next and that we are enjoying at the moment, I might add, until I knew for certain how the Ogilvies had fared. So we slipped away by ourselves early one morning. (I'll not say here how we managed that, it would need its own letter.) Anyway we boarded a tramcar to the Lower East Side. After walking some distance, we found Orchard Street. Don't ask why it's called that, because it's the furthest thing from an orchard I've yet to see.

" 'We trudged up and down what seemed like a million stairs (thank God, they are having what is termed an Indian Summer here, extremely hot days and cool nights), until at last we found the Ogilvies. The wee family was in dire straits again. Virginia's uncle—I'm told he was aye the black sheep of that family—had not waited the week for them to get off the boat and through the registry. The man would not have known that they had no money left and didn't know how to get to his farm in the southern part of the state of New Jersey. (Not all young men go west, Peter, old chap.) The man had good intentions, mind, but he didn't dream the family would have no money at all.

" 'Kirsty got busy cleaning and comforting, and she took charge of baby Christina, while we sent Garnett out to buy some food. What a gem my wife is, Peter, but I believe I've mentioned that to you before now.

" 'Garnett came back with the food, already cooked, from a German place called a delicatessen. We soon assured him that our own relatives would know how to get them to Glassboro, and although Garnett was thrawn about taking money from us, I told him he could pay it back by joining a kirk and tithing, the minute he found one and had earned a dollar or two.' "

Again Peter stopped speaking to glare about him, daring anyone to make fun of his show of emotion. No one did, and so he blew his nose heartily and wiped his eyes before declaring, "Somebody else's turn, the rest of this I'll be keeping to myself." Beulah rocked silently for a moment. Then she said, "Jamie can you read for me, and then Mary Jean can you share from your letter?"

Bruce's beloved daughter nodded. Her own feelings were very mixed concerning her father's shattering news.

Jamie glanced quickly at his volatile wife, but he made no remarks as he took the letter from Beulah and placed his finger where she had indeed marked the place. He started quoting at once: " '. . . Well, Granny Mac, I knew I would miss all my dear ones in Scotland, and I'm glad I'm not here to stay, although it is a grand country, and if I could bring myself to leave Scotland, this is where I would reside. What I never realized is how much I am missing the pulpit. I got my chance, though, this morning. The big kirk here in New Bothwell has four ministers. The senior one has been away, but when he came home and heard we were staying with the Fairbanks family, he asked if I would take the pulpit for a Sunday. Being a bit out of practice at the preaching—' "

Again a noise from Peter interrupted, and this time George echoed the sound as Peter said, "Aye, that'll be the day, when the MacAlister forgets how to preach!"

Jamie, carefully keeping his finger on the place, glanced up briefly, but he went on without comment: " 'Anyway, I took the pulpit and said my piece. Kirsty, bless her (you were right about her Granny, I did pick a winner), had warned me to do no casting up about steerage passengers or Ellis Island. But as you know, Granny, I never take advantage of the pulpit for airing such matters. I spoke on Philippians, the fourth chapter, and expounded a bit on the verse where Paul exhorts us to think on the best things, like love and honor and good report; och, you know the place. The folk were most polite and receptive and I got a surprise when they not only clapped their hands but stood up to do it as I left the podium.

" 'To tell the truth, Granny, I'm anxious to come home and get back to work now that—' "

"Jamie!" Beulah rattled her walking stick at her great-grandson-in-law, and he stopped at once.

"Sorry, Granny, I nearly missed your mark."

Nobody else spoke then, so Mary Jean opened her reticule and removed her own precious missive. Taking her time to withdraw the finely penned sheets from their envelope, she said, "I'll not read the whole thing either, as some of it is repeating what we've already heard, and some more is just answering what we wrote to him last month, which you all know as well." She, too, glanced about as heads nodded in agreement. She caught a movement at the green baize door leading to the kitchen, and she smiled. Of course Betsy and the others wanted to know everything about her daddy and his escapades.

She continued her aside, "He expressed his delight that Mrs. Nellie Brodie has accepted the Savior and that she is following through with it and going to kirk with the Livingstones in Motherwell. By the way, we're all to keep praying for Maimie Dickson. Daddy says . . . well, he says Kirsty did write to her mother, saying how pleased they both are."

Everyone in Granny Mac's drawing room and those crowding at the swinging doors waited with tightly held breaths. Would Mary Jean never get to the bit that would confirm or deny their suspicions? "They are both pleased, too, that the plans for Nellie's sweet shop are going well." Again Mary Jean paused, and what could be described only as a groan escaped Peter. Jamie moved toward his wife and bent to whisper in her ear.

She nodded again. "Yes, Jamie, I'm getting to it. Here then is the most important part of our letter. The *great announcement*. I'm to have a wee brother or sister, April or May, they say, but—" Her next words were drowned out as Peter gave a great whoop and everyone began to speak at once. Only Beulah had known this for certain, as Bruce had wished Mary Jean to be first with the news.

An excited Betsy burst through the doors and made a beeline for her mistress. All this commotion might. . . . But Beulah sat calmly in the midst of the turmoil of happy reactions. She whispered to Betsy, "Bring wee Jason to me, Betsy."

Without question Betsy obeyed. After handing her mistress the baby, she leaned closer to receive another order. A moment later the company froze in amazement as the clangor of the great dinner gong, unused for many months, rang through the room.

Beulah spoke now, with tears streaming through her smile as she held up her great-great-grandson: "Well, Jason Philip Douglass, what do you say to that? You'll have an aunty or uncle on this side of the family, for a change, and younger than you to boot."

The little boy gurgled his delight and promptly spoke his first phrase, "Gran'da, Da-da!"

The group exploded again at this gem, which would surely go down in the history of the MacAlister saga.

A different set of people, with the same goal in mind had gathered in the living room of Raju and Faye Felicity Singh Smith, in the prosperous town of Cairnglen in the heart of the Trossachs. Faye had served a meal after church service, and the replete company sat round her handsome room, where one wall, completely made of glass, gave them a glorious view of the Dochart Falls. Trees on either side of the tumbling cascade had not yet shed their leaves, so the glowing colors, ranging from pale yellow to a deep glowing red, soothed and delighted every eye.

Barnie Hill broke the comfortable silence, "If we're going to have

some reading of letters, I vote we make a start, then, before somebody goes to sleep."

His wife smiled at him, knowing he was the most likely to fall
asleep. Although her father, Dr. Peter Blair, Senior, should have
been the one to do that, the elderly gentleman was wide awake. He
stirred in the comfortable armchair.

"I second that, Barnie," the doctor ordered. "No sleep till we've
heard all the hielandman's news."

Barnie began to unfold the letter he had just removed from his
pocket. "I don't know about the rest of you, but I've been a bit
leery that the so-called promised land might be luring Bruce away."

Dr. Blair interjected, "Not me! I've nothing against America,
mind you, but our Bruce MacAlister's no' so easy lured, eh,
Hamish?"

Hamish turned from where he had been standing, admiring the
rushing water. "Right, Doctor, he'll be back and afore too much
longer." Bruce's half-brother had just completed a lengthy assign-
ment with the brotherhood, and he was spending his few days of
freedom with the Singhs.

Barnie stared at Hamish. "He's given you a date when he'll be
back, then, Hamish?"

"No' a date but A just ken."

They accepted this as Barnie began again, "I'll just read bits
then, as I know everybody here has received a communication of
some kind." He bent his head to the closely written sheets. " 'I've
not been too successful in finding a photo factory, but as you can
tell we've been very busy otherwise. Maybe this coming week,
when we take train to Pennsylvania, we'll find something along
that line for the Phoenix Photo Factory researcher—meaning yourself, Barnie. As it is, I *have* come across some excellent pictures of
various landmarks, not just the usual postcard views either. You'll
know that Kirsty and I have been sending a constant stream of that
kind all over Scotland this last while. The ones I mention now are
true works of art, done by a person who is not just an amateur at
snapping pictures, but a real camera artist like yourself.' "

Unabashed, Barnie grinned smugly before continuing, " 'I also
discovered some works by what we call in Glasgow a pavement

artist, but here, of course, it's *sidewalk impresario*. We bought up his entire stock, and we'll be bringing it all home to share with our artistic friends. The man is a genius. His drawings of folk walking about on the famous Boardwalk of Atlantic City are so real that you wait for one of them to jump out and say hello, or "Hi," as it would be here. The masterpiece I managed to persuade him to part with is a charcoal drawing of a great cathedral in New York, Saint Patrick's. We visited it one day, and this drawing is more real than the original. . . .' "

Barnie sighed deeply as he shuffled the sheets, but he continued to quote: " 'We'll be home before Christmas, Barnie and Deb. Our regards to Dr. Blair and—' " He stopped to gaze round the room at his avid listeners. "The rest is more salutations!"

Raju sat up straight. He would be next. "After his letters about the poor conditions for some on board the ship and then the one about the slums, we hardly knew what to expect. I wondered if he would want to stay and start a revival or what, but no, that hasn't been his call, it seems. Here's what he had to say to us about that. 'My heart has always been to bring the Gospel to my ain folk, Raju, my friend, so if nothing else, this journey has made me realize how much I love my Scotland, my highlands and islands. For a while the desire of my heart was to get back on the *Revelation* and continue to answer my call to the isles. However, discovering that my dear Kirsty has, or I should say had, a terrible fear of the open water, made me look at other alternatives for our future.

" ' I may as well tell you we have been offered a living here in this bonny land and if—oh, well, no *if onlys*—specifically in a town called New Bothwell, population 30,000, with about a tenth of them worshipers at the church where I was offered the pulpit. 'Tis even on a George Street, believe it or not! There's a braw fountain in Livingstone Square. So many reminders of home and so many folk who come and tell us how their parents or grandparents or roots from even further back are Scottish, and they don't seem ashamed to admit it either!

" 'The town is very modern, with a tramway on the main thoroughfare, telephones everywhere, and many big motorcars. The church itself is quite recent, having been built in 1879, so it's not as old as most of ours.

" 'I'll not say we weren't tempted. Anyway Kirsty liked it a lot and taking into consideration her fear of the water and facing the boat trip home, I nearly said yes to a trial period. That's when she surprised me again. "Bruce MacAlister, you do believe in miracles, do you not?" What else could my answer be, but indeed and I do that, seeing I've experienced more than a few. She had guessed the reasoning behind my near decision. She was quiet for a wee while and just sat there, looking at me with those big, green eyes. Then it dawned on me, she wanted me to pray for a miracle for her to be healed of her fear of the water!' "

Raju stopped reading and pushed a sinewy brown hand through the lock of hair that had fallen forward in front of his face. The others waited patiently, miracles being nothing new or strange to anyone present. Raju resumed, " 'We were seated on a bench outside the kirk, and I had just told the board of deacons I would consider their offer. We'd been given the grand tour of the town and had been left to make our final decision. The fountain splashed away in the background, and the trees had begun to shed a few leaves. Your daft friend here got on his knees and began to pray for Kirsty's miracle. Thank the Lord, no one was about. To cut this short then, the Holy Spirit gave me a powerful prayer from all the "fear nots" in the Bible. After we both said amen, Kirsty stepped over to where the water spilled over into the pool. Reaching in, she scooped up a handful and let it run through her fingers before she spoke. "We have our miracle, Bruce. As you prayed I suddenly saw that the waters I've feared so much are only made up of millions of these wee drops. Och, I know the ocean is not to be compared, but the picture that came to my mind was Jesus walking on the Sea of Galilee. That was the moment you said in your prayer, 'Fear not, I am with you alway.' If that's the case, then what have I got to fear?" ' "

The reading halted again, and still no one else spoke in the Singhs' room as they all gazed out at the waterfall. The sun was sinking behind it, and the droplets sparkled like diamonds.

Raju glanced back at the letter. " 'Anyway, Raju, I hope you can make sense of this, as my emotions are a bit mixed up, so this letter must be, too. Tell everybody we'll be home by Christmas; then, after the blessed event of the birth of our child, we'll be outfitting the *Revelation* for another stint through the isles of the sea. I'm picturing you all as you read this, Raju, with Barnie and Deb, Dr. Blair and of course my namesake. We'll be there soon enough, and tell Brucie I've something special for him, as well, but he'll have to wait and see.' "

Raju glanced round again as his son made a gesture of complaint. "I believe the remainder is private."

The room's occupants fell silent again as the sun disappeared, then Deborah Hill stood up. "Time to go, Barnie, or dear knows what the dogs will be doing."

Tensions eased, and they all laughed, knowing how Barnie's family of purebred King Charles spaniels would never do anything undignified. The two men lingered as the women moved toward the door.

Young Brucie hovered close to Hamish. "Uncle Bruce wouldn't know you were here, Uncle Hamish!"

Hamish smiled at the lad as he placed his hand on the shining head. "He wouldna ken because no' many folk ken my movements, Brucie. I hardly ken mysel' whiles. But dinna worry, my ain letters had much the same news. He sends them to Strathcona House for me to collect when I'm in Glesca." Intrigued at what he considered must be an exciting life led by his father's friend Hamish Cormack, Brucie knew better than ask any more questions of this silent man.

The Hills were leaving now. "He'll be here by Christmas, Raj. Isn't that just grand? He'll be stopping here for a day or two before they're off to Aribaig?"

"Yes, Barnie, it is just grand as you say, and another MacAlister on the way. All is well!"

"Aye, it is so. We'll see you at the office, in the morning then."

30

The dogs at the Mains had no dignity to uphold. Their usual welcome to Taylor the Post resounded across the steading and over the fields, calling all and sundry to come to the big house for the morning tea break. This might be the Cormack Homes now, but the traditions at the Mains stayed much the same. Taylor had not been round for two days, so that made him all the more welcome to Papa and Mama Ward. Jeremy had been a bit anxious that his friend Taylor might still be suffering from the slight accident he'd had on the bowling green on Saturday, but the sight of that individual leaping from his bicycle and almost running, with his big postie's bag overflowing, reassured him.

"We've a lot for you the day, Jeremy. Some from America!" Although this normally reticent representative of Her Majesty's Royal Mail would never go as far as his predecessor and try to guess the contents of letters, once in a while he did take the liberty of noting where one came from.

Jeremy answered, "Aye, that's good, you'll bide for a sup of tea and a scone whilst we read Bruce's letter then?"

"I will, and thank ye. I've had a braw postcard mysel'. Oor Fergie's been that excitit aboot the stamps for his collection."

"In you go then, and we'll see what else you have."

Whatever else would come forth from Taylor's bag would be ignored for the time being as the extended family settled round the immense table for the ritual. Not all those gathered had met the Reverend Bruce MacAlister or his missus in person, but all knew the stories well and would quietly munch on Dorrie's delicious scones and sup from bowls of fresh frothy milk while Papa Ward read to them. The hum subsided as Jeremy got ready to begin. Postcards for Dorrie Henderson and her brother Jimmy had been handed over as well as a small packet for their father, Jake. These were held unopened, as that trio also waited and watched. The schoolhouse mail had been given to Rob Heriot, but he, too, had no intention of reading his until Jeremy shared from the main missive. No one fidgeted as Wee Howie, now grown quite a bit taller and wider, waited Papa's signal. Howie was Jeremy's official letter opener, and he guarded the position proudly.

Rob Heriot smiled at his prize pupil. Only a few weeks ago, all had despaired of his ever learning to talk, but all that had changed. Now the youngster could say plenty when it suited him.

"Right, you are, Howie." The lad stuck the blunt edge of the opener under the flap of the envelope, and the gathered company let out their breaths, as Jeremy began to read.

Mama Ward glanced round the group as her husband read out the names of those being greeted. Hannah and Howie, Rosie and Wattie, and any new members of the family since Bruce's last visit, more than six months ago now. Everyone living in the Cormack Homes must be included, and Liz smiled her satisfaction. All was well with her world. Hearing her own name, she began to pay more attention: " 'Mama Liz, you will be gratified to know that even if some of the children's homes we've visited may be bigger and better equipped than the Cormack, none we saw could be compared for the quality of food and the just plainly happy folk.' " She smiled at the praise, but she could honestly admit the MacAlister's influence on her husband and on herself had produced the ability to foster the right environment for such happy people.

Embarrassed, as the tableful of these same happy ones had turned to gaze at her in awe, Liz began to fiddle with some of the other mail. One from Blodwin. *Thank God I've come to be truly glad about that situation, too*, she thought. *I'll read it after everybody goes back to work or school.* Another letter showed Hamish Cormack's bold writing. This was addressed to Jeremy of course, but as word from that rather dour character came seldom, she knew it would have something significant to say. The next envelope puzzled her.

It was pale blue and had some fancy writing on it. Not Mary Jean, who did incline toward fancy notepaper, because Liz did not recognize the writing. Postmarked *Motherwell*—she would need to wait to find out more.

Jeremy was drawing to a close as Howie held up the final sheet. " 'So, we'll see you all at Christmas. We'll have a grand big soiree—that's if the customs and excise officers let us through with the boxes and trunks of "stuff" that wife of mine keeps buying for you all. Now, until then, the Lord bless you and keep you; the Lord make His face to shine upon you and keep you safe till He comes. Amen!' " With excited shouts and even some whoops, the children, closely followed by the equally pleased and excited adults, trooped out of the house. Within moments Liz and Jeremy sat alone.

"Did you hear the bit about the *Revelation?*"

Liz look flustered. "Forgive me, Jeremy, I was daydreaming a bit. What about the boat then?"

"Hamish will be coming to see aboot its restoration. Jake and Jimmy will be asked to help him, before they go off to Cairnglen for Christmas and the New Year. My, but it's goin' to be grand to have them here; this is still Bruce's home, you know, however far away he might travel at times. But they've that many places they could be goin' to. Now, what about our other news?"

She held up the bundle of letters. "One from the MacKinnons!"

Jeremy turned away to hide his glee. She had never referred to Blodwin as a MacKinnon before. "They've had their own correspondence from the reverend, of course. Apparently he's been telling Thomas quite a lot about the crime problem in New York. I wonder if it can be worse there than it is in Glasgow or London?"

He did not answer, knowing quite a lot about the underworld of Glasgow from his own early life.

"Anyway Thomas is talking about taking some time off to cross the ocean and see for himself. Oh my goodness, I hope Blod is not considering . . . but surely not with all the children and another one coming?"

Again Jeremy refrained from asking questions. Long ago he and Liz had sorted out their own differences about family, deciding with no difficulty that the Cormack Homes would suffice. Now it appeared that his wife's hard feelings toward her relatives had been healed. "Who's that fancy letter from? 'Tis not Mary Jean's writing!"

"It's from a Carrie Livingstone. Remember the couple who took Kirsty in when—?"

He remembered, but knowing the subject still held pain for Liz, he merely nodded. She continued, "Well, Mistress Livingstone wanted us to know that she and her husband, Harry, inspired by what they'd heard from Thomas—and Bruce and Kirsty, too, of course—about the Cormack Homes, have decided to take in one or two needy children to their own home. Not necessarily orphans and not for adoption, but children in temporary need. Can you imagine that they want advice from us . . . ? Jeremy?"

He glanced up from the illustrated paper he had been scanning. She didn't use that tone unless she considered it serious.

"Could we maybe visit this Carrie sometime? I like the sound of the Livingstones. Or maybe we should invite them here."

He dropped the paper and came to stand behind her chair. Gently he placed his better hand on her shoulder. "You do need a friend like that, my dear, don't you? Yes, we could invite them here, Liz, and I suppose we could go there, too, sometime, as long as we don't go near Glasgow!"

They both laughed, then she said, "And what does Hamish have to say?"

"Och, I nearly forgot. Will you open it?"

Once more the trusty MacAlister heirloom opener came into use, and a single sheet fell from the envelope. The letter was short and crisp: "Dear Jeremy: I'll be at the Mains by Thursday or Friday to start on the boat. Ask Taylor to let the polisman know. Bruce'll be home ere long. Christmas, he says. Is that not just grand?"

Amazement at the last sentence made the couple stare at each other.

"Hamish must miss him a lot more than we know!"

"Aye, he must. If Taylor doesny come in the morrow, I'll go to Aribaig mysel' and tell Neal. He's had charge of the boat, but anyway, the whole town should be told he's not goin' to stay in America."

Friday morning dawned bright and clear. Jeremy and Hamish had mounted the horses and ridden to the loch side. Neal Mac-Leod was coming by the water and would be meeting them on the *Revelation*. As they still had some time, both men stood gazing down the scree cliff at the battered boat. The hatches remained intact, as Hamish had left them in the spring, but the two men shared thoughts that went much further back than that. Neither said anything for a while, and then they both spoke at once.

"Do you mind thon time, Hamish . . . ?"

"We've all come a long road, Jeremy."

They looked fondly at each other. A long road indeed, in more than one way. Jeremy's thoughts lingered on the night when Hamish had chased and caught him as he ran from he knew not what. Many times he thanked God that he had been caught, because that had been the night he had been saved, and Hamish had taught him many things. Then Bruce had taught him, too, and Bruce's mam, Elspeth, and her husband, Andrew. But best of all had been Gran'pa Bruce's loving guidance. Aye, it had been a long way indeed, but a good way, and Jeremy had come to know the only true Way. He turned to Hamish again. "You've missed Bruce a lot, haven't you, Hamish?"

Hamish gazed out across the water, calm on this bonny late-autumn day. His voice sounded choked: "Aye, but the Lord has gien us all our own work for His Kingdom." They viewed their small corner of creation for another few minutes as a stray cloud hovered across the sun, until finally Hamish moved toward the path.

"We should get on then and take they measurements, for Jake and the lads. I see the polisman's boat yonder."

"Wait just a bit, Hamish. Look at the sky." The clouds had

opened again, and as clouds will, they had begun to form a pattern. "It's the shape of a sail, Hamish."

The other man squinted upward. He smiled. "Aye, a sail, and the other bits of clouds are just like islands in the sky. Bruce would say it's a sign of his 'isles of the sea.' " He placed his hand on Jeremy's elbow, and together they made their way down the slope toward the sparkling water.